CREDO'S BONES

ALISON NAOMI HOLT

Denabi Publishing

CHAPTER 1

T oday, I can honestly say, is the first time I've wondered what the hell I was thinking when I decided to become a cop. At the moment, my partner, Casey Bowman and I were on our knees in a sweltering, dilapidated old camper that had been abandoned on a property that bisected the line between the City of Tucson and Pima County.

Not only did the property bisect the line, but the camper did as well. To our great misfortune, the part that contained the toilet with the human femur sticking out of it just happened to be located in the city. So, since it was a very old bone and the homicide detectives were supposedly too busy to come take a look, our sergeant, Kate Brannigan, agreed to have Casey and me dig around to see what else we could find under the toilet, beneath the rat droppings and around the cholla cactus some packrat had dragged in.

My name is Alexandra Wolfe. I'm a detective with the Tucson Police Department assigned to the Special Crimes Unit. I'm twenty-nine and stand about five-foot seven. My eyes are brown, as is my hair, which is short, and usually a mess since I never learned how to properly use a blow dryer.

I adjusted the facemask covering my nose and mouth to allow a tiny bit of air to circulate around my face. Major mistake. The smell of packrat urine and decades old decay overwhelmed my senses. My eyes even began to water, which surprised me. In the desert, it's generally so dry in the summer any liquid my body might produce usually evaporates into the sweltering 115-degree heat. My hands, however, were drenched and chafing. The rubber gloves were fulfilling their purpose: no fluids in or out.

"Here, hold this." Casey had managed to dislodge the remainder of the bone from the depths of the holding tank. She handed it back to me with the proper care and dignity she felt any dead body part deserved. This was hardly textbook evidence collection. But then, getting one of our departments to actually claim the crime scene demanded we pull out the bone to see what we had.

I, who hate dead bodies, looked at the white scepter she was passing with undisguised disgust. "Explain to me again why we can't just put the whole camper on a tow truck and take it to the station so the people in the crime lab can dismantle the thing piece-by-piece in the cool air-conditioned garage?" I gingerly took the bone between thumb and forefinger and set it down on a clean sheet.

Kate stuck her head in the door. She'd been outside arguing with the supervisor from the Sheriff's Department over whose jurisdiction the camper fell under. "Believe me, Alex, if I could get just one commander from either department to lay claim to the crime scene, then we could move the damn thing. As it is, both departments want to know what we have before either of them will take it."

She carefully picked up the bone and began to examine the shaft. "That's why the three of us are sitting out here in the middle of this Godforsaken field rummaging through years of garbage and filth."

Casey reached into the toilet again. I leaned over and watched as she gingerly poked the disposal flap open with one finger. She clicked on her mini-mag flashlight and pointed it into the hole, trying to see if there was anything else of interest down there.

When we'd first arrived, we took a cursory walk around the camper. Sometime after the camper was abandoned, some rocket scientist removed the pipes leading to the black water waste valve, and shoved a large, galvanized livestock watering tank directly under the toilet hole.

They'd screwed the top flanges around the edge of the tank directly to the bottom of the camper so the only way to empty the damn thing was to unscrew it and tip it to the side, letting all the effluent run down the nearby hill. Little holes had been poked in the sides of the stock tank, probably in an effort to vent the methane gas that would otherwise seep back up into the camper with such a harebrained invention.

Casey sat back on her heels and absently rubbed her forehead with the upper part of her sleeve. "Whoa."

Kate and I spoke at the same time "Whoa?"

Casey's jaw tightened over the edge of her mask. "Lots of desiccated poop with what looks to be chunks of bones embedded in it." She glanced back at Kate. "And I think I could make out parts of three orbital sockets."

Kate stepped up onto the rusted step we'd managed to tug out from under the door and pulled herself inside. "Let me take a look."

Casey stood and made a beeline for the door. "It's all yours. It may be 115 outside, but that's still cooler than in here."

I got up to leave as well, but Kate had other ideas. "Hold it, Alex. I want you to take a look after I do so we can all compare notes on what's down there."

Sighing, I dutifully waited for her to look down the hole. When she'd finished, I took the proffered flashlight and slowly lowered my free hand down into the toilet, feeling the morning's chorizo and eggs making their way back up from where they'd only just recently gone down.

"Kate," I cleared my throat in an effort to not sound so pathetic. "You know I hate dead bodies. In fact, didn't I tell you that if you ever wanted to get rid of me, all you have to do is transfer me into homicide? Dead bodies are so... dead. They stink, the old ones look really slimy and—"

"Everything's dried up. There's no odor of decaying flesh, and no slime. Now, are you going to look down there? Because if you're not, I happen to know they need a new patrol officer out at the landfill."

I knew it was an empty threat. But I also knew Kate had some very creative ways of handling discipline and I'd never particularly cared for any of them. "Fine." I wedged myself back into the tiny bathroom, pushed open the flapper at the bottom of the bowl and shined my light down the hole.

I'll dispense with describing the piles of desiccated filth, but I could definitely see the three pieces of orbital bone Casey had mentioned. I couldn't tell if they were three pieces of two eye sockets, thus possibly belonging to only one person, or three separate sockets from two, or maybe three, distinct skulls. I say three pieces of two sockets, because I could clearly make out the outside curve of the orbital bone on two of the pieces, but I couldn't tell if the third circular piece was from an eye socket or something else entirely. The forensic people would have to figure that out.

The little I could see had grabbed my interest though, and I completely forgot that my head was down inside a fifty-year-old, much used and little cleaned, toilet bowl. Sharp fragments of bone lay interspersed among the dried and flaking contents of the tank.

Someone had gone to great effort to reduce the various skeletal parts to sizes that would fit through the three-inch opening. My guess was it would take the lab quite a while to piece together the human puzzle those fragments represented.

As I was about to pull my head out and close the flap, my light glinted off a shiny object almost completely buried in the debris off to the right side of the tank. I studied it a minute, then sat back and blinked, trying to reconcile what I thought I'd seen with where we were and what we were doing.

Kate squatted down next to me. "What?"

I glanced over my shoulder at the county deputy and sergeant who were both poking their heads into the camper through the tight doorway. I looked back at Kate and shrugged. "Nothin'." I wasn't sure I wanted to say what I thought I'd seen in front of the deputies, so I stood up and motioned to the two men. "Excuse me. I need to get out for some fresh air."

Before I stepped down from the camper, Kate stopped me. "Alex." She held out her hand, indicating the flashlight with a waggle of her fingers. I handed it to her and watched as she squatted down and pushed open the flange.

I hadn't realized just how hot I'd gotten until I descended the rickety step into the fresh air, tore off my facemask and took a deep breath of cool, 115-degree, desert air.

Casey walked over with two bottles of water. She handed me one, then poured part of the other over the top of my head. "Here, your face has gone past red. Cool yourself down before you end up with heat stroke." She pulled a third bottle out of her back pocket and handed it to Kate when she joined us.

Kate's far-off expression told me she'd seen what I thought I'd seen. She held my gaze for a second, very clearly telling me to keep my mouth shut, then turned to the sheriff's deputies. "I'm going to make an executive decision on this one, Mike, and cut out the command staff completely. We'll take the case, but you guys owe us one." She flashed him a winning smile while pulling off her rubber gloves and holding out her hand as a gesture of goodwill.

The sergeant, a rather portly man whose belly completely covered most of his duty belt, shook her hand genially. He wasn't wearing a bulletproof vest, but his tan uniform shirt was soaked through and rivulets of sweat were pouring down his face and dripping onto the dirt at his feet. I guess the evaporation theory doesn't hold true for truly obese people. Whatever was happening, he didn't look like he should be out here in this heat much longer.

Kate graciously pulled back her hand, which was now covered with a slick sheen of sweat that had transferred from his meaty palm to hers.

Obviously relieved that we'd taken the scene, Sergeant Mike chuckled and started walking toward his air-conditioned car. In answer to my question, he turned and called over his shoulder. "Who knows why these grungies do what they do? Probably using the place as a hotbox or something." Grungies was the term most cops used for the dirty, mostly young street people who wouldn't take a job or a shower if it were handed to them on a silver platter. A hotbox is a sealed, air-tight room, or in this case, camper, where pot smokers go to smoke their joints. The exhaled smoke stays in the air so they can breathe it in again in order to get full use of their joint.

Casey pulled a travel package of hand wipes from her pocket and handed one to Kate, who took it with a nod and motioned to a nearby palo verde tree. "Let's get into the shade where we can talk without passing out from the heat."

We followed her to what little shade the branches provided. The tree was aptly named, as palo verde literally means, "green stick" in Spanish. The canopy consisted of hundreds of intertwined sticks that grudgingly offered a pittance of shade to the truly desperate.

Kate pulled a small notepad out of her back pocket, along with a pen, and looked at Casey and me. "All right, let's see what we have. Casey, what did you see down there?"

Casey stared off into the distance, apparently trying to picture what she'd seen. "Fragments of bones in among the filth. I'm no expert, but it looked as though someone had tried to break them up enough to be able to stuff them down the toilet. I saw what I think were the bones that go around the eye sockets, and—" She glanced at Kate. "I think I saw three of them, which means—maybe there was more than one skeleton?"

Kate was jotting something on her notepad. She spoke as she scribbled one last thought. "I don't mind you making guesses at this point. I want your first impressions, not ideas that have been filtered through your logical mind." She looked up from the paper. "Anything else?"

Nodding, Casey pulled off her sunglasses and began wiping sweat off the lenses as she tried to remember every detail. "The femur I pulled out was stuck about three-quarters of the way in. I had to twist it a little to get it out and I'm not sure if I scraped it up or not. Really, the forensic folks should have come taken it out, or the department should have had it towed in. I think it sucks that they'd have us do it just so they or the S.O. can decide if it's worth claiming the scene or if it might be a political hot potato."

I raised my brows in surprise. That was one of the longest speeches I've ever heard Casey give. I glanced at Kate, who was studying Casey with a similar expression. Her lips twitched as she tried to hide her amusement.

Kate nodded, "I agree, except the way that tank was screwed on under the camper and the way they dumped the excrement over the hill means someone is going to have to disassemble it and sort through the refuse before calling a tow truck to take it to the station anyway." She held her pen poised over her notes. "Okay, what else?"

"That's about all I saw." Now that was more like the Casey I knew. Short, succinct, and to the point.

Kate thought for a second, tapping her pen on her notepad a couple of times before motioning for me to take up the narrative.

"Well, I think I saw a T.P.D. badge."

Casey's head jerked up and she squinted at me for a second before replacing the sunglasses on her nose. "A badge?"

"Yeah. I only saw it for a second, but it looked like it might have been an older style, you know, the kind with the numbers on the front?"

I glanced over at Kate who seemed reluctant to add her two cents. It wasn't my place to get her to talk, so I held my tongue and waited. It was close to four o'clock and the sun was still beating down on us pretty hard. I lifted the water bottle to my lips while I watched Kate over its length.

Something that happens to a person's eyes when their mind takes a journey. It doesn't matter if they're thinking about the vagaries of the past or the possibilities of the future. It's different than what happens the moment people die. When someone's soul, or whatever you want to call it, leaves their body, their eyes just kind of go empty—the light goes out. Conversely, when a person becomes lost in memories, they're gone, but the light's still on. Kate had disappeared somewhere deep inside herself.

I glanced over at Casey who raised her eyebrows. This was definitely not normal Kate-like behavior.

When she came back, Kate shook her head. For just an instant, she seemed surprised to see Casey and me standing with her under the tree. She absently tapped her pant leg several times, smiling at something only she could appreciate. Collecting herself, she shook her head again and glanced over at the camper. "Sorry, just some very old memories resurfacing. I can't be one hundred percent certain because a lot of the badge was covered and it was obviously corroded, but it looked to me like the number could have been 68."

She looked first at me, and then at Casey to see if that pronouncement meant anything to either of us. It didn't, so both of us shrugged. She flipped her notebook closed and slid it into the back pocket of her Dockers. "When I first hired on, there were only a few women officers on the department.

"A lot of the male officers resented us, and tried to make our work lives miserable. But I discovered a whole other group of men who believed women could be just as good and, at times, better than their male counterparts. Micah Maloney was one of them. Badge number 68 belonged to his father, Seamus, who died in the line of duty. When Micah joined the department a year later, he was given permission to use his father's badge."

She took out her cell phone and began searching through her contact list.

I knew there had to be more to the story. "And?"

But she just looked up at me and put the phone to her ear.

When someone answered, her brows came down low and she quickly checked the number she'd dialed. Satisfied that she hadn't hit the wrong person in her contact list, she put the phone back to her ear. "Deputy Chief Pardo, please."

I shifted further into the shade and sighed, anxious to either get back to my much cooler car or, better yet, back to the overly air-conditioned office.

Kate pulled her sunglasses down slightly and peered over the top of them. "Something the matter, Alex?"

Shaking my head, I adjusted the holster of my Glock to a more comfortable position and listened to her side of the conversation.

"X? Why do you have your cell phone forwarded to the secretaries?"

I glanced over at Casey, who shrugged. "X" was Xavier Pardo, the second highest ranking officer on the department. Kate had not only called him by a nickname only a very small minority ever dared use, but she was questioning his phone practices as well. "I know, hey listen. I'm at a camper that has several very old bone fragments and — Oh, you've heard about it? Well, I think you need to get down here."

She listened for a second. "Yeah, I know, but I don't think you'll melt." She glanced up at us and rolled her eyes. "Okay, we'll wait for you here."

"Wait for him? I'm waitin' in my car then. It's too friggin' hot out here." The words spilled from my mouth before I had a chance to stop them.

Shaking her head, Kate pulled out her notebook again. "Actually Alex, you're in luck. I need you to check out that house on the other side of the property and find out who owns this land and the camper."

I looked to where she was pointing and could just barely make out the outlines of a few buildings across the cactus strewn desert. My guess was they were about a hundred and fifty yards away, and they appeared to warp in and out of alignment as the heat waves rising off the ground made the buildings dance beneath the sweltering summer sun. I nodded and headed toward my car.

Kate stopped me before I'd taken more than a few steps. "Actually, I need you to walk there and keep your eyes open for any other bones or signs of criminal activity along the way. Head there in a fairly straight line though. I'm going to call out one of the cadaver dogs to see what he can come up with."

I turned and glared at her, certain I shouldn't say what was going through my little pea brain right about then.

Casey went to her car and pulled out three more bottles of cold water from her cooler. She came back and handed one to both Kate and me. She kept the other for herself, grinning with half her mouth, as she often did when something I did amused her. "C'mon. I'll go with you. Ya gotta love workin' in Arizona in the middle of the summer."

She started out across the desert and I threw one last irritated glance at Kate before joining her. As per instructions, we walked straight toward the buildings without deviating to the left or right. I concentrated on looking for anything out of the ordinary—like a human skeleton hanging from an arm of a saguaro cactus, for instance.

As we approached the buildings, I began to make out one main house with two large sheds angled so that they formed a semi-circle around the house and one stand-alone three car garage to the rear. The buzz of an electric sander reverberated off the walls of the nearest building, so I walked up to the open garage door and stuck my head inside to take a look. A man in his early to mid-sixties stood holding a sander against the side of a really old camper similar to the one we'd just left.

There were actually four old trailers in various stages of restoration: aluminum completely off, aluminum still on with the original cracked and peeling paint still visible (this was the one the man was sanding), and two where the aluminum had already been sprayed with a coat of glossy new paint. I stepped inside the relatively cool interior and called out a greeting. "Hello."

There wasn't any real chance of him hearing me since the noise from the sander reverberated off the metal, and he was wearing a pair of acoustic earmuffs to muffle the sound. On top of that, a radio was blasting Dolly Parton and Kenny Rogers singing Islands in the Stream. To make matters worse, a rotating fan, obviously set on the highest setting possible, rotated back and forth on its base.

I walked over and flipped off the radio, which finally got the man's attention.

He whipped the muffs from his head, spun around and was in the process of drawing a pistol from the front of his pants.

Casey yelled, "Gun!" and we both pulled our weapons as we hit the ground.

I rolled behind the tires of a faded red camper and peeked under the chassis to get my bearings.

The man knelt on one knee with his pistol pointed at the ground. He was looking squarely in my direction. I was lying on my belly, gun held straight out in front of me. I brought the front site up until it was level with his chest.

Casey yelled from where she'd taken cover behind a pile of discarded portable air-conditioners. "Tucson Police. Drop the gun! Now!"

The guy's shoulders drooped as he let out a disgusted sigh. "Police? Don't tell me, that toothless old bugger who's started sleeping in my camper out there—uninvited I might add—called the cops?" He lifted his shirt and shoved the .22 back down into the front of his faded, well-patched blue jeans. I pushed to my feet and edged around the side of the camper, my Glock at the ready just in case.

The slightly amused curl of his lip as he followed my progress made me wonder if my zipper was down or something. I discretely felt the front of my Dockers, thinking somewhere in the back of my mind that I didn't want to get shot with my pants undone.

Shaking his head, he made a shooing motion with his hands, palms down, fingers brushing the air, before turning to pick up and switch off the still running sander. He set it carefully on a rickety card table, which was piled with various discarded items.

I automatically catalogued each one in case any of them could be used as a weapon. There were several orange teardrop-shaped running lights, a cardboard box full of round, red tail lights, a battery powered drill, several screwdrivers and a huge assortment of rusty screws scattered about.

I walked over and motioned for him to move his hands away from his body. "I'm just gonna take your gun while we talk. I'll give it back when we're done."

"Aw for crap sake." A dramatic sigh accompanied his grudging assent as he held his arms out to his side. He had a short, compact body, and what little neck he had was solid and covered with a healthy spread of neck hair to match the grey, three-day stubble adorning his cheeks and chin. I slipped the revolver out of his waistband and stepped back a few paces.

Casey holstered her weapon and walked over to join me. "In answer to your question, the call to 911 was made anonymously from a public phone, so I'm not sure exactly who called us. Why do you think it was the man you described?"

"Because I've run him off my property more times than I care to count. I figure he thinks calling the cops is some kind of revenge." He shrugged and pointed to his pistol, which I'd unloaded and set on the table behind us. "Sorry about that. Mostly the people who come around unannounced are the troublemaking types who think stealing what they consider junk isn't really stealing at all." He squinted, his gaze moving from Casey to me and back to her again. "So what'd he say? That I threatened him? I did. That I threw him off my property? Guilty."

The air from the fan felt good, and each time it turned my way I discretely held my arms away from my body to try to cool myself.

Casey rested her forearm on the handle of a moving dolly and propped her other hand on her hip. "No, we're here because of the bone sticking out of the toilet in that camper over there." She halfway turned and pointed toward the other side of the property.

"Oh that." He waved dismissively. "Been there almost fifteen years. That bone was part of an old bull of mine that died some years ago. He got caught in some barbed wire fencing. Dumb thing strangled himself before I found him."

He gestured to the southwest corner of the pasture with a lift of his chin. "I just left the carcass out there for the coyotes, and some smartass stuffed one of the legs down inside her hole." He shrugged, "Haven't given much thought to it since."

Neither Casey nor I corrected him on the error of his skeletal identification.

Casey tilted her head just a fraction. "Her?"

"Yeah, the camper. She was my first. At least the first one I bought on my own. My wife, Ella, and I traveled all over the country in her. After Ella passed, I never could bring myself to take another trip in that particular camper, so I parked her." He lifted one shoulder as he spoke. "S'pose I should'a fixed her up instead of just letting her rot over there. I let some bum live in it for a while, but I haven't been over to see her in God knows how long."

He looked wistfully across to his first love, then moved his head forward and squinted. He'd apparently just noticed the attention the little trailer was getting and his voice rose several octaves. "Who the hell is muckin' around in my camper?" He threw down a rag he'd been using to wipe his hands and strode out of the shed with a determined gait.

Casey caught up to him and I grudgingly followed, reluctant to exchange the relatively cooler interior of the shed for the baking oven of the desert landscape. Casey was trying to explain Kate's presence. I missed his growling reply.

When a K9 SUV pulled onto the property, the man pulled back his shoulders and began waving his hands back and forth in wide, exaggerated motions. His pace quickened to as fast as his short legs would carry him. "Oh no. Hell no! You are not making a circus out of my place." He grabbed his sagging, slightly over-sized jeans as he yelled across the last twenty yards to Kate. "Hey lady! Keep your grubby mitts off my camper! You have no cause to be messin' around in her! Get away from there!"

He strode angrily up to Kate and began poking at her chest with a crooked finger, never quite touching, but getting his point across just the same. "This is my property. You can't just drive in here slick as you please and start messin' with stuff. You can't!"

Kate took a defensive step backward. "Unfortunately, Mr...?" She waited for him to fill in the blank.

"Never you mind that. Just pack your stuff and go." He made a beeline for the crime scene tape Kate had put up.

I've never understood how Kate can growl loud enough to make the words sound like a barked command, but she did. "That's far enough!"

As anyone who's ever been the recipient of that particular tone does, he obeyed, but the glare he turned her way said he wasn't happy about it. The green flecks in his eyes flashed as his lips curled into an angry snarl. "She's mine, and you're trespassing."

Kate rested her fists on her hips and leaned forward slightly. "She's a crime scene now, unless the 'she' you're talking about is the person whose femur was stuffed down the toilet, in which case we have a hell lot more to say to each other."

"I'm talkin' 'bout my camper, and unless you have a warrant, you can pack up and leave."

Kate shook her head. "This camper is abandoned on public property. I don't need a warrant."

"This is my property, and I'm tellin' you to leave!" He angrily poked his finger about an inch from her chest, his raised eyebrows and pinched lips a sure sign that he was expecting some type of reaction. When Kate silently turned her back to him to study the camper, he jerked his hand back down to his side.

I wasn't too worried about Kate's safety. What I was most

concerned about was the bulging vein in the man's temple that had begun pulsing dangerously fast.

The way Kate stared at the little camper made me wonder if she'd been bluffing about the land the camper was parked on. After a short time, she turned back to him, pulling herself up a little straighter and giving him "the look" that I'm all too familiar with—chin down, eyes locked on his.

She spoke quietly, putting more meaning into her words than if she'd been yelling at him. "I'm not one to play games, Mr...." She paused, searching around for a name she'd never been given. "What is your name, anyway?"

"None of your business." He turned and spat to the side to emphasize his point.

"Fine." Kate reached behind her back and pulled out a set of handcuffs.

He'd obviously been acquainted with them on previous occasions, because he immediately put his hands up and backed away. "Okay, okay, no need for that. I'm Jepson, Tom Jepson." He nervously eyed the cuffs.

Kate nodded. "Okay, Mr. Jepson. We both know your property ends just to the right of that power line. If you care to continue to dispute that fact, you can do so from the back of a patrol car as you're on your way to the jail for obstructing a police investigation."

Casey and I glanced at the power line. Since the jurisdiction of the camper had come into question, I was sure Kate had the dispatchers studying the boundary lines of the area and therefore knew exactly what she was talking about.

His whining response, combined with his nasal intonation wasn't a pleasant combination. "But the camper's mine."

Kate relaxed slightly. "And we'll try to return it to you in one piece. In the meantime, you need to go with Detective Bowman and tell her what you know about the contents of this trailer." Fully expecting to be obeyed, Kate turned away and addressed the K9 officer, who stood a few yards off patiently awaiting his orders.

"Sam, take Alex and see what Lido turns up. She'll fill you in on the way."

Lido, a loveable, sad-eyed bloodhound, was the department's part-time cadaver dog and full-time ambassador of good will.

His handler, Samuel Yazzie, had spent the last twenty of his thirty-five years on the department in the K9 unit. Everyone knew he was more or less retired-on-duty, but he was one of the best trackers in the country, and I'm sure the chief's chest swelled more than a few inches whenever various law enforcement agencies from around the world called requesting Sam's assistance.

Sam waved me over to his vehicle where he opened one of the rear doors and snapped a leash onto Lido's collar. As soon as he hooked up the big dog, the happy tail wagging stopped and Lido morphed into the professional cadaver dog who'd found more dead bodies than any other dog in the State of Arizona. Sam's shelf life may have expired as far as chasing bad guys was concerned, but he was still an exceptional K9 trainer and tracker.

We began crisscrossing the desert between the camper and the house, pausing every now and again to inspect some white object that may or may not have been a bone.

Sam pulled a handkerchief out of his back pocket. He shook it open and wiped his sun-browned forehead. His big, barrel chest tugged at the buttons on his shirt, but it still didn't rival his ever-expanding girth falling down over his utility belt. He spoke with a slow, guttural drawl common to many Native Americans. I swear there are times when I could hear a touch of a Scottish Brogue as well. "So, what's the story? Obviously we're looking for a body. What's the rest of it?"

I kicked at a three-inch seedpod that had dropped from the branches of a sprawling mesquite tree. "There was a human femur, just the white bone, no muscle or skin, sticking out of the toilet in the camper, and some bone fragments in the holding tank."

He grunted as though that was an everyday occurrence, which, to him, I suppose it was. "So I'm looking for old bones instead of a fresh body?"

I nodded, thankful that the sun was on its way toward the horizon. "Yeah."

The desert here was mostly made up of mesquite, ironwood and palo verde trees with the occasional cholla or barrel cactus thrown in.

We wound around them, every now and then stopping in the shade for a break.

Sam wasn't much of a talker, and I was too hot to make small talk, so our conversation was minimal.

After one particularly short shade break, Sam and I started out again, but Lido continued to sit where he was. Sam commanded the dog to search and Lido turned his head away and ignored him.

The big man watched his partner for few seconds.

I glanced back and forth between the two of them, and couldn't help notice how Sam's droopy jowls had an uncanny resemblance to Lido's.

"Hmph." He walked back to where Lido sat and began slowly gazing around, obviously searching the ground around the big hound for bones.

I watched Lido, who had begun staring at Sam with an intense gaze, seemingly willing his partner to understand what he was trying to tell him.

I walked around the base of the tree, kicking apart anthills and poking aside bushes with the toe of my shoe. "I don't see anything. Maybe he's just hot and doesn't want to go any farther."

Shaking his head, Sam stepped out from under the tree's canopy, pulling gently on the leash. "Sook."

"That means track, right?"

"Yeah. Lido, sook." The bloodhound stubbornly refused to move.

Even though the temperature had dropped a few degrees, I still expected to see birds using potholders to pull the worms out of the ground. Out of frustration, I waved an arm in a wide arc, trying to get the dog to move. "Sook, for cripes sake. Sook!"

Sam walked back and knelt next to his hound. He gently gathered Lido's oversized ear in the palm of his hand and bent to look him in the eye. "What is it, buddy? What do you smell?"

Lido sat up a little straighter, turning his head slightly to pull his ear away from Sam's hand. He seemed a little affronted, as though reminding Sam that they were working a case and this was no time for a friendly caress.

Sam nodded and let his hand drop. "Okay, Buddy, you're right." He unhooked his keys from his duty belt and handed them to me. "Would you mind going back to my SUV and getting my shovel out from behind the seat?"

I glanced at the vehicles parked some two hundred yards away, then sighed dramatically before taking his keys and starting the slow trek through the overheated air. Usually, I enjoy working with the K9 unit, but today was just too damn hot to be out traipsing around looking for old bones.

Kate, Casey and Deputy Chief Pardo were standing in a semi-circle next to the camper, with Jepson facing them. His side was to me and he was gesticulating wildly, his arms moving up and down and back and forth. I guessed he was once again ordering them off his property.

As I wiped the sweat from my brow, I heard a pop and the unmistakable sound of glass shattering.

From the left side of my vision, glass sprayed outwards from the windshield of Pardo's vehicle. Tiny flecks of sunlight glinted off the shards as they spread outward from the vehicle in a conical shaped explosion.

Simultaneously, or so it seemed to me, blood burst from Jepson's chest, spraying Kate and Casey with bright, crimson spatters.

While the blood was still airborne, Deputy Chief Pardo staggered backward as though he'd been punched. He grabbed the right side of his chest, looking down at his fist as it crumpled his white commander's uniform. For the briefest second, his terrified gaze caught my own shocked expression before he too fell; first to his knees, then over onto his side in a modified fetal position, one leg pulled up to his chest, the other feebly kicking, trying to join its mate.

The bullet had come from my left, so I tore my gaze from the tableau in front of me and searched the desert in that direction.

Sam Yazzie yelled my name, and I spun around to see him lumbering our way with Lido close at his side. Sam was pointing to an area farther left than I'd originally looked, toward a cluster of green mesquite trees I'd missed on my first glance west.

A figure stood silhouetted against the sun, moving quickly to shoulder the sling of his rifle across his chest. I assumed it was a he— from a hundred yards I really couldn't tell because the sun had sunk lower in the sky directly behind him. The distance was too great to make out any real details.

Casey and Kate would help the chief, so I sprinted toward the shooter, drawing my weapon as I ran.

The silhouette quickly knelt to retrieve some type of pack, then turned and disappeared into the thicket of mesquites.

I caught occasional glimpses of him through the trees. I know the desert, and I'm fast, but I didn't seem able to close the gap between us. He already had a huge head start. The fact that he was outdistancing me with a rifle slung across his back carrying some type of canvas bag tucked under his right arm told me I was going to have a heck of a time trying to catch him.

He reappeared for a brief second as he dodged around a towering saguaro and then suddenly dropped out of sight.

As I redoubled my effort, my TPD baseball hat caught on an overhead branch and flew off my head. I fervently hoped it hadn't fallen into the pile of cholla I'd just skirted.

The smell of creosote wafted through the air, and I saw several broken stalks hanging loosely from three or four tiny-leafed creosote bushes.

The man had run straight through them, crushing the plants in his rush to get away.

I dodged around each bush he'd barreled through, my feet slipping slightly on loose rocks scattered on the hard-packed dirt. When I came close to where he'd disappeared, I slowed, trying to silence the sound of my rasping breath as I moved about ten yards south of where I'd lost sight of him.

I'd come to the edge of a ravine, and understood why he'd suddenly vanished. I bent over and braced my hands on my knees, consciously expanding my lungs, all the while keeping my throat as open and relaxed as possible to minimize any sound.

There was a more than an even chance he'd be kneeling in the wash with his finger on the trigger waiting for me to stick my head over the edge.

Slowly and carefully, I lowered myself to my belly and peered down into the arroyo.

The sand-filled wash ran from north-to-south about five feet below the jagged, irregular lip I was lying on. Hard-packed dirt made up the walls of the ravine where years of flash floods had carved deep channels through the desert with torrents of rushing water and debris.

When I saw deep footprints heading across the ravine, I holstered my Glock and leapt down into the wash, nearly falling on my face as my feet sank into the soft sand and stayed there while my momentum carried me forward. I caught myself on my hands, pushed up and began running, occasionally slipping to my knees whenever the sand shifted unexpectedly under my feet.

After about twenty-five yards, I saw where the shooter had climbed out by grabbing onto small plants that sporadically dotted the arroyo wall. He'd pulled several loose in his haste, and now they littered the area around where his tracks left the wash.

It was easy enough to clamber up after him, even though the walls were five or six feet high. I rolled up and over the lip in one swift movement, actually rolling onto the man's tracks, which continued south from where I lay. I glanced back the way I'd come, hoping and expecting to see Casey following, but the desert was empty.

I pushed to my feet and took off running again. After about a hundred yards, my calf muscles tightened painfully and I worried they'd cramp before I caught the bastard. By the time I'd gone another hundred yards, my quadriceps were burning and my breath had become ragged and loud.

The stern visage of my friend, Mr. Myung, flashed before me, quietly telling me to quiet my breathing before my enemy silenced it for me.

I stopped and once more braced my hands on my knees, taking a moment to catch my breath. As I practiced what Mr. Myung preached, I scanned the area ahead, looking for any movement that would give away the man's location.

Myung had also taught me some tricks about concealment and positional awareness. Instead of looking for a person's whole body, he told me to look for something that doesn't belong. A hand, a foot, maybe a boot. He said if your brain is focused solely on seeing an entire body, you'll miss the only part of the person that isn't concealed.

Luck was with me on this one.

About seventy-five yards away, with his back to me and his lower body concealed behind a creosote bush, the man was down on one knee, chest heaving as he studied me over his left shoulder.

The rifle still hung on his back, secured by the leather strap slung across his chest. We stared at one another, both of us catching our breath before the final push. He was a fleeing felon who'd just murdered in cold blood and I had every right to shoot him if he took off running again. I drew my Glock and aimed for his shoulder, the largest part of his body I could actually see. There was no way I'd be able to hit him at this distance, but I thought I'd try to bluff him into surrendering. I cupped my free hand to my mouth, hoping my words would carry from this distance. "Tucson Police! Stand up with your hands in the air."

I saw a quick flash of teeth as he grinned. He glanced down and I had the vague impression he was checking his watch.

I was too far away to make out any distinct facial features. Since my bluff had done nothing more than amuse him, I holstered my weapon, pulled in all my reserves and began sprinting in his direction.

He'd apparently recovered more quickly than I had because he took off running at a steady, ground-pounding lope. I heard an engine off in the distance and hoped it was the cavalry coming to back me up.

Unfortunately, a green, newer model Toyota Land Cruiser came skidding down a dirt road, moving in an intercept course toward the shooter. Great plumes of dust followed in its wake and when it neared him, it skidded in a semi-circle before coming to rest in the center of a self-induced dust storm.

The man disappeared into the brown cloud and seconds later the vehicle tore away from the area at a high rate of speed.

As I stood watching him go, a tangled knot formed in my stomach. I thought of the frightened look on Chief Pardo's face just before he fell and I committed everything I'd just seen and heard to memory.

I'd forgotten about the heat during my adrenaline-fueled run across the desert, and as I stood watching the Land Cruiser speed away, my vision gradually blurred. I felt suddenly, incredibly weak. I dropped to one knee, slightly confused as to where I was and what my next move should be. Bracing my arm on my knee, I looked around, hoping for a clue about where I should go to get under some shade and find a big bottle of water.

Off in the distance, I heard the braying bark of a hound on the hunt. As I turned to look, the world began spinning, then turned black as I corkscrewed to the ground.

CHAPTER 2

Water splashed onto my face. Great war drums pounded in my head and my cheek hurt where it had apparently bounced off the hard desert floor.

"Open your eyes, Alex. You need to drink." Casey ran her hands under my shoulders and pulled me into a sitting position, supporting my back with one of her legs. "Here, drink." She pushed a bottle into my mouth and the second the water touched my tongue, my body knew what to do.

I grabbed it and began guzzling, letting the liquid flow down my throat unchecked until Casey pulled the bottle away from me.

"Whoa, easy now. Not too fast. Sam's bringing his SUV and some more water." Opening the collar of my shirt, she poured the cool liquid down my chest and then up over my head. "I just happened to have this bottle in my hand when I took off running after you."

I heard heavy panting next to my ear. I swiveled around to see Lido sitting next to me, drooling happily and glancing curiously between Casey and me. When he looked at me, his left eyebrow lifted, and when he shifted his gaze to Casey, the right one shot up in an arch. My voice slurred as I once again focused on the bottle of water. "Why's

Lido here but Sam's bringing his SUV? He never goes anywhere without Lido."

"Here, drink some more, but *slowly*." She dragged out the last word to emphasize her point, then brought me up to speed on what had been going on. "Jepson's dead. Same bullet got Pardo in the chest. I had to stay with Kate to try to stabilize him, so I couldn't follow you right away.

"Sam saw the direction you'd run, and he started after you with Lido. He ran about twenty-five yards before he had to stop." She shook her head. "Way too overweight and way too hot. That man's a stroke waiting to happen." She glanced toward the road. "Here he comes now."

In the time it took him to get to us, Casey finished her narrative. "Kate ordered me to come find you, and she ordered Sam to get back to help her. When I met him returning to the camper, he shoved the baseball cap you dropped under Lido's nose and told him to search. Then he threw me the leash and told me to follow." She shrugged. "Never seen a dog handler do that before, but then, these weren't exactly ordinary circumstances."

Still feeling kind of woozy, I watched as the Explorer came to a halt. Sam slid out, ran to the rear and flipped up the back hatch. He grabbed some water bottles and hurried to where I'd fallen. "Here, Alex." His thick eyebrows drew together in the middle of his forehead. "I'm sorry I couldn't follow you. Damn old legs gave out. Lido find you okay?"

I cut a quick glance at his protruding belly, thinking he'd been lucky it hadn't been his heart that had given out. I looked up before he could take offense. Taking the proffered bottle, I twisted off the cap. "Lido was a champ. I think." I looked to Casey for confirmation.

She smiled and laid a hand on the bloodhound's head. "Came straight to her, no hesitation whatsoever."

Sam pulled a bowl out from under his arm and filled it with water. He slid it in front of Lido and the big bloodhound lapped it up. "It was an easy track for him. I didn't think he'd have any trouble." The eyebrows drew together again. "I'm wondering if maybe it isn't time to hang up the leash. You needed me, and I couldn't keep up. I'm real sorry, Alex."

I took a long, slow drink before pouring more water over my head. "Don't quit on my account, Sam. I don't know any other handler who'd let someone else work their hound. And it says something about your training ability that Lido did his job whether you tagged along or not. We need you here to keep the rest of the K9 unit trained and inline. I'd take one of you over ten of those guys." I smiled at the red tint that began at his collar and rapidly rose into his cheeks.

Casey helped me to my feet and we watched as Sam gathered up Lido and his bowl and put both into the back seat of his vehicle.

Casey climbed in after Lido, graciously surrendering the front passenger seat to me. "I assume the shooter got away?"

I nodded as I climbed in. "Yup." I gave her the description of the Land Cruiser, which she relayed to dispatch. We drove back to the camper where the EMTs were just loading Pardo into the ambulance.

The red blotches covering Kate's white polo shirt were a gruesome reminder of how rapidly a routine investigation had turned tragic. Her cheeks were wet with tears, and when she saw me staring, she reached up to wipe them away. Her hand halted midway to her face when she realized there wasn't a clean spot showing through the blood on her hands.

I quickly reached into the ambulance to grab a towel before the driver shut the rear doors. When I turned back, Kate was rubbing her face on the inside of her shoulder. I walked over and handed her the towel.

She accepted it with a nod and wiped her cheeks before holding her hands out for Casey to pour water over them.

"I assume he got away?" Kate had regained her equilibrium, and I found myself relaxing now that we were back on familiar ground. I'd never seen her cry before, and the quick glimpse I'd gotten of her humanity had unnerved me more than I cared to admit. She was my rock. As long as she was confident, I was confident, and I didn't want that to change. When I nodded, the muscle in her jaw flexed. "Did you get a good look at him? Or her?"

"Just enough to know it was a man. I couldn't tell his height, but I can make a guess."

She raised her chin slightly, prompting me to continue.

"He seemed a little taller than average. Maybe six feet, a hundred and eighty pounds, muscular."

Casey added her two cents. "Lido found his tracks when we were looking for Alex. I'd say he wears a size ten boot. We'll have to take photos and measure them, but that's my best guess. There were also some distinctive wear marks on the sole, and a brand name I didn't have time to get."

Kate pulled in a long breath and slowly let it out again. Her voice still shook slightly when she spoke. "Obviously we're going to have to work overtime." We all watched as a caravan of vehicles carrying detectives, crime scene techs and commanders descended on the scene.

Sergeant Logan, the supervisor of the homicide unit, Chief Sepe and Assistant Chief Morneaux joined us near the camper. The chief placed a hand on Kate's shoulder. "Are you okay, Kate? I don't mind you handing this off to someone else if you think you need to." The look Kate turned on him would have made a grizzly bear flinch, and he got the message loud and clear. "I didn't think so. So tell me what happened."

Kate must have asked Nate to find something to cover the bloodstains on her shirt, because he jogged up and handed her a blue windbreaker. She nodded her thanks as she pulled on the jacket.

There wasn't much point in me hanging around while Kate filled in the brass, so I started to move away to see if I could help anyone with their part of the investigation.

Kate stopped me with a hand on my arm and held a finger up to Chief Sepe. "Just a minute, Chief." She turned to me. "Alex, you and Casey get a search warrant for Jepson's home and garages. I want to know everything about our camper man you can find. Wives, ex-wives, hobbies, military service...everything." She turned back to the Chief. "I thought we'd keep the bone in the camper part of this investigation and help Jon and his crew with Jepson's homicide and AC Pardo's aggravated assault, if that's alright with you?"

Being around commanders gave me the willies so I was grateful to

Kate for giving me a job about as far away from them as I could get. I didn't wait around to hear Sepe's answer.

The area had quickly filled with people, and Casey and I had to dodge several box-carrying detectives, a bevy of crime scene techs and one brazen reporter who was trying to sneak onto the scene without being noticed. I stopped her with a hand to the front of her chest. "Can I help you?"

The woman brushed a strand of glossy black hair behind her ear. "I'm Amanda Kellworth, six o'clock news?"

"Is that a question, because it sure isn't an answer to mine." With very few exceptions, the press had never been complimentary of me, more often than not demonizing me at every possible opportunity. I was a favorite target of theirs, and Kate had specifically ordered me not to talk to them.

Amanda Kellworth, six o'clock news, moved in close and spoke quietly so that only I could hear. "Can you tell me what's going on? I'd appreciate anything you can give me. It'd be completely off the record and I'll return the favor sometime."

I glanced back at Kate, who was staring at me while she filled the chief in on what had taken place. There was nothing I'd like more than to bodily throw this woman out of the crime scene, but I also knew Kate would probably frown on that. I motioned with my hand that Amanda was to precede me and escorted her to the perimeter tape where I held the yellow ribbon high enough for her to duck under. "No comment."

Undaunted, she continued to question me as I turned and began walking away. "Detective Wolfe, I've heard you've been spending a lot of time with Gianina Angelino lately. Can you tell me anything about that?" Her voice carried across the crime scene. Completely taken off guard, I took a stutter step before slowly turning to face her again.

Casey, who'd continued to her vehicle while I took care of Miss Kellworth, started back to try to intercept me. Fat chance of that. This lady was mine.

Before I'd taken two steps, Kate called out, "Alex."

Casey may not have had the power to stop me, but Kate certainly did. I stopped and quietly waited, my glare boring a hole through Ms. Kellworth, who stood patiently with an expectant look on her face.

Kate took my arm and moved me out of Kellworth's hearing. "How many times have I told you not to react to the press? They love to goad you because your friendship with Gia makes a great story for the news and a coronary for the chief."

We both glanced at Chief Sepe, who'd turned his back to us and had begun speaking to Jon Logan.

Trying a different tack, Amanda called out to Kate. "Sergeant Brannigan, can you tell me what happened here today? Whose blood is that on your shirt? Will Chief Sepe be giving a press conference anytime soon?"

Kate casually brushed the dirt from her pants. As she walked over to the crime scene tape, she pulled up the zipper of the windbreaker, effectively covering any trace of the red smears covering the front of her shirt. I'm sure the last thing she wanted was for a picture of her covered in AC Pardo's blood to be splashed across the six o'clock news or all over the front page of the newspaper.

I started to follow, but Casey put her arm across my shoulders and redirected me toward our cars. There was no love lost between Casey and the press. In fact, she always said the only thing she hated about working with me was the amount of times she had to get near the cameras. "C'mon. Don't let her get to you. You know they just want you to react."

"I know. She caught me off guard, that's all. How the hell does she know how much time Gia and I have been spending together?"

"Have you been?"

"Have I been what?"

"Spending a lot of time with her."

We'd arrived at my car and I rummaged around in my briefcase looking for a blank warrant template. "I've been spending a lot of time with Shelley. We've been going to the Angelino's horse farm down in Sonoita to see Legacy and just hang out together." Shelley Greer was Gia's grand niece, her dead twin brother's granddaughter, and Legacy was a beautiful, midnight-black racehorse Gia had given us about a year ago.

"Do you think that's such a good idea? The brass is already pissed about your friendship with the head of the Angelino crime family. Obviously the press is drooling for a juicy story about you and Gia."

I couldn't find a pen anywhere.

Casey produced one that was bent like a person's spinal column. The writing on the side was fuzzy, obviously a bad batch from the printer.

She handed it to me and I held it at arm's length. "What the hell's this?"

"I got it from my chiropractor. She knows I go through a lot of pens, and this batch was bad so she couldn't use 'em. I've got about a hundred if you want one."

I stared at her a few seconds before I began filling in the warrant. "Anyway, nobody's gonna tell me who I can be friends with. Not the media and not the brass. If Gia's ever convicted of a felony, well, okay then, they can tell me to steer clear. In the meantime—" I let the end of the sentence hang since Casey already knew what I was going to say.

After I finished filling out the form, it took about a half-hour to find a judge who was willing to listen to our telephonic warrant granting us access to Jepson's home and outbuildings. In addition to the garage where we'd first met Tom, there were two other buildings beside the house.

Once we'd obtained the warrant, searching his home seemed like the logical place to start. Casey knocked on the front door while I announced to what was probably an empty house that we were coming in. With all the commotion out by the camper, if there had been someone inside, they would have come out by now. "Tucson Police. We have a warrant to search these premises, open the door." We waited the requisite ten seconds, then let ourselves in.

The front door opened onto a tiled living room full of furniture that at one time would have been considered quasi-elegant. Now, the yellow antique sofa and chairs, end tables and coffee table were piled high with old trailer lights, rusty camper stovetops, rounded hubcaps and numerous other miscellaneous parts.

I picked up a hubcap and held it under a light trying to decipher the letters written in the center. Ruddy brown rust pitted the surface and I had a difficult time making out the letters. I used a towel I found draped across one of the chairs to wipe off some of the corrosion and discovered red letters circling the center. "S...E...something, something, O. And then S...C...O..."

"Scotty." Casey poked around in some boxes of junk Jepson had lying around. "Serro Scotty. We used to have one when I was a kid. Believe it or not, my parents and the five of us kids traveled around Colorado, Wyoming, Montana—all over the place—in a fifteen foot camper."

"Sounds like a nightmare." I set the hubcap down and circled the room, looking for anything that would give us a clue as to why Jepson had a human leg stuck in the toilet of one of his campers and why someone had just blown a hole through his chest.

"Naw, it was heaven for a relatively poor family of seven. All the kids slept in tents. We only took one vacation a year...well, other than the occasional weekend trips, but both my mom and dad made sure our one big vacation was special. I remember my dad bringing home pamphlets his buddies brought back with them from various tourist destinations after they'd had a run. He was a bug slinger on the Missouri Pacific railroad."

"A what?"

Chuckling, she set the box she'd been searching on the ground and began rummaging through another one. "A switchman—the guy who moves the cars to various locations in the yard. Anyway, he'd bring us whatever brochures the guys found on their trips around the country." She pulled an empty holster out of the box and set it to the side. "And then my mom used to scour old magazines people would save for her. You know, like when her friend, Lucy, was done with the magazines in her hair salon, she'd give 'em to my mom, or sometimes the guy at the gas station had old magazines left over and he'd save 'em for her. She loved to search 'em for travel pictures of wherever they planned to take us that year."

Casey always became uncharacteristically chatty whenever the topic of her family came up. They'd been relatively poor, but she'd been surrounded by a loving family that I envied whenever she told her stories.

I walked over to an alcove that contained a smallish, upright piano. Like every other flat surface, camper parts and old rags covered the lid and keyboard. Above it, a shadow box hung on the alcove wall and I had to stretch to take it down. Inside were four military medals and their accompanying ribbons. "Look at these."

Casey came over and took the shadowbox from me to study the medals. She flipped up the silver latch holding the glass door closed and carefully opened the lid. Lifting one of the medals off the blue velvet padding, she turned it around to see what, if anything was written on the back. "My dad had this one, The National Defense Service Medal." She set it down and picked up two others. "He had this one too, and here's the Vietnam Service Medal." She held up one attached to a yellow ribbon with red and green stripes. "At least we know that he or someone else who lived here was in the service and what war he was in." She glanced at the nail where the box had hung on the wall. "We'll have to get his service record and see if there's anything interesting in there."

I watched her reverently put the medals back in the shadowbox, carefully smoothing out the ribbons so they hung just right. "Here." She handed it to me and watched as I rehung it on the wall.

Next to it, a professionally framed vintage poster from the White Star Lines hung slightly askew. I tilted the bottom to the left, then back to the right. When I had it perfectly balanced, I took a moment to study the picture.

Apparently, the White Star Line owned several luxury passenger steamships. An impressive one, The Republic, featured prominently in the background of the drawing. In the lower left, a man in a rowboat pulled diligently at his oars. A woman stood in the prow, offering up a loaf of bread to the passengers leaning over the railing of the ship. The towering Republic dwarfed the tiny rowboat. Large text promised untold adventure for those who traveled from the Mediterranean to the Orient, or from Boston to the Azores.

Looking over my shoulder, Casey asked, "Where are the Azores?"

I shrugged. "I think they're a bunch of islands somewhere around Portugal or Europe or something."

"That'd be a long trip, Boston to Portugal."

"Yeah I guess so, but maybe not so bad if you're traveling on a luxury steamship. Might be kinda nice." A strange sensation swept over me as I stared into the water surrounding the boat. An almost indiscernible wave of nausea came over me, like I was actually floating among the strands of seaweed. I shook my head slightly to dispel the feeling.

There didn't seem to be much else I wanted to see in the living room, so while Casey continued her search, I went into the bedroom to take a quick look around. Jepson had told us his wife had died, but I wondered whether he'd remarried or if maybe he had a female friend staying with him in the home.

Inside the closet, assorted men's clothing hung haphazardly on plastic hangers, many of which had fallen to the floor. Old, dirty shoes had been carelessly tossed about, most of them lying in a jumble of sneakers, work boots and men's sandals. Just as I was about to shut the door, I saw a gallon-sized Ziploc bag partially buried under dirty clothing. I knelt and began tossing stuff off the bag.

When one of the shoes landed in a back corner, a distinctive, buzzing rattle activated every internal alarm I possessed. I looked up to see two beady, really pissed-off eyes glaring at me out of a triangular head. Tiny horns stuck up from its eye ridges, giving the snake an evil, Tyrannosaurus Rex kind of look.

My focus zeroed in on the prehistoric scales covering the flat area between its eyes, with each scale gradually getting larger and more pronounced as they flowed backward onto its coiled, diamond-backed body. We stared at each other a few milliseconds; me, frozen on my knees just inside the door, and it, flicking its tongue in and out in the snaky equivalent of smacking its lips.

I didn't blink. In fact, I'm not sure I could have if I'd wanted to. As the buzzing intensified, adrenaline pumped through my veins, twisting my intestines into a knot. Through my peripheral vision, I watched the rattles blur as they clacked together in the center of the coiled body.

The instant my brain registered some miniscule, indefinable change in its eyes, I leapt backward, barely avoiding being skewered by half-inch fangs. "Shit!"

I landed on my butt and scrambled backward like a crab, putting as much distance between me and the snake as I could. As soon as I thought I had enough room, I flipped over, jumped to my feet and flew through the bedroom door, slamming it shut as I ran.

When I burst into the living room, Casey spun around, spewing the fingerprint powder she'd been holding all over the white tile floor. Her free hand went to the grip of her Glock, pulling it halfway from its holster. When no obvious threat presented itself, she scanned the room, trying to figure out what the hell was wrong with me and why I was acting like a panicked fool.

Not stopping for explanations, I ran to the laundry and grabbed a towel. On my way back to the living room, I twisted it into a tight roll and when I reached the door, I shoved it into the gap along the floor. That done, I stepped back and drew my Glock, aiming it at the brightly colored towel and waiting for the snake to push its evil snout through the cloth. "Shit, shit, shit, shit!"

I shifted from a two-handed grip and used my free hand to feel the pulse at my neck. The rapid pounding of my heart beat so loudly against my fingers that I barely heard Kate's droll voice over the roaring in my ears.

"Problems, Alex?" She stood in the front door, arms crossed, eyebrows raised.

I shot a quick glance her way before immediately returning my attention to the towel. When nothing came slithering out, I lowered my Glock and backed toward the sofa. Suddenly, I imagined snakes hiding under every surface and curled in every dark corner. "Demon from hell, boss."

"Demon from—" She glanced at Casey while I holstered my gun and got down on my hands and knees to check under the sofa.

Casey chuckled, rubbing her eyes with her thumb and forefinger. "Snake?" She knew I was not overly fond of venomous things ever since a rattler had tried to kill me as a kid. When it struck, I'd managed to move fast enough that he'd barely grazed my leg, but my calf had still painfully swollen to three times its normal size. To add insult to injury, I'd had a reaction to the first type of anti-venom they'd given me and had ended up staying in the hospital for two weeks. I've been terrified of getting bitten ever since.

Kate sighed.

I looked up in time to see her going back out the door, shaking her head as she took Chief Sepe's arm and steered him away from the front porch. "They're not quite finished yet, Chief. Let's give them a little time to sort things out."

Sepe allowed her to lead him away, but as his head swiveled around, he caught me watching him. I can't be absolutely certain, but by God I could have sworn I saw an amused glint in his eyes before he turned back and listened to whatever Kate was telling him.

Casey stepped through the swinging door into the kitchen. I listened to her rattle around until she came back holding a long pole with a rope attached. The rope had a loop at one end, with the rest trailing down the length of the shaft. When I saw what she held in her hands, I blurted out, "A snake stick? Where'd you get a snake stick?"

She pointed back over her shoulder. "I saw one in the pantry when I was searching the kitchen. Finding snakes in his house must have been a pretty common occurrence for old Tommy boy. Not everybody keeps one of these hanging in their broom closet."

"You know how to use one of those things?"

"I live so far out in the desert, Alex, I find snakes around my property all the time. Mostly they're king snakes, which I leave alone since they prey on rattlesnakes, but occasionally they miss one and I have to capture and release it a couple miles from my house." She pointed to the door knob. "Can you open it for me, please?"

"The door?" I had no intention of going anywhere near the door.

One eyebrow edged upwards as she cocked her head, waiting for me to move. I sighed, took a deep breath and then forced myself forward, keeping my eyes on the towel, halfway expecting a pink, forked tongue to zip out from where I hadn't quite pushed the roll all the way to the floor. I licked my lips, which had suddenly gone completely dry. "You know, I searched pretty well in there. We can probably just leave well enough alone."

"It's better if *you* open the door so I can hold the pole ready. It takes two hands to operate this thing, and if I have one hand on the doorknob, well, you never know what a pissed off snake might do."

Unfortunately, that made sense. Tentatively edging forward, I stopped about three feet away, leaned over and braced myself on the wall with one hand while I took a firm grip around the doorknob with the other. The second I felt the catch release, I pushed it open and shoved it inward, then rapidly high-stepped across the living room floor, poised and ready to run out the open front door.

Casey burst out laughing. "Where's my camera when I need it?"

I opened my eyes wide and motioned toward the bedroom with little rolling hand gestures, wanting her to get the damn snake and take it as far away from me as possible.

Still grinning, she pushed the door open farther with the stick, glancing around the room trying to locate my attacker. "I don't see her." Moving a little into the room, she spoke in a hushed tone. "Where was she when you first saw her?"

"Her? It's an it! A maniacal, evil-eyed it!" I growled a little as I pointed to the right. "Over there, in the corner of the closet." Casey slowly moved into the room and I jumped when the familiar rattling started. Panicked, I searched the living room, just knowing it had snuck out and was somehow hunting me out here while Casey was hunting it in there.

Casey must have spotted it because she started cooing to the damn thing. "There you are. I wondered where you'd gotten to." She stepped toward the dresser on the left side of the room. "Easy now, I'm not gonna hurt you."

"Would you quit talking to that thing like it's one of your kittens?"

She spoke slowly and quietly as she inched to within lasso range. "Tom built his house right in the middle of this gal's habitat. She probably wandered in by mistake and couldn't find her way out. Not her fault."

Slowly lowering the pole, she brought it to within six inches of the head, then with a quick flip of her wrist, expertly tossed the rope and slipped it around the leviathan's neck; if you can call what snakes have a neck. She'd managed to put the coil just behind the triangular head and had it cinched up tight.

Carefully lifting the pole, she studied the dangling snake with a critical eye. "You're pretty lucky she missed, Alex. She's about three and a half feet long, and when they uncoil, they can leap about half their body length."

I watched as she carried it through the living room, out the front door and past Kate, who was returning to the house alone. I guessed that the chief had probably gone to the hospital to check on Pardo.

She motioned for Casey to wait, then casually examined the snake. There was a short list of things that scared Kate, and apparently rattlesnakes weren't on it. When she'd finished, she motioned Casey on before coming in to talk to me. "That's a good-sized rattler."

"Any rattlesnake's too big for me. I don't mind the non-poisonous snakes so much, but rattlesnakes just feel evil."

"Where was it?"

I pointed toward the bedroom. "In the closet."

"Did you see anything interesting in there before the snake attacked you?"

I studied her, wondering if she was making fun of me. "I have no clue whether there's anything interesting in there or not. I was moving some shoes off a plastic bag when the snake started rattling."

Nodding, she jutted her chin out while she thought. "Do you think he put the snake in there on purpose?"

"What? Hell no! Who'd do that? Who'd even *think* of something as asinine as that?"

Kate tilted her head and glared at me until I realized what I'd just said.

"Well, I mean, I know *you* just thought of it, but nobody in their right mind— I mean, not that *you're* not in your right mind, but—"

She raised a gloved hand. "Enough, Alex."

Casey chose that moment to come through the door still holding her now empty stick. I waved at the closet. "Want to shake that thing around a little bit in there to see if anything bites?"

After grinning and tossing the stick my way, Casey returned to the living room.

Kate started for the door. "We don't have all day, Alex. We still have several sheds and garages to search before we go home. Finish with that closet and meet Casey and me outside when you're done."

Reluctantly, I lowered myself to my knees and stared at the top of the plastic bag poking out from under the clothing. Once more I shoved the stick in and began flicking shoes this way and that, wanting to uncover the bag before sticking my hand in and grabbing it.

What I found surprised me. I didn't figure Jepson to be much of a family man, but there, encased in a Ziploc bag, were several pages, maybe fifty in all, of what looked to be fairly detailed genealogical research. I grabbed the baggie, walked into the living room, and set it on the table.

"Bag it and tag it, Alex." Kate came back inside and walked to the coffee table. She turned the paperwork toward her with tip of her gloved finger. "Let's get whatever prints we can before we take a look inside. We can have the techs dust it back at the office."

Casey had brought in several brown paper evidence bags. I grabbed one and shook it open, placed the baggie with the papers inside, folded the top over several times and taped it shut by running a piece of evidence tape completely across the folded edge. I wrote my name across the tape so I'd know if anyone else opened the bag, and then filled out an evidence form.

When we'd finally finished with the main house, Casey and I stepped outside to see where the other detectives in our unit were searching. Nate Drewery and Allen Brodie stepped out of one of the side buildings toting several evidence bags, so Casey and I headed to the final structure, which looked more like a modern day carriage house than a garage or shed.

The front of the building had two sets of garage doors, each with a row of elongated hexagonal windows in the top third of the door. The opening of the one on the left rose about one and a half times higher than would be necessary for standard sized cars or trucks. There appeared to be only one floor to the building, even though two dormer windows were set under the eaves of a shingled, sharply-pitched roof.

The sun had gone behind the mountains while we'd been searching the house. Across the field, lights had been set up near where Jepson and Pardo had been shot.

Another set of lights glowed off to the right near the mesquite tree where Lido had refused to move when Sam ordered him to track. Sam watched Detective Tony Rico as he dug several test holes to see if anything unusual showed up. Lido watched as well.

I often wonder what goes on in the minds of police dogs. They're definitely a notch above most other dogs in intelligence, and sometimes when I watch one working I know the dog's just happy that their handler has finally come to the same conclusion it had come to fifteen minutes earlier.

Lido seemed to be that type of hound, and as I watched him sitting next to Sam, I wondered what he was thinking, and what he would tell Sam if he could talk.

"What's the matter?" Casey, who'd stopped next to me, followed my line of sight.

"Nothing. I'm just wondering what Lido knows that we don't, and how long it's gonna take us to figure out what it is."

"Hm." Casey grunted. There wasn't much she didn't know about animals. Not in the training sense of the word, but in the literal. She *knew* dogs. She understood them, almost better than she understood people. "Well, if anyone can figure it out, it's Sam. C'mon, we have to search this last building before we can head to the hospital to see how AC Pardo's doing."

"Have you heard anything?"

"Kate's been in contact with some commander at the hospital. Pardo's in surgery. We'll know more when they get done."

We left the evidence bags in her trunk, grabbed some more supplies and entered the large garage.

When we stepped through the door, Casey stopped and let out a low whistle. "Would you look at that?"

In the center of an immaculately organized garage, a show-quality vintage camper stood sentinel behind a beautifully restored antique car.

Nate stepped in after us and I heard his breath catch. His whispered exclamation had a rapturous quality about it. "Oh my God! Would you look at that?"

He slowly walked over to the car and let the palm of his hand hover about an inch above the hood. "What a beauty!"

He eased around to the front, reverently moving his hand along the lines of the fenders, never touching the paint, but hovering just above, as though feeling an aura emanating from within the soul of the machine. He followed the fender's curve, which swooshed from the rear wheel, continued along the bottom of the door and gracefully rose to finally cover the front tire.

I followed and peeked in through the passenger door. "I take it you like old cars?"

He shot me a look of incredulity. "*Old car?* Do you even know what this is?"

I took a step back and studied the vehicle. "Well, it's a car. An old car, like I said before."

His eyebrows morphed into a pained, long-suffering grimace.

I shrugged. "Hey, classic cars are cool, but it seems like every family on the south side has one in their back yard."

He swept his arms wide. "This is a 1937 Mercedes-Benz 540K Special Roadster. It's a very special car. There were only, I don't know, maybe thirty to fifty of these cars ever made. Have you heard of the Blue Goose?"

Both of us shook our heads.

"Well, Reichsmarschall Hermann Göring, the Nazi bastard who started the Gestapo, had one. And one just like it, a 1936, I think, just sold for over eleven million dollars."

I blinked. "Eleven—"

He nodded. "Million."

Casey walked to the trunk of the car, "So, how do you know so much about classic cars?"

A smile lit his face. "Oh, my dad's been rebuilding classics for fifty years. His dad, my grandfather, worked for Ford Motor Company in the thirties and forties, and the two of them used to restore old cars in the back yard. When I came along, they had a wrench and screwdriver in my hand by the time I was three. We'd go to car shows and auctions."

His sigh was so wistful, it made me wonder if I was the only person on the planet who hadn't had a fairytale childhood. He air-wiped a non-existent smudge off the chrome bumper. "Those are the best memories of my childhood. Right now my dad and I are working on an old boat-tail Barchetta we pulled out of an abandoned garage outside of Thatcher. Dad's in his late seventies, but he still keeps up with who's buying what and what vintage cars come onto the market."

Casey stood and patted the camper. "Know anything about this beauty? I've never seen this design before."

Surprised, Nate grudgingly took his eyes off the Roadster, obviously just noticing the camper for the first time. "Nope, sorry. I'm not into campers." He returned to eyeing the Roadster.

I took a minute to look around.

The first building where we'd met Jepson had been in complete disarray, with tools lying haphazardly about and discarded paint cans strewn around the dirty cement floor.

But this building couldn't have been cleaner or more organized.

Instead of a cement floor, white and grey tiles had been laid out in a checkerboard pattern similar to ones I'd seen in some of the old fifties magazines my mom had squirreled away in her library. Stainless steel office furniture took up one corner of the room. There was a glass-topped writing desk with perfectly placed leather desk accessories, and an expensive mahogany and leather chair with silver, nailhead trim on the back and arms. A lavish floor lamp—that if I had to guess, was made from plated nickel and cut crystal—had been placed near the back corner of the desk. Definitely not your everyday garage decor.

I heard Casey snapping on some fresh gloves so I pulled a new pair out of my back pocket and did the same.

A five-drawer mahogany filing cabinet sat in an alcove behind and to the right of the desk. I figured that was as good a place to start as any. Each drawer had an embossed leather card inserted into silver brackets on the front panel and all of them had a small lock seated next to the drawer handle. I tried one of the drawers and discovered it was locked. I called over to Casey, who was in the process of opening the camper door. "Hey, can you toss me the keys?"

She tossed them. "Here you go."

I tried five different keys before one slid in and turned. I opened the top drawer and riffled through several file folders. I didn't find anything particularly interesting, just sales receipts, eBay ads for vintage campers currently on the market and other material necessary to a vintage camper restoration business. Drawers two, three and four were all empty.

In the bottom one, I found a leather-bound ledger, with a large letter J surrounded by a T and an M embossed in gold in the center of the cover. The inscription inside the cover identified the owner as Thomas M. Jepson. A flip of the first page showed that the first entry had been made on February, 12, 1979. The record showed the sale of two vintage Aladdin, indoor, brass, propane lamps which Mr. Jepson had purchased for twenty dollars each from a private party in North Carolina.

Four entries down, he'd sold the lamps for five hundred dollars each to M.B. Stanton-Wald, who lived in Stamford, Connecticut. "Whoa, I am definitely in the wrong business. This guy made, let me see..." I did some calculating on my fingers. "Almost a twenty-four hundred percent increase on some vintage lights. And that was back in 1979."

Nate stopped ogling the car and came to look over my shoulder. "Sounds too good to be true, or legit. How many entries are in the book?"

"I don't know. It starts in 1979, and ends in..." I flipped to the last page. "It ends in 1987." I checked the file drawer where I'd originally gotten the ledger, but it was empty.

Nate and I began searching the room with a purpose now, looking for ledgers that would bring us forward thirty-three years to the present. There weren't any obvious places where a person could hide a safe in the building; no pictures that swung out to reveal a tumbler-locked door, no hidden floor panels opening to a cement-embedded lockbox, and no vaults hidden behind closet doors.

Casey poked her head out of the camper. "Hey, you guys have to see this. It's ten times fancier than my house. Who puts this kind of money into cars and campers?"

As Nate and then I climbed the gold-studded, retractable step that led into the camper, I ran my fingers over an embossed metal plate mounted to the left of the door. The silver, top half of the plate depicted a covered wagon being pulled by two oxen. The brown, checkerboard lower half read The Covered Wagon, Mt. Clemens, Michigan.

Nate whistled as he stepped inside.

When I followed him in I experienced an unaccustomed, almost painful realization that there was my version of a comfortable existence, and then there was a whole other strata of society where the word "money" has no basis in reality.

Awestruck, I ogled the absolutely stunning interior. Glowing maple paneling covered the walls and ceiling. Everywhere you'd expect a hard edge or corner, the walls had been rounded into continuous, flowing contours of grace and refinement. Elegant, hand-woven, silk drapes framed the windows, the deep folds in the gold-flecked material sweeping down to just above the walnut-inlaid, cherry wood flooring.

One of the most intriguing details was the matching set of silk curtains that hung in semi-circular patterns to form a partition between the bedroom and the living area. I pulled my glove off and ran my hand down the material, getting an almost sensual feeling from the soft, gossamer fabric.

Casey's voice startled me out of my revelry. "Watch this."

She flipped a switch.

"Whoa." I stepped over and caressed the brown and crème, semi-transparent countertop that was now backlit by a series of lights shining up from inside the custom designed cabinet. "What's this made of?"

Casey bent to examine the circular patterns embedded in the stone slab. "I'm not sure." She pointed to a framed brochure standing upright in a bracket on the countertop. "That might tell you."

I turned the frame my way so that I could read the description aloud. "Let's see, says here this is a 1937 Deluxe Model 18' Covered Wagon that was custom ordered by Holly Marceau, heiress to the Marceau shipping dynasty."

I skimmed through the pamphlet until I came to the part about the kitchen area. "The elegantly appointed kitchen includes backlit, agate slab countertops, a hammered-copper, under-mount sink along with a matching copper faucet and soap dispenser. It says this same model of camper was once used by Audrey Hepburn as a dressing room on some of her movie sets." I glanced up at Casey. "You think that's true? I wonder if Jepson owned this. Or do you think he just worked on this stuff for other people?"

Casey shrugged. "I don't know. The Jepson we met sure doesn't fit the profile of someone who'd own a multi-million dollar vintage car and camper like this. I think Kate needs to see this place and tell us what she wants done with it."

Casey took out her cell and called Kate, asking her to join us. When she walked in, we climbed out of the camper to meet her.

Nate motioned her over to the Roadster while I returned to the desk to get the ledger and bag it as evidence. Granted, it was more likely to be evidence in Jepson's murder than in our bone in the toilet investigation, but I wanted to have a chance to read through it to see what other information might be hidden among the pages. If homicide got their hands on it first, it'd be months before I saw it again.

There wasn't much evidence to be gathered in this building. "Sparsely elegant" would be a good description of both the furnishings and the contents of the drawers and cabinets.

Kate was in the middle of questioning Nate when I walked up. "Do we know who the vehicle's registered to?"

Nate's blank look was all the answer any of us needed. He'd completely forgotten this was a crime scene, given his excitement at seeing a Roadster in such mint condition. "Uh, no, sorry. I, uh, didn't want to open the door in case I smudged the gloss on the paint. I mean, look! It's like a mirror. You can see yourself!" His excitement flared again as he knelt down and studied his reflection in the highly polished burgundy exterior.

I could hear the slight exasperation in Kate's voice when she asked, "Do these things have a glove box or a trunk?" She opened the passenger door and slid inside where she found and opened a small door in the dashboard and pulled out the registration. "Thomas M. Jepson II. Do we know if the man who was just killed was Jepson the second or the third?"

When we all shook our heads, she turned to me. "Okay, I'm sure homicide will get that all sorted out. Let's wrap things up in here and get the evidence back to the station. Tony dug up a several bones under that mesquite tree, so you two are going to meet back here in the morning to do more digging and sifting. Make sure you bring shovels and rakes. Casey, bring whatever tools you think you'll need to take that holding tank off the camper. Tony volunteered to stand guard tonight to maintain the integrity of the scene."

"I'll be happy to stay here tonight, boss. I don't mind." I'd be happy all right, happy to stay here in the coolness of the night instead of working tomorrow in the heat of the day.

"Tony beat you to it, Alex, but nice try. Once you and Casey get this stuff put into evidence, get a goodnight's sleep and meet back here in the morning."

There wasn't much sense in arguing, so I grabbed all the bags and followed Casey out to the cars. The place was still a hive of activity, so I threw the evidence into the trunk and headed back to the station.

CHAPTER 3

After Casey and I finished bagging and tagging the evidence, we closed up shop and headed down to the garage. I hadn't had any dinner, so on the way home, I stopped at a local burger joint to pick up my usual; one regular-sized burger and two smaller ones for my "kids"— Tessa, who is a white and tan mutt with silky fur and a non-stop tongue, and Jynx, my little Papillion-Chihuahua mix who won't even touch a hamburger if it doesn't have extra pickles loaded on.

I gave my order to the voice in the little box, and when I pulled up to the window, a heavy-set, African American woman I'd come to know as Luvenia was standing at the window waiting to take my money. When she saw me, the sides of her mouth pulled back slightly in what I knew was her version of a hearty welcome.

"That's ten dollars and seventy-six cents." She held out her hand, leaning slightly out the window so I wouldn't accidentally drop the money. "Where's your red-headed frien'?"

She was referring to my best friend since we were in daycare, Megan O'Reilly, who'd actually gotten Luvenia to lift up her shirt and show us her huge stomach and breasts to prove she was much, much heavier than Megan could ever hope to be. In Luvenia's opinion,

Megan didn't hold a candle to her in the beautiful, large woman category.

"Megan? She's at her house, I guess. I'm just getting off work and heading home to the pups. Don't forget Jynx's extra pickles. He'll be really pissed if they aren't there."

Luvenia took my money and counted out my change. "When you gonna bring that little one back here for a visit?"

"Who, Megan or Jynx?"

Her lips twitched again. She had beautiful, brooding brown eyes surrounded by long, black lashes. I squinted slightly, trying to picture her as a young woman. The high cheekbones and contoured lips made it obvious that she'd been a ravishing beauty back in the day. "That little dynamite you brought in that one time. The one with the big ears."

I grinned. "That could still describe either one, but I'm gonna go out on a limb here and assume you're talking about Jynx."

She left the window for a second, then returned with a white paper bag, which she held out to me. "I put some fries in for him. He loved them fries last time."

"Yes he did. Thanks. I'll bring him by sometime to say hello."

She nodded, then got a far-off look in her eyes, probably listening to someone else giving their order. She adjusted the microphone that snaked around from her ear to her mouth. "Welcome to the Patty Palace. Can I take your order?"

I started to drive away, but she held up a finger, asking me to stay a second. When she'd finished with the next customer, she crossed her arms and rested them on the windowsill, her voluminous breasts completely obscuring her forearms as she leaned toward me. "Is Tommy okay?"

That brought me up short. I stared at her a minute, trying to figure out how to answer without compromising the investigation. "Tommy?"

She narrowed her eyes and gave me a no-nonsense glare. "Don't even try to bullshit me, Detective Wolfe. I've been bullshitted by the best of 'em, and you ain't it."

"There's a lot of Tommies in the world, Luvenia. You're gonna have to be a little more specific than that."

"We heard somebody was shot and loaded into an am-bu-lance out near Tommy's place. That true?"

"Well, yeah, someone was shot this afternoon, but I can't say who until we notify next of kin."

Her eyes popped open into wide, startled circles. She straightened up so quickly the headset slipped off her head and landed with a sharp clack on the stainless steel countertop. Looking around wildly, she tore off her Patty Palace apron, threw it at a young man who was filling soda orders and came charging out the side door into the parking lot. She ran—well her feet ran, and her breasts bounced—to my passenger side door. She flipped the handle, expecting it to be unlocked. It wasn't, but as soon as I pushed the unlock button, she threw open the door and slid in.

The car behind me honked, and Luvenia twisted around in her seat, giving the man an evil eye.

I looked in in my rearview mirror. He was holding up his hands in a frightened apology.

Mission accomplished, Luvenia swung back around. "Pull over there." She pointed to an empty parking space to the right of the building.

To say that Luvenia and I were friends would be stretching it. Quite a bit. I turned and glared at her. "Excuse me? I'm the cop, you're the...well, you're not the cop. I'm the one who says pull over, not you."

The guy who'd taken her place in the window yelled across me. "Hey Luvenia, we gettin' backed up. You' blockin' the lane."

She turned the same evil eye on me that she'd just given the guy behind us. I pulled forward, but made sure I didn't park in the spot she'd indicated. Heck, I barely listened to Kate when she ordered me around, and I'd be damned if Luvenia was going to tell me what to do. When I'd thrown the gearshift into park, she started right in. "He's dead? Tommy's dead?"

"How did you hear that someone named Tommy had been shot?"

Her nostrils flared. "Is...he...dead?"

"Answer my question and maybe I'll answer yours. How did you hear that someone named Tommy was shot?"

She sat back in the seat and stared out of the windshield. We were facing an ice cream shop with our trunk angled toward the Patty Palace, and we watched as several pre-teen girls loaded into an SUV, each one holding a double- or triple-scoop cone. "A lady came in, one of our reg'lars. Said she was driving by Tommy's place and saw an ambu-lance and a shitload of cop cars parked next to the ol' camper. She said they was loadin' somebody in the back." She turned to me again. "Now you answer me, Detective Wolfe. I gotta know. Is Tommy dead or not?"

I rubbed my eyes. I could smell the hamburgers. I hadn't eaten since early that morning, and I wanted nothing more than to take my burgers home, feed one to Tessa and one to Jynx and climb happily into bed. "Look, I promise I'll answer your question, but first, I need to know how you know this Tommy person, and what his last name is."

Her nostrils flared again, and I swiveled around so I could put my hand on her shoulder. "I'm not trying to jerk you around, Luvenia. I'm a cop in the middle of an investigation, and there's a certain way I have to do things."

Her lips disappeared inside her mouth while she digested all that. "Tommy 'n me, we been close sometimes." She turned and held my gaze, and I couldn't help looking down at the small diamond she wore on her left ring finger.

"*Close* close?"

"That surprise you? You think men don't like plus-sized women?"

"Actually, that hadn't even crossed my mind." I indicated her left hand with a lift of my chin. "Your wedding ring is what crossed my mind."

She twisted the ring around her finger, absently playing with it while she once more stared at the people coming and going from the ice cream shop. She spoke so softly, I almost couldn't catch her words. "His last name's Jepson." Her eyes became misty and she swiped at a tear before it could roll down her cheek.

I blew out a breath. "Yeah. He was killed today. I'm sorry."

The people at the shop next door continued going in empty-handed and coming out with scoops of pink, green, brown or blue ice cream. Two little girls wearing matching pink-striped pants and pink shirts with pink and purple wings sewn onto the back went in and ordered, each one accepting their cone with a giggle and a curtsy. Life just seems to go on no matter how many tragedies occur. While these people were enjoying their ice cream, Tom Jepson was lying on a coroner's slab, Pardo was in surgery fighting for his life, and the dispatcher was sending units to an armed robbery that had just happened down the street.

I listened to the radio chatter while we sat in my car, Luvenia trying to hold back her tears and me fervently hoping she'd succeed. "Did your husband know about you and Tom?"

Her eyes narrowed as she once more turned an icy glare in my direction.

That didn't particularly bother me, since what I was interested in finding out was whether she or her husband had a reason to want Tom Jepson dead. "Okay, then answer me this. How long have you known Tom?"

"We both grew up in this neighborhood. I've known him all my life. His daddy was rich, and mine ran out on my momma and me when I was three. But honestly? I'm not sure whether Tom or me got the worser deal as far as daddies go."

"And your husband? Did he know Tom as well?"

She nodded, finally looking out the front window again. "Malcolm an' him was best friends. We all grew up t'gether. Malcolm's daddy worked for Mr. Jepson like my momma did. When I say Mr. Jepson, I mean Tom's father." Her mouth crinkled in disgust. "Basta'd that he was. The world's a better place with that old man dead, gone and buried."

"Is it a better place with his son dead, too?"

"No, no, no. No way." She shook her head back and forth for emphasis. "Tom fixed up a trailer for Malcolm and me and didn't charge us a penny. That's what he did, fix up trailers for folks. It's supposedly how his grandaddy made all his money but I didn't buy it then and I don't believe it now."

"Why not?"

"Cuz one day they was middleclass, nothin' special, and th' next they was buildin' them buildin's and buyin' expensive cars and other stuff."

"When was this?"

"Oh I don't know, we was around seven I guess."

I pulled a fry out of the bag and bit off an end. "Look, Luvenia, I need to know if your husband knew about you and Tom. I can tell you don't want to talk about this, but unfortunately it's either talk to me now, or the homicide detectives will pull you and Malcolm downtown for questioning."

She put her head against the headrest and sighed. "He knew." She turned toward me. "You gonna think it's screwed up, but he didn't care. Malcolm, well, sometimes—" Her cheeks turned a darker shade of mahogany, and I realized, somewhat inappropriately for this particular moment, that an African American's physiological response is exactly the same as a Caucasian's, so of course they'd blush when they were embarrassed.

"Sometimes what?"

She didn't answer, so I thought I'd help her out. "Look, I've been a cop long enough to have seen just about everything you can imagine, so if you think you're gonna shock me, or if you're worried I'm gonna judge you—well, you won't, and I won't."

She tried again. "Well, sometimes—" She shrugged, then indicated her belly with a sweep of her hands. "Look at me, Detective Wolfe. You think they's enough of me to go around for more than one man?"

I looked away to try to hide a smile, but then gave up and grinned at her. "Don't forget I saw your breasts when you flashed Megan. You've got enough for two people per breast and more besides."

All of a sudden tears began running down her face.

"Oh shoot. I'm sorry, Luvenia. That wasn't called for."

The side of her mouth quirked up. "That's not why I'm cryin', Detective. I'm gonna miss him, that's all. You right. One on each breast and another doin' a southie besides." She shook her head. "Lord, we gonna miss that man."

CHAPTER 4

I finally made it home around midnight. Luvenia had grabbed the bag with my now-cold hamburgers and had returned to her position at the cashier's window. She sent the young man who'd taken over for her out with a bag of fresh burgers, a full order of fries, two apple turnovers, and a large drink.

After I settled in the kitchen and unwrapped the burgers, Tessa gobbled hers so fast I doubt she even tasted the special secret sauce that came standard on every burger.

Jynx did what he always did when I treated him to one of the Palace's burgers. He set the whole thing on the floor, tipped off the top bun and carefully ate all his pickles. Then, after he'd gobbled up the meat and bottom part of the bun, he jumped on the top part with both front feet and began sliding around the tiled kitchen floor. He especially loved it when they put on enough extra sauce to allow him to take a running leap and pounce on the bread with enough momentum to send him scooting half-way across the room. Of course, Tessa followed behind licking up whatever mustard tracks Jynx left behind.

I left them playing in the kitchen and walked to my bedroom with what was left of my food. I'm not sure if it was the near brush with heat stroke, the carbs in the burger and fries or just the fact that it was after midnight, but the next thing I knew I was waking up to my alarm. The french fry container, several decimated ketchup packets and the white paper bag were shredded into tiny pieces, all of which now lay scattered on my sheets and bedspread.

Tessa, who rested comfortably on one of my pillows, had a red band of ketchup lining her hairy white jowls.

Sighing, I lifted the bedspread where I knew I'd find Jynx. He tended to be a little cold-blooded, and I could always count on him burrowing under the covers at some point during the night, rain or shine, summer or winter, full bed or not. His little lips puffed out every time he exhaled, which was a sure sign he was still asleep. But instead of using a pillow to rest his head, he was using the top bun of my hamburger that he'd carefully placed with the secret sauce side-down.

It was obvious what had happened. He and Tessa had gone on a quiet feeding frenzy after I'd fallen asleep without finishing my dinner. Since Jynx's stomach is so small, he'd filled up before she did. I'm sure he'd grabbed the bun and scurried under the covers, determined to make sure that if he couldn't finish it, Tessa wouldn't get it either.

After a quick shower and breakfast, I headed back to the camper to meet up with Casey. On the way, I called my friend, Ruthanne Stall, who was one of the homicide detectives working on Jepson's murder. I filled her in on my conversation with Luvenia and gave her the contact information.

When I hung up, my phone immediately rang with Kate's siren ring. "Alex, I just had a call from a woman who knew Tom Jepson. She said she and her friends have some information we might want. When I told her we were working on a different case and that she should call Jon Logan or Ruthanne, she asked if our case had anything to do with the old camper. I told her I'd send you over to take her statement."

"Okay, hang on a second." I pulled into a toy store parking lot and took a notebook out of my back pocket. After fruitlessly rummaging around in my briefcase for a pen, I dumped the contents onto the passenger seat. Old notebooks, file folders, a tape recorder and other miscellaneous junk tumbled out in a disorganized pile. I heard Kate's voice coming from my cell phone, which I'd unceremoniously thrown onto the dashboard.

"Take your time, Alex. It's not like I have anything else planned for the day."

"Hang on, Boss. I know I've got a pen here somewhere."

"Pick up the phone, Alex." When I did, she spoke as though she was explaining the concept of Legos to a seven year old. "Do you remember me telling you to download the Sticky Notes app onto your cell phone? Now would be the time to use it." She paused, waiting for me to find the app. After several seconds, she let out an irritated sigh. "Never mind. I'll just text the information instead of waiting for you to find the damn app."

I saw the end of a pen sticking out of a notebook and grabbed it. "Got a pen boss. What's the address?" I heard the text notification on my phone, and realized she'd already hung up and texted the information. I read the address she'd sent and tossed the phone back onto the dash before pulling out into traffic and heading into Midtown.

The home where Kate had sent me was in the same upscale neighborhood as my mafia friend, Gianina Angelino. At one time, these million dollar homes had been built on the outskirts of town, but over the years, urban sprawl had not only surrounded the area, but had continued east for another thirty miles or so.

I turned onto one of the avenues that led into the enclave, and followed the twisting roads as they wound this way and that, with none of them following any real, logical pattern. My guess was the people who'd originally built in this area weren't interested in what the city engineers thought about logical road development and infrastructure. They'd had enough money to grease the palms of the most influential men at the city planning office and, judging by the complete lack of organized transit, had dropped their homes wherever they wanted and let the engineers worry about how to build the roads around them, instead of the other way around.

Imported palms lined several driveways, their ninety-foot trunks dwarfing the smaller citrus trees planted in many of the artfully landscaped front yards. I pulled around a corner and was surprised to see five beautifully renovated vintage campers lined up along the edge of the road. The smaller ones were hitched to sedans while the longer and heavier ones were pulled by trucks or SUVs.

A group of five women sat on lawn chairs in one of the yards. I quickly checked Kate's text for the address and confirmed that the large, ranch-style home was where I was supposed to meet the lady. Kate hadn't mentioned there were going to be five of them, and I hoped I wouldn't need to spend the entire morning talking to all of them.

I pulled to a stop behind a small camper, the lower half of which was painted a glossy, mint green while the upper half was a dirty cream that reminded me of an old, lacy curtain that's been stored away in some trunk for the last hundred years or so.

As I got out of my car, five heads swiveled my way. I shut my door just as a woman in her mid-sixties started toward me. I stepped around the front of my car to greet her. "Mrs. Ketterly?"

The crags and valleys in her forehead deepened as she squinted through heavily-lidded eyes. She wore a white cotton blouse over a green tank top, jeans, and leather, closed-toed sandals. She kind of reminded me of a cocky little Marine drill instructor who stood five-four but who looked six feet tall to her terrified recruits.

"That's me." Her gaze roamed from my head down to my shoes before finally coming to rest on my badge. "You look too young to be a detective. How long have you been on the department?"

I shrugged. "Long enough I guess."

"For what?"

I smiled at the lady, recognizing her attempt to take charge and direct the interview from the get go. "You told my sergeant you had some information for us." I lifted my hands, palms up. "Here I am."

A second woman stood and pointed at me. "Hey. You're the cop who's friends with Gianina Angelino. I've seen your picture on the news." She glanced around at the other ladies who held various drinks that, judging by the flushed cheeks and silly grins, were laced with more than lemonade.

I glanced at my watch. Ten o'clock and already a bit tipsy. Sounded like a club Megan might enjoy.

The second woman continued speaking. "The Angelinos have lived in this neighborhood—" She paused and glanced at Mrs. Ketterly.

"What do you think, Phyla? Thirty years?" She waited for Mrs. Ketterly to answer.

The older woman simply lifted one shoulder.

The other lady took that as a yes and continued. "And that woman's never so much as spoken to any one of us. Like she's too good to even bother." She pinched her thin lips together as she studied me, her eyes roving up and down in critical assessment. "I don't see what you have that we don't. Why would she even give someone like you the time of day?"

I took a small step backward, surprised at the unexpected verbal assault. I studied her a little more closely after that volley of good cheer. If the first woman could be described as lithe and stalwart, the best words I could come up with for the second was podgy and slightly...oily. There was something rat-like about the way her eyes darted between me and the other women, looking for some hint of approval from her friends. I had no intentions of getting into a conversation about me and Gia, so I turned back to Mrs. Ketterly. "Is there someplace we can speak in private?"

Before she could answer, the second woman scurried over. "Oh, we all intend to help you find out what's been going on at Tom's place. I always thought he—"

"Darla. Go sit down. Please."

Darla blinked at Mrs. Ketterly, who lowered her chin and stared pointedly at her. "Darla" must have gotten the message because she obediently returned to the circle of women, stopping momentarily at a red and white cooler to pull out a can of Hatch Light beer.

I grimaced when I saw what she'd chosen. "Ugh."

I didn't think I'd said it out loud, but I heard Mrs. Ketterly mumble under her breath. "No kidding. A can of piss would taste better as far as I'm concerned."

I answered back just as quietly. "If you pour it into a glass, that's exactly what it looks like."

She snorted quietly, then patted me on the back and pointed to a glossy red two-door camper. "That's mine. We can talk in there." She walked over to the cooler and pulled out two hard lemonades. "Want one?"

The heat already had the birds sitting in the shade with their little beaks hanging open. There's nothing I'd have liked more than to kick back and have a cold one. I eyed the bottle longingly. "I wish, but I'm on duty." I craned my neck to see what else she had in there. "A diet soda would be great, though."

Smiling slightly, she nestled the second hard lemonade back into the ice and pulled out a bottle of diet root beer. She held it up, silently asking if that would do.

I took it from her. "That'd be great. Thanks."

All of the women were looking at us expectantly, and Mrs. Ketterly obliged them with a quick round of introductions. "Detective Wolfe, these are some of the ladies in our camper club. The blonde over there is Leslie Schuman."

A small-waisted woman wearing a cheery yellow striped shirt over yellow cotton pedal pushers beamed at me with a mouthful of brilliant white teeth.

I nodded to her as Ketterly moved on and pointed to a rather short, stout woman who could have had a job as the dwarf Gimli's wife in *The Lord of the Rings*. "This is Agnes St. Germaine, the club's historian."

Agnes gave me a friendly wave and I nodded to her as well.

Mrs. Ketterly's voice dropped to a monotone. "You've met Darla England."

I nodded. I didn't want to give Darla any chance to start talking about Gia again, so I quickly looked toward the final woman, hoping Ketterly would catch the hint and move on. Darla opened her mouth to speak, and I felt a surge of gratitude when Ketterly immediately walked over and rested her hand on the final woman's shoulder. "And this is Sonya Walks With Bears."

Sonya was a strikingly exotic Native American whose eyes sparkled with mischief and good humor. She wore her short, black hair spiked in the front, giving her just a hint of attitude to go with her slightly bemused expression.

Ketterly pointed to her camper. "Now that we've gotten that out of the way, let's go talk."

Her camper was larger than the others with two doors instead of one. Each door had a porthole window set into it and there were retractable steps below. The rear end of the camper flared out slightly, probably to give a few extra inches of space on the inside. She'd painted the body a deep, glossy red and the roof some type of off white.

"This camper's different from the others. What kind is it?"

She beamed with pride. "This is a collector's piece. There are only a few of her kind known to still exist." She patted the skin affectionately. "She's a 1950 Liberty Coach. Her skin is made from Masonite, so most of this type of camper rotted away after about 15 years. This one was kept as a cottage and they built walls and a roof around it."

Seeing the gleam in her eye I expected her to lean in and kiss the door, but she climbed onto the step and pulled herself inside instead. When I stepped through the camper door, I was surprised to see that the interior was almost as nice as the one in Tom's showroom, just not quite as flamboyant. The paneling was some type of highly polished, light-colored wood. The front dinette, where she indicated I should sit, was a small table off the back side of the island counter. Three chairs were arranged around it, so I squeezed in so my back was to the wall, screwed the top off my soda and drank deeply.

Mrs. Ketterly sat across from me and did the same with her hard lemonade.

I set the bottle down on the coaster she provided and after getting the preliminaries out of the way—like address and phone number—I started in on my questions. "So, you guys are in some kind of camper club?" I'd drunk the root beer way too fast. An uncomfortable bubble of gas was rising in my throat. I gritted my teeth to try to hold it in, but she knew immediately what I was doing.

"Go ahead. Let it out. Better out than in I always say."

I put my fist to my mouth and tried to burp as quietly as I could.

Her leathery cheek pulled up in a half smile. "In answer to your question, we're all Camp Vamps. We're a nationwide club of vintage camper owners. Mostly women, but some husbands tag along. There are about seventy members, and it all started right here in Tucson." She made a point to catch my eye. "Tom renovated about half of the campers in the club."

"So he was a friend?"

She puffed some air out of her nose, then tapped the bottom edge of her bottle on the table. "No, actually, he was a son of a bitch who treated most people with unbridled contempt. I don't know of a single Vamp he hasn't insulted or angered at one time or another."

"Do you think any of them were angry enough to kill him?"

"No. We may get a little rowdy at some of our rallies and campouts, but none of us even come close to being killers." She wrinkled her brow. "Some of the husbands on the other hand—" She paused to think about that for a second. "No, I can't picture any of them killing him either. But I thought Sergeant Brannigan said your squad wasn't investigating his murder."

"Well, we're working alongside the homicide unit, helping out where we can. So when you called you said you had some information about the old camper we found in the field close to his property."

There wasn't an odor of stale cigarette smoke in the air, so I was a little surprised when she pulled a pack of Virginia Slims out of a hidden compartment concealed in the paneling just above the little table where we sat.

The swiveling drawer was actually kind of ingenious. When she tapped the wall just above the table, a three by five inch portion of the paneling swung inward on hidden hinges, allowing the top part to swing out. Tucked inside was a cavity large enough to hold a pack of cigarettes, or a small derringer, whichever you preferred.

She tapped the pack against her fingers, and then offered me one.

I shook my head.

Pulling one out for herself, she began rapping the filtered end on the table. "Mind if I have one, then?"

Second hand smoke always made me slightly queasy, but I didn't think I had much choice, so I shrugged. "It's your camper."

She studied me a minute while she continued to tap the cigarette on the table, giving it a little bounce every third tap or so. "I know whose camper it is. That's not what I asked."

Not many people were abrupt and to the point anymore, and I found her no-nonsense way of communicating refreshing. "Okay then.

Yes, I mind. Smoke makes me sick to my stomach, and I hate smelling like formaldehyde and gasoline for the rest of the day."

She looked slightly confused so I explained.

"I had a seventh grade science teacher who made us learn what the manufacturers put in cigarettes. Formaldehyde, which they use to embalm people, Benzene, found in gasoline, Polonium 210 which is radioactive and toxic, arsenic, and lead cadmium. There are a lot more, but that list was enough to turn me off the little bastards."

She stuffed it back in the carton. "Fair enough." Apparently she not only spoke bluntly to people, but appreciated the same in return. She plopped the pack back into the secret drawer and pushed it closed. "The reason I contacted your sergeant was because I received a call from a woman in our club who said she'd heard Tom had been shot."

Her unconcerned shrug confirmed just how much she really didn't care that the man was dead. "Not a loss to humanity, but a loss to the vintage camping community. He knew his stuff as far as restoration goes. Most people specialize in one or two manufacturers. Shasta or maybe a Scotty or one of the others. Tom could work on them all. Yellowstone, Trotwood, Airstream, Vagabond—you name it, he or his father restored at least one of every kind out there."

She looked out the window at the circle of women. "In fact, he restored all of our group's campers, mine included. What a waste for a scabrous blight on humanity's arse to be gifted with such an incredible, God-given talent."

I was torn between needing to hurry her along, and wanting her to talk my ears off, because she kept the interior of her camper at what felt like a cool seventy degrees. All in all, sitting in a comfortable camper and drinking an ice-cold root beer won out over meeting Casey and tearing apart the old camper. Silence is usually an effective interviewing technique, so I nodded and waited for her to continue, which she did.

"He's probably renovated hundreds of campers in his lifetime, more if you count the ones he helped his father rebuild when he was growing up." She sat forward, leaning her forearms on the tabletop and lacing her fingers together. "I was best friends with his wife, Ella. They bought that little camper you're talking about the same year they were married. I think that was right around 1974. The two of them, and me and my wife, used to travel all around the country together."

I blinked. The part about the wife kinda threw me. "Your...wife?"

Nodding, she cocked her head and studied me. "You have a problem with that?"

I quickly held up my hands. "No! Not at all, but women couldn't get married thirty years ago. Well, not to another woman anyway."

"Not legally. But she was my wife just the same. Anyway, when Ella died, he parked that camper and never touched it again. He just let it rot." She sat back and rested her arm across the back of her seat. "Does that strike you as a little odd for a man who makes a living restoring and selling old campers?"

"Not really. If the camper reminded him of her, I could see why he'd want to hold onto it. And I'd understand not wanting to work on it if doing so reminded him of someone he'd loved and lost."

She snorted. "Hardly loved and lost. They hated each other. Traveling with them was a nightmare, and the only reason Kelly and I did it was because Ella asked us to. She was afraid of him, and she was absolutely terrified of his father."

"Why did they go camping together, then?"

"Because his father made them. That was supposedly how he—" She wiggled two fingers on each hand indicating quotation marks. "Made his money. Tom and Ella would travel to camping jamborees and shows in their renovated campers and people would go gaga over them. Orders would pile in after they'd been to a show."

"Why do you say, supposedly? And I thought you said they travelled around in that little camper that's parked in the field, not in campers they'd renovated."

The ladies outside were starting to get loud.

Ketterly listened to them for a while, tapping her fingers on the table to a song only she could hear. "All I can tell you for sure, Detective Wolfe, is nothing was as it seemed with the Jepsons. Ella used to say if Tom's mouth was open, he was lying about something. She also said if Mick Jepson's mouth was open, he was hurting someone and making a buck doing it."

She brushed a fly away from her hair. "As far as why they needed the little camper, if they didn't have one ready to show, they'd take it to an event and pin pictures of some of the campers they'd already sold on a corkboard."

"Call me Alex. Who's Mick Jepson? Tom's father?"

"Then you call me Phyllis, or Phyla. That's what my friends usually shorten it to. And yes, Mick was Tom's father. It's what people called him anyway. His real name was Thomas Michael Jepson II. I once saw him ram a man's head through the rungs of a ladder and kick the ladder over because the man accused Mick of lying. Another time, Ella showed up at my door with two teeth knocked out. She said she'd accidentally tripped over a gallon of special order paint and Mick had grabbed the can and smashed it into her face."

She glowered at the bottle in her hand before setting it to her lips and taking a long, slow drink. She eased it down onto the table, turning it while she gathered her thoughts. "When I saw what he'd done to her, when she held her fist out to me and dropped her teeth into my hand, I wanted to kill him."

She raised her gaze from the table and leaned toward me. "She'd shut down. Her entire face was covered in blood, from the top of her forehead to the bottom of her chin. If I'd have had the guts, or the opportunity—" She rubbed her eyes with her thumb and forefinger, gathering in her emotions with an effort. "Ah well, they're all three dead now, I guess. No use wasting my time getting angry all over again."

Thinking about her friend reminded me of all the women I'd spoken to who'd been missing teeth or patches of hair or worse. I leaned back in my seat. "I'm going to ask you a question, but I need you to keep what I say confidential, okay?"

"Sure." Her eyes crinkled again. "You're gonna have a three-ringed circus here pretty soon anyway. You don't need me adding to it."

I looked at her suspiciously. "Why?"

"I told you, there are close to seventy members in the Camp Vamps Vintage Camper Club. Most of us are retired and bored, so the chance to help solve a murder of one of our own— Well, let's just say they're circling the wagons and heading to town."

I sat back and rubbed my eyes. "Oh my God." There's nothing

worse than having people who don't know what they're doing trying to help you solve a crime. More often than not, they destroy evidence and screw up interviews. I stared at her for a moment, wondering how Kate was going to contain seventy bored, intoxicated, wannabe investigators. "Seventy?"

"Well, I think only about twenty or so will actually show up." She let me stew on that awhile before asking, "So what was your question?"

"Only twenty." I rolled my eyes. "That's just great. Okay, anyway, I wanted to ask you if you'd ever seen anything...out of the ordinary in the old camper."

She shook her head. "No. Not when Ella was alive, and I haven't been in it since he parked it."

"How did Ella die?"

"Waldenström Macroglobulinemia." At my blank look, she added, "Lymphoma."

"How the hell do you remember Waldenström whatever it was you just said?"

"Waldenström Macroglobulinemia. I was a cancer research specialist in another life. I retired about ten years ago. I got tired of big pharmaceuticals buying the patents to all the major cancer breakthroughs so they could continue to make billions by selling people chemo drugs that don't work." She sighed. "But don't get me started. What else do you want to know?"

I filed away *cancer researcher* and *really, really smart* in the back of my mind before asking, "Did Tom's wife have an open or closed casket?" Now it was her turn to look blank. I held up a finger asking for patience. "Humor me."

It was obvious she was trying to figure out where I was going with my question. Her brows came down as she stared into my eyes. "She was cremated."

Okay, that meant the femur probably hadn't been hers. "Here's the part you need to keep to yourself. What's the first thing that comes to mind when I say we found old human bones in the camper?"

Phyla crossed her arms and leaned back into the cushion, squinting slightly as she stared at me for a few seconds. "Human?" Her gaze rapidly tracked back and forth while she thought about what I'd just said.

There's such a huge difference between interviewing someone with a sharp, quick mind, and interviewing a drug-addled low life who can't even focus on a hand held directly in front of his nose. When asked a question, an addict's eyes might track to the left, then slowly up so he can contemplate the pretty patterns in the ceiling tiles, before finally coming back full circle to rest on me. Then, more often than not, he'll ask me to repeat the question and the process begins all over again.

Not Phyla. She considered my question, took just long enough to gather her thoughts, and formulated an answer. "The first thing I think of is that one time, Tom had a cookout for the Vamps on his property. Some of the ladies wandered over to see the old camper and came back with a story about seeing a bone stuffed down the toilet.

"By that time, Tom was working on his sixth or seventh Jack and Coke, and he started in about an old brahma bull he used to keep in his pasture to warn off people who thought stealing trailer parts from his stockpile would be a walk in the park." She lifted her hands in a gesture of surrender. "He regales us with that idiotic story every time he gets drunk, and if I have to hear him tell it one more time—"

She paused, suddenly remembering the man was dead and no longer capable of telling anybody anything. "Well anyway, he *used* to go on about how many people his gray demon—" She rolled her eyes. "That's what he called the bull, his gray demon. So, anyhow, he'd brag about how many people the bull had chased from his property.

"At some point, the animal apparently strangled itself in some strands of fencing wire, and Tom said he just left it out in the field. He said one day he'd noticed someone had stuffed part of his dead bull down the toilet." She lowered her chin and held my gaze. "Now you're saying it's a human bone, not a bull's?"

"Any ideas about whose bones they might be?"

"Absolutely none."

"Is Tom's mother still alive?"

"So they're women's bones."

This lady was quick. "Actually, I don't know if they're male or female. I'm just trying to account for all the people who may have lived on the property since Tom parked the camper."

"Tom's mother was Linda Jepson, Mick's first wife. She died in a commercial airliner crash when Tom was, I think, about five or six. I don't imagine they found any bones to bury. Mick remarried. It was a perfect match. She's a real witch."

I was feeling pretty comfortable around her, so I thought I'd clarify. "A nasty piece of work, huh?"

She chuckled and shook her head, then tossed back another swallow of the hard lemonade. Humor sparkled in her eyes as she looked at me down the barrel of the bottle. When she finished, she wiped her mouth with a napkin before reaching over to set the empty bottle onto her red laminate countertop. "No, I meant what I said. She really is a witch. He met her on a trip to the Andes when Tom, Ella and I were still in middle school. She was apparently a very powerful village bruja, or witch. Back then, she was stunningly beautiful, in a dark, exotic kind of way. She still is as far as that goes.

"Mick decided he had to have her. He basically kidnapped her and brought her back to the States with him. She absolutely loathed him, and never missed an opportunity to call down curses on him and Tom."

Sometimes, I loved my job. Where else would you hear the kind of stories I'd been hearing about Tom Jepson and his family? "So what happened to her? Is she still alive?"

"She is. In fact, she's one of the charter members of our club. Word travels pretty fast among the Vamps. She'll be here in a few days. She said she was driving down from Yellowstone to do a celebration dance on the spot where Tom died."

She grinned. "I watched her do one on Mick's grave after most of the mourners had left the cemetery. She did some kind of intricate dance steps around the grave for about five minutes, then stood right over the open hole, lifted her skirts and pissed down onto the coffin." Laughter kind of bubbled up from somewhere deep inside her chest, which took me completely by surprise since she hadn't shown much of a reaction to anything we'd talked about so far.

She leaned forward on her forearms again. "And you know what? Ella, my wife, Kelly, and I all joined her!" She sat back and smiled, obviously lost in a pleasant memory. "Best purification ritual I've ever seen. Cleanses the soul, by God."

While I digested that little gem, someone knocked on the camper door. Before we could respond, Darla pulled it open and stuck her head in. "Rhonda and Amy just arrived. They're going to set up out at Catalina State Park. I thought you might want to say hi before they left."

Phyla nodded and slid out of the booth. I handed her my business card, which she stuck on the door of her refrigerator with a pink flamingo magnet. I indicated the card with a lift of my chin. "Call me if you think of anything. And when Mick's widow gets here, would you give her my number and ask her to call me as well?"

She reached over to a shelf just above the little sofa at the back of the camper and took a card off the top of a pile. "Sure. Here's my card if you need to contact me for any reason. And if I hear any interesting stories around the campfire once all the gals get here, I'll let you know. I think you'd like most of the people in the Vamps. We come from all walks of life: a former zoo keeper, a paleontologist, a cowboy." She stopped and indicated my badge. "Heck, Sonya Walks With Bears is a major in the Army Reserve. She's in military intelligence. You'd like her. Very down to earth."

I nodded. "Maybe someday when I'm not working a case. But in the meantime, I need to get back to work." I slipped past Darla and headed for my car. Another camper had pulled up behind me, and I looked back at the circle of folding chairs on the lawn.

Two more women had joined the group and were happily chatting away with their friends. As I watched, one of the women glanced casually in my direction. When she saw me watching her, she nodded once and winked, then smiled before turning back to the group.

I needed to get going, but I decided I wanted to pass around my business card just in case anyone else had something interesting to say. I walked over to the group and laid a pile of cards on an outdoor camping table, said my goodbyes and left.

CHAPTER 5

As I drove away, I checked my watch to see if I had enough time to stop by Gia's home since I was already in the neighborhood and had something I wanted to talk to her about. I figured Casey wouldn't mind working alone for a little while longer, so I turned onto Gia's street and thought about the many changes she'd made to her home since the first time I'd come for a visit.

Several months earlier, a rival mafia hit squad had shot their way into the home and killed her father. Since then, a black Cadillac Escalade constantly patrolled the nearby streets, and armed guards were stationed at strategic locations around the front and back patio walls.

The local homeowners association had started a petition to force Gia out of the neighborhood, but she refused to let anyone tell her where she could or could not live. Honestly, she had too much pull within the local government to worry about any kind of petition having a snowball's chance in hell, but her neighbors hadn't let that stop them from trying.

Gia's guards were used to seeing my car by now, so when I pulled up in front of her home, all I got was a raised chin from Luca, one of the men in the Suburban, as it drove by.

A six-foot adobe wall surrounded the front yard, and one of the most dangerous looking men I'd ever known met me at the door to the inner courtyard. His full name is Agapito, which, absurd as it may seem, means, "beloved," in Italian. Pito's slicked-back hair, scarred lip, pockmarked face and left eyebrow that had been re-arranged by a nasty set of brass knuckles all combined into one mean looking dude. An unfortunate set of familial genes had given him what my grandmother used to call an eagle-beaked nose, one that slanted down from between his eyes to a point where it dramatically hooked south, stopping just short of his upper lip.

He was thirty-two, had grown up in Chicago, been arrested four times, acquitted three, and on the fourth had spent five years in the medium security Mahoney State Correctional Institution in Frackville, Pennsylvania on manslaughter charges. Apparently, a Pennsylvania jury had thought "accidentally" running down a man in the street, and then "accidentally" backing over him again to "go back to make sure he was okay" was a viable enough explanation to knock the charge down from first-degree murder to manslaughter. No hint of a mob payoff in that little jury box, now was there?

How do I know all this? Because the little gnome who sits on my shoulder had started jumping up and down and pulling my hair the very first time I'd laid eyes on the guy. I'd run a complete background check. I never turned my back on him, but neither did I give him even the slightest hint that his macho posturing or his not-so-veiled imbecilic threats bothered me.

He stood in the entrance to the courtyard with his legs apart and arms crossed, effectively blocking my way into the inner sanctum. I could have ordered him to move, but I decided to wait and see if he'd to step aside on his own.

"Mith Angelino didn't thay you wath comin'." The v-shaped scar that bisected his lower lip made it impossible for him to pronounce esses. I'd heard that when he was a kid, a bullet had ricocheted off a rock, pierced his lip, taken out three of his lower teeth along with part of his tongue and lodged in his upper palate. Pretty damn lucky, if you consider the bullet had been on a direct course for his very small, mostly empty, brain pan.

I crossed my arms. "So?" Obviously, he and I had never really bonded. Like most of Gia's employees, he was the son of one of her father's goons. The older crime syndicates like to ensure the loyalty of their employees by keeping it in the family. He'd worked for the Angelinos for the last fifteen years, but never as one of Gia's bodyguards until a few months ago.

"Tho, y'ain't comin' in."

I wasn't in the mood for games. I shoved him aside with a forearm to his chest, but he grabbed my throat and slammed me into the wrought-iron gate.

He kept his pistol in a holster down the front of his pants, and while he was grabbing me, I hooked the grip with my thumb, pulled the gun out and poked the barrel into his right eye far enough so he knew it was there. "You wanna go back to prison, Asshole?"

He squeezed my neck a little harder, and I squeezed the trigger just enough so he could see the hammer slowly moving back into the firing position. He quickly let go and stepped back, holding his arms out to the side to show he wasn't really going to hurt me after all.

I continued to aim at his head until Gia's personal bodyguard, Gabe, stepped out of the front door and slowly walked our way, glancing sideways at the goon before turning a deadpan expression my way. "Ms. A said she'd appreciate it if you didn't hurt him this time, Alex. He was out two weeks after you popped his thumb the last time."

Truth be told, I hadn't meant to really hurt the guy the last time we'd gotten into a shoving match. I'd used a martial arts technique Mr. Myung and I had been practicing. When I'd leveraged Pito's momentum, he'd gone flying over my shoulder, landing face first in the dirt. I guess Mr. Myung should have told me to let go of the guy's thumb as he sailed through the air, since I nearly amputated it when he landed.

I lowered the Berretta, released the magazine, which I pocketed, and cleared the chamber. I pocketed that round as well. Gabe watched as I field stripped the gun, systematically throwing the pieces around the yard as I came to them. The recoil spring went into the middle of the rose garden, the barrel I tossed up into the branches of a lemon tree.

I handed the frame back to Pito. "Here. You'll get the bullets back when I leave." At any other time, I'd throw his ass in prison for assaulting a cop, but Gia was in the middle of a turf war and needed all the feral dogs she could muster.

We glared at each other, both knowing that if the other wasn't under Gia's protection, it'd be all-out war. I shoved past him and walked up the path to the front door.

Gabe moved around in front of me and, like the gentleman he is, opened the door and waited for me to enter before following and motioning toward the kitchen. "Ms. A's in a meeting. You're gonna have to wait in here."

I looked toward the end of the hallway where the living room was located. I vaguely heard Gia speaking.

The easily recognizable basso profundo voice of William Silverton, her attorney, responded.

A second man, whose voice sounded vaguely familiar, said something I couldn't quite make out.

I stepped into the kitchen where Gia's twelve-year-old great niece, Shelley Greer, was busily mixing two glasses of chocolate milk.

"Hi Alex!" She turned and glanced at me with carbon copies of Gia's sparkling grey eyes.

"Hi yourself." I pulled out a stool and sat at the island where bowls of mixed nuts and various dried fruits had been set out.

Shelley set one of the glasses of milk down in front of me, then climbed onto the other stool. Her dog, Muddy, snoozed on his doggy bed in the corner. She pointed to his front leg, which was sheathed in a bright purple cast. "The vet said his leg's getting better. I don't think he's gonna chase anymore race horses."

"What happened?" I slid off the stool so I could kneel down and examine the cast.

"I took Muddy with me when me and Gia went to Sonoita." Sonoita is where Gia has her race horse training facility. The barns are ten times nicer than the house I live in. "Muddy got too close to Gia's newest horse, Credo's Bones, and he kicked him in the leg. The vet said he has a crack in his leg bone, but he'll be okay."

"Well, that's good. How about you? Everything going okay for you the last couple of days?"

She shrugged and looked down at her glass. "I don't like having all these guys around all the time, and I don't like being followed wherever I go. Aunt Gia says it's the way it's gotta be for now." She rested her temple on her fist and sighed. "I wish things could go back the way they were before Great Grandpa was killed. I can't go to summer school, I can't go to the park alone, and nobody'll hang out with me 'cause they're too scared of whatever chump is guarding me. I hate it."

"Have you talked to Gia?"

Her face darkened into a scowl. "She doesn't have time anymore. She's always in some kind of meeting or down at her office or something." She glanced around to see if anybody was listening.

I did too, even though I knew we were alone.

"I heard her tell Mr. Silverton to get the best deal he could for somebody, and to make sure the man's family has enough money to live on, 'cause we take care of our own." She lowered her voice to a whisper. "I think the guy killed somebody."

I nodded, knowing full well who and what she was talking about. From what I'd heard from the organized crime detectives, bodies have been piling up on both sides of the turf war. I studied her a minute, wondering if this little girl would one day step into Gia's very big shoes. Shelley's intelligence—her emotional intelligence—was off the charts. She'd had to deal with so much in her short life, and she'd done an excellent job with what she'd been given.

Born to a prostitute with no father in the picture, she'd been shuttled from one foster home to another, eventually moving into the tunnels under the city to live with a schizophrenic, mostly caring old lady who'd beat her with a stick one minute for sitting on her imaginary friend, then turn around and teach her classic literature the next.

We heard voices on the other side of the door, and I realized that Gia and her guests were coming down the hall.

Shelley jumped down from her stool and hurried to the swinging door, pulling it open just in time for me to see Gia, Silverton, and a very shocked Teddy Langston, who, when he saw me, quickly turned his back and let himself out the front door.

Two months earlier, I'd been on a protection detail for James Kootenai, the illustrious, arrogant, and sanctimonious mayor of

Phoenix. He and twenty other Arizona mayors had come to Tucson to attend a special conference on immigration. Several detectives from each division had been called in and assigned as extra protection since Tucson's mayor didn't want any untoward incidents in his fair town.

Casey and I had been assigned to Mayor Kootenai, and I recognized Langston as one of the his aides. Langston was a minor player in Kootenai's entourage, but he nevertheless treated our protection detail with the disdain many politicians have for us working class slobs. Seeing him here with Gia certainly gave me pause.

Shelley had no idea anything was amiss and she quickly announced the obvious to Gia and Silverton. "Alex is here!"

Silverton always treated me with the utmost respect, but then I think he dealt with pretty much everyone with an equal amount of civility regardless of their lot in life. He always spoke quietly, followed Gia's orders to a tee, could wreak havoc in the lives of judges and felons alike and had a grace under pressure I envied. The man was just plain brilliant; one of those unsung geniuses who are always two or three steps ahead of whomever they're dealing with. Well, with the exception of maybe Gia, whom I'd come to recognize as a gifted tactician whose talents would have rivaled even the ancient imperators of Rome.

Silverton accepted his hat from Gabe, who waited by the door to let him out. As he placed the old style fedora on his head, he raised his gaze to meet my own. "I don't think I need to remind you to be discreet, Detective Wolfe."

I considered his words a minute, not sure whether he was attempting to give me an order, or whether he was simply reassuring himself of my intentions. "No, you don't. I mean, who would care that Mayor Kootenai's aide was visiting Gianina Angelino, anyway?"

Gia impaled me with the glare that had become commonplace over the last few months. It'd been a while since I'd seen her soft side, and I suddenly realized I missed it.

After her father had been killed, she'd pulled back into her armored shell, directing her toy soldiers from within her citadel, holding her councils of war in the living room where she kept her stash of the best Scotch I'd ever had the pleasure of tasting. "Don't worry,

Gia. I'm not naïve enough to think our politicians aren't just as dirty as ninety percent of the felons we put into prison."

When Gabe rolled his eyes, I realized what I'd just said. "Well, I didn't exactly mean that like it came out. Just because he's meeting with you doesn't mean he's doing something criminal. You guys could be discussing global warming or immigration or—"

"Enough, Alex." Gia sounded irritated and tired all at the same time. She patted Silverton on the shoulder. "We both know Alex is discreet, Bill. Thanks for coming. We'll talk again tomorrow."

Silverton held my gaze a moment, which made me want to clarify my stance on the matter. "Discreet, Mr. Silverton, but not bought and paid for."

He settled his hat a little more firmly, nodded slightly and smiled before stepping out the front door.

Without saying a word, Gia turned and walked back to the living room. Shelley and I followed her down the hall.

There used to be priceless paintings hanging in the hallway, but when the shootout happened, the goons had sprayed bullets everywhere, trying to hit anything that moved. They'd indiscriminately shot holes in a Monet she'd just bought at an auction in Paris, and had completely destroyed a painting by an Italian painter I'd never heard of, but who was apparently one of Gia's favorites.

When the smoke had settled, she'd taken any undamaged works of art and placed them in various museums around the world. Now the walls were bare and sterile looking, hardly the type of home a little girl should grow up in.

I stepped into the living room and motioned for Shelley to make herself scarce.

Like I said, she's a bright kid. She immediately knew I wanted to talk to Gia alone. She ran over and grabbed a book from the coffee table, then pulled open a door at the end of the living room and disappeared up the stairs to the second floor.

I watched Gia as she poured two glasses of Scotch and offered me one. I waved it away with a flip of my hand. "I can't have anything yet, I'm still on duty. But thanks. I'd love a rain check, though."

She re-corked the bottle and picked up one of the glasses.

Sounding incredibly tired, she said, "Sorry, I wasn't thinking. There's a soda in the fridge." She motioned to a mini-fridge under the bar and then lowered herself down onto the dark brown leather sofa.

I grabbed a non-alcoholic ginger beer and sat down next to her. "Problems?" I knew that sounded lame given the current events in her life, but I'd tried all the psychological hoodoo I knew on previous visits and nothing had helped open her up.

She looked at me over her Glenlivet, and for the first time in months I saw the beginnings of the mischievous sparkle that had been missing from her latest arsenal of expressions. "Yes, Alex. Problems. Ones that I can talk to you about? No. Ones that you can help me with? No."

Before Gia and her father had been attacked by the Andrulis Mafia —one of the most brutal crime syndicates ever to come out of Lithuania—we'd had a fairly relaxed relationship. We rarely spoke of our professional lives and for the most part enjoyed each other's company.

I had something specific on my mind, though, and I dove right in, hoping she'd hear me out. "Shelley tells me she's still not back in school. I know summer school started a few weeks ago because I had a case involving a student last Thursday." I absently wiped droplets of water off the bottle I held in my lap. "I'm not sure it's such a good idea to keep her so isolated."

Gia set down her snifter and opened a camel-brown box Gabe always kept close to whatever chair she was seated in at the time. Earlier in the year, a senator from Michigan had sent her a luxury humidor full of her favorite cigars. I'd been visiting when the package arrived. Gia had admired the workmanship, but had been preoccupied at the time and had discarded the accompanying brochure.

My family is firmly ensconced in the "white bread middle-class" as my grandmother used to say, and anything as flamboyant and extrava-gant as the little cigar chest absolutely fascinated me.

I'd retrieved the brochure from the trash and had discovered that the box had been crafted from the staves of an antique whiskey barrel, purportedly salvaged from the Westmorland, a nineteenth century steamer that had sunk in 1854 off the coast of the Lake Michigan shoreline. The corners of the humidor were capped with gold that had also been salvaged from the wreck. The ship had supposedly been on a run to supply the payroll for an army garrison on Mackinac Island, and a $20 double eagle gold piece recovered from the sunken treasure had been inset into the center of the humidor's lid.

Kiln dried Spanish cedar lined the interior, which had a good selection of her imported cigar collection nestled inside. Each of the hand-rolled cigars appeared identical to my untrained eye, but she quickly flicked through them and pulled out one that met with her approval. She used her twenty-karat gold tip cutter to snip off the end.

I waited impatiently while she coaxed the cigar to life. "Gia, she's a kid. Kids need friends. A social life. You can't keep her locked away for the rest of her life."

She managed to get an even burn, then tilted her head back and slowly blew out a thin trickle of smoke. She didn't say anything for a minute and I sat watching her, wondering what she was thinking behind her inscrutable poker face.

Just as my thoughts began to wander, she stretched her neck to the side and rubbed tense muscles. "And just where can she go, Alex? The park? To a friend's house? The Andrulis Mafia intends to destroy me and my family. I intend to destroy them first. Just where do you see Shelley going where she'll be safe?"

I had known she'd ask that question and I'd been preparing for it all week. "Have you ever heard of the Regency Academy? It's an elite, international school located in rural Kentucky. It's for kids who are high-profile targets. Some of the parents are politicians or celebrities, some are tycoons, and probably some are just plain paranoid. The school sits in the middle of thirty fenced acres and there are armed patrols twenty-four hours a day, seven days a week." I pulled a folded brochure from my pocket. "Here, I brought this for you to look at."

Gia set down the cigar and picked up the snifter again before taking the pamphlet from me. She skimmed it, then set it in her lap. "Alex, I appreciate what you're trying to do, but be realistic. Shelley has never completed a full year in the same school. She was either pulled out by her mother who couldn't stay in one place for more than three months, or bounced around from one foster home to another, none of which were ever in the same school district as the previous home."

"She's smart, Gia. She'll adapt." I picked up the pamphlet and pointed to the third paragraph. "Look, they have tutors if she's behind her age group. They also have an indoor arena where the kids learn dressage or jumping." I batted the page. "Shoot, they even have kids who've brought their own cutting horses and take lessons in that. And she can take Muddy with her. They have kennels and special rooms for kids with pets."

I handed her the paper again. "Just think about it, okay? You can't hold her prisoner here. You know as well as I do she might decide this isn't for her and take off again. She's comfortable in the streets. You don't want that, do you?"

That kindled a spark of interest in her eyes, which was better than no interest at all.

"I went to the school once with Casey to interview some students when we were investigating a child sex ring here in Tucson involving children of very wealthy parents. We met some of the staff, administrators, teachers and security people. They seemed very bright, very accepting, and most importantly, competent and caring. I think Shelley would do well there."

My cellphone rang. I stood and walked to the window before answering. "Hey Kate, what's up?"

"I just spoke to Phyllis Ketterly. She said you left about forty minutes ago. Are you on your way to meet Casey?"

"Well...kind of." I fidgeted at Kate's prolonged silence. "Okay, yes, I'm definitely on my way. Tell Casey I'll be there in about twenty minutes."

I disconnected and turned back to Gia. Considering her initial cold reaction to sending Shelley to the Regency Academy, I was gratified to find her studying the pamphlet.

She set the brochure on the coffee table and slowly raised her eyes to meet mine. She lifted the cigar to her lips, then patted the seat next to her. "Come sit a minute, Alex. There's something we need to talk about."

I hated getting into situations where Kate wants me to do one thing and Gia another. I shook my head once, aware that I was one of only a handful of people who dared say no to Gia. "I have to meet Casey at a crime scene. I told Kate I'd be right there." I stepped closer and rested a hand on the back of the leather sofa. "I can come back later if—"

The clicking of heels coming down the hallway accompanied an unfamiliar voice. The honeyed tones echoed throughout the home. "Gianina, my love! Gabe said you were busy, but I knew you wouldn't—"

I turned in time to see an elegant, dark-haired woman come sailing into the room.

When she noticed me, she paused just a fraction before striding confidently up to Gia, leaning over the back of the sofa and giving her a passionate, and what seemed to me proprietary, kiss on the lips.

I blinked several times before my brain kicked back into normal and told me to stop behaving like a voyeur. Blushing, I picked up a magazine from a half-circular arrangement neatly stacked on the end table and flipped it open.

I felt Gia watching me, and when I looked up, she caught and held my gaze. Amusement crinkled the corners of her eyes. The corner of her lip turned up slightly, and after a few seconds, she stood and walked around the sofa to stand next to the woman. "Aisla Westhaven, this is my good friend, Alexandra Wolfe. Alex, Aisla Westhaven."

Aisla had on form-fitting designer jeans and a starched, white cotton blouse that only buttoned up as far as her cleavage. The resulting V opened wide to reveal perfectly shaped clavicles and a long, graceful neck. Her short-cropped, impeccably styled hair had just the right touch of messy chic, and her dark eyes and sensual lips would have fit on any runway model, anywhere in the world. Even at fifty plus, she was stunning.

She studied me with the same disdain with which a wolf would regard a Pekinese. After a short pause, she deigned to grace me with a tight, thin-lipped smile. "This must be your little pet detective I've heard so much about."

I bristled, then stilled, subconsciously readying myself for a verbal confrontation.

Gia's reaction was even more telling than mine. Her eyes flashed a dangerous, steely gray as she slowly turned and pinned Aisla with her glare.

Aisla, for her part, never missed a beat. She had the superior confidence many of the wealthy, overbred elite ooze from every pore. Moving in close enough for their waists to touch, she pulled Gia even closer and purred, "Now, now, my love, you know how that angry, bossy look of yours always affects me."

Gia pushed her away, but stayed close enough that her hand remained resting on Aisla's hip before turning to face me, "Alex, Aisla and I need to have a little talk. You and I can continue our discussion another time."

My gaze locked onto Aisla's, every cell in my body wanting to rip the smug smile off her tanned, deceptively beautiful face.

When I didn't move, Aisla raised one sculpted eyebrow and spoke to Gia as though I were just another part of the furniture. "She's not very well trained, is she? Maybe you should— "

She sucked in a startled breath as Gia's hand constricted painfully on her waist.

The woman I rarely saw—the mafia doña who ruled her empire with uncompromising power and, at times, a vicious, bloody brutality —locked hardened, steel grey eyes onto her prey.

Obviously shaken, Aisla darted a quick glance toward me before carefully pushing Gia's hand off of her body. Her voice shook slightly as she moved toward the bar. "Really, Gia. What's gotten into you? Why don't I just pour us both a drink?"

A tiny stab of fear ran through me as Gia turned "the look" on me. When I automatically moved into a defensive stance, she must have realized she hadn't tamped down her fury before turning my way. Her features softened as she put her hand on my shoulder, gently turning me toward the door to the hallway. "I'll have Bill Silverton research that school, Alex, and I'll call you when I make a decision." She chuckled as we walked out of the library. "Breathe. Your shoulders are as hard as a rock."

My usual fight or flight mode was ninety-nine percent fight, one percent flight, and it wasn't easy to relax when what I really wanted to do was put my fist through Aisla's perfectly whitened teeth. I pulled in a deep breath while I made a conscious effort to loosen the muscles in my neck and back. I turned and looked directly into Gia's eyes, not sure what I expected to find there. "She's your lover?"

The amused glint returned and she lifted a shoulder. "Every now and again. Does that shock you?"

I held her gaze a while before answering. "It worries me."

Her eyes unfocused a moment while she considered my words. Then she put her hand on my cheek and said softly, "No worries, Alex. I'll be all right." With that, she left me standing in the hall as she returned to the library and quietly shut the door.

CHAPTER 6

B y the time I got to the camper, Casey had already unfastened the tank from beneath the camper and was carefully troweling its contents into a bucket a little bit at a time before emptying the scraps and bits onto a manual sieve.

The department's sieve wasn't anything to crow about. It had probably been built in the early seventies by some detective who'd needed it for one of his cases. It consisted of a metal, bottomless box that set about waist high on an x-frame of aluminum poles. A fine, metal mesh stretched across the top of the square. Since it actually got very little use, the department had never seen fit to replace it for a newer model, so here was Casey, laboriously loading up the mesh with the detritus she'd found in the tank.

She looked up and wiped her forehead with the top of her sleeve. "Glad you could make it. I think it's hotter today than yesterday, and it's still only, what, around noon?" She started to reach for her cellphone in her back pocket, realized where her gloved hands had been, and thought better of it.

I checked my cell and nodded. "Yeah."

She sighed. "Well, grab some gloves. I'd double-glove if I were you. It's hotter that way, but with the stuff we're sifting through, I'd hate to have a tear at a bad time, ya know?" She pointed to an open box sitting on the hood of her car. "I stopped and got some industrial strength ones. They seem to work pretty well, 'cause I haven't had any rips yet."

I peeked over the edge of the trough. "Why are *we* doing this instead of the crime lab? Doesn't it make more sense for them to do it?"

"Because Kate wants us in on every aspect of the case, and I don't think she wants it to get around that there was a badge rotting away in here." To emphasize her point, she gingerly picked up a badge from a folding table next to her. She held it carefully between her thumb and forefinger. There was still mud—and I hate to think of what else— sticking to it, but I could plainly see the letters T, S, O, and N, from the word Tucson, and P, L, C, and E from police. The number 68 stood out in clear relief.

I grabbed some gloves from the box, doubling them up like she'd suggested, put on a facemask, picked up a trowel and began shoveling. Luckily, the contents were completely dried up. For whatever reason, someone had also poured dirt into the mix, possibly to hide the odor. As I dug, I found more dirt and bones in the tank than anything else. When the debris began overflowing the rim of my bucket, I carried it to the sieve and waited for Casey to finish brushing the last of the previous load back and forth on the mesh with her little 3" paint brush.

Some items were big enough to find without using the sieve, so when I emptied the bucket onto the mesh, I automatically picked out various bone fragments and a cat's eye marble.

She pointed to a stack of paper bags on the table. "Unrecognizable bone fragments go into this bag. If you get anything where you can tell what it is, like the orbital bones here, it goes in in its own paper bag and then gets put into this box."

"And stuff like the marble?"

She held up a tiny paper bag and waggled it at me before holding it open. I carefully dropped the marble into it, sealed it with evidence tape, and gave it an ID number.

We worked in silence for a while, unfortunately not coming up with very much in the way of interesting or helpful evidence.

Until Casey picked up what looked like a piece of skull and began turning it this way and that. She took off her sunglasses and squinted at it. "Look at this. It kinda looks like something's been carved into it. An S or maybe a 5?"

She handed the fragment to me and I wiped it with a rag to get some of the dirt off. "It could either be 1s or 15. Wait, I don't think that dot in front of the first letter is part of the natural pitting. It's too deep."

Casey moved behind me so she could peer over my shoulder. "Maybe it's .15."

I turned to look at her over my shoulder. "What the heck?"

Both of us began pulling the flat skull pieces out of the evidence bags. We examined each one carefully. Most were blank. Those we replaced and resealed in the bags.

"Here's something." I pointed to some marks on the latest piece I'd pulled out. "This looks like LC kind of, but maybe not."

She took it from me and flipped it upside down. "No, if you—" She stopped and polished it with her thumb. "If you count that line and turn it upside down, that makes it a 2 instead of a C."

"So it's a 27. And look, another dot, but after the numbers this time." I picked up the first bone fragment and held it next to the one Casey had. "Nope. I thought maybe they'd fit together."

She shook her head. "Not even close." When she set hers on the table, I put mine down next to it. We went through all the rest that we'd located so far. There weren't anymore numbers so we picked up our tools and began the tedious work of sifting through Jepson's—well, I hated to think about what exactly I was sifting through.

I had just loaded another trowel full of dirt into my bucket when a movement in the distance caught my attention. I glanced up, but the only things even remotely moving were the heat waves floating above the desert floor. I continued watching for a moment, staring into the distance and not really focusing on anything in particular.

Casey stopped brushing and followed my gaze eastward. "What?"

I shook my head. "I don't know, I thought I saw something move." I studied the relatively open desert. When nothing stirred except a small dust devil, I shrugged and moved back to the trough, my trowel and bucket at the ready. "Probably a coyote or something."

We returned to our individual jobs—me scooping, carrying and pouring, and Casey sifting. Every now and again I'd glance up and search the desert. I'd seen movement. If I was patient enough, whatever it was would show itself. After about five minutes, my stubborn curiosity paid off. "I knew it."

"What?" Casey shielded her eyes as she looked out over the desert again.

I kept my attention riveted to the spot where I'd seen some movement, pulled off my gloves and dust mask and began walking directly toward the barely perceptible hump lying in the dirt.

Casey dropped her brush and discarded all her safety gear before falling into step beside me. "What do you see?"

I gently pushed her away from me, and she moved a short distance away. If we somehow became targets, it'd be more difficult for a shooter to hit both of us with one volley of shots.

She moved about five yards away, scanning the desert as she walked with her hand on the grip of her holstered weapon. We advanced cautiously, every now and again glancing behind us to make sure no one was circling around to the camper while we directed our attention elsewhere.

We came to within twenty yards of the mound, which had begun to look like nothing more than a wrinkled, brown blanket discarded in the dirt. When I saw it move slightly, I held up a hand.

Casey immediately froze.

We watched as the blanket lifted a few inches off the ground and moved forward a few feet before settling back down into the dust.

Both Casey and I knelt down. I hadn't yet drawn my weapon since I didn't know exactly what I'd seen, but I drew it now and pointed it at the hump.

Casey glanced at me to make sure I was ready and then shouted, "Tucson Police. Don't move!"

In the time it took for Casey to finish the command, a woman who'd been hiding under the blanket threw it off, leapt to her feet, and took off with an awkward, hop-skipping run toward Jepson's cluster of buildings.

We were both so startled to see a lady pop out that it took us a few seconds to gather our wits and follow. I've always been the faster runner, but Casey had a head start, so when the woman skidded around the far corner of Jepson's home, Casey was close on her heels.

I veered off to the left and circled to the other side to cut her off.

The woman rounded the far corner at the same time I did. When she saw me, she threw up her hands and began to laugh. "Okay, okay, you got me."

The grin slowly faded when Casey came up behind her, pulled one of her arms behind her back and ratcheted on a handcuff. "Wait—wait, wait. You're making a mistake! I haven't done anything. Ask Alex! She knows me."

She tried to turn, but Casey twisted the cuff she'd already put on, forcing the woman back around so she could put the second cuff on her free arm. "Ouch! Hey! You can't arrest me. I haven't done anything illegal."

I recognized her immediately as the dwarfish looking brunette from the camper club. I mean really, how many five foot women with thick eyebrows and big-boned eye ridges can there be in the world?

I began ticking off offenses with my fingers. "Let's see, we can start with trespassing, entering a crime scene without permission, failing to obey a lawful order given by an officer of the law." I looked up at the woman, eyebrows raised. "Would you like me to continue?"

She made a stab at an ingratiating grin. "Look, me'n the ladies were talkin' about Tom, and we were talkin' about how he got killed and all, and one thing led to another, and well—" A blush crept up her stumpy little neck. "I kinda bragged that I could solve his murder quicker'n you guys since I've worked a little with Tom on his campers and I'd know what to look for. You know, if anything was out of place, or if you overlooked some vital piece of evidence."

Casey pulled a wallet out of the woman's pocket, looked at it, then held it open for me to see. "A private investigator."

I took the wallet from her and pulled out the I.D. card. "Heller School of Investigation-Certificate of Completion."

We both knew that over the last several years, a glut of online "colleges" had begun offering courses in crime scene investigation with some interview and interrogation classes thrown in. A few even pretended to actually know enough to teach criminal law. They were usually shady, fly-by-night operations that granted a private investigators license to anyone who could come up with a pocketful of cash.

I held up the certificate. "You do realize it's illegal to work as a private investigator without first being registered by the state of Arizona, right?" I made a show of searching through her wallet. "Nope, no official P.I. license hiding in here." I raised my eyebrows, silently asking her to produce one.

She colored to an even darker shade of red, suddenly finding the tops of her red sneakers particularly interesting. "Well, I guess I'm not really a P.I." She nodded toward the certificate with her chin. "I just got that online to impress the Vamps."

Casey rolled her eyes. "So why were you hiding under a blanket in 115 degree weather?"

By this time, the blush had crept up all the way past her bushy eyebrows. "I don't know." She shook her head. "Well, yeah I do. My friends are always teasing me about the P.I. license, and they started razzing me about how I couldn't even get into the crime scene, let alone solve the crime. I bet them I could sneak right past you guys without you even knowing I was here." She shrugged. "I watch that show, *Soldier, Sailor, Sniper*, all the time, and figured I'd do what they do when they're sneaking up on people."

Casey and I exchanged looks. Neither of us really wanted to take the time to arrest the lady, and Casey raised her eyebrows silently asking me what I wanted to do. I decided to verify her story. If it checked out, I'd let her go. I slipped Phyllis Ketterly's card out of my pocket and walked a short distance away where my conversation wouldn't be overheard.

When Ketterly answered, she sounded slightly out of breath. "Yeah?"

"Phyla? This is Alex Wolfe. Sounds like I caught you at a bad time."

"No, I'm just helping a friend unpack her camping gear out at the campground. What's up?"

I realized I didn't remember our mutual "friend's" name, so I twisted the wallet around with one hand in order to read the name on the certificate. "Do you know Agnes St. Germaine?"

I knew she did since she'd introduced her to me earlier in the day, so it was kind of a rhetorical question.

"Yes, of course I know her. She's one of the Vamps you met this morning. What'd she do now?" Phyla didn't sound amused.

"She tried to sneak into our crime scene unnoticed."

Phyla let out a long sigh. "Oh good God. I heard the ladies goading her on, but I never for a minute believed she'd be gullible enough to try to pull something like that." She paused briefly, then continued. "Do you need me to do something? I guess I can pick her up at the jail if that's where you're taking her, but she's gonna have to wait until I finish here."

I glanced back at Casey, who was running her hand through her hair and wondering, I'm sure, how the hell I knew Agnes and what I intended to do with her.

As for the dwarf, she had big tears streaming down her face, several of which were clinging precariously to the tip of her slightly hairy chin.

"No, I'm not gonna waste our time arresting her. I don't see it, but I'm guessing she parked her car somewhere around here." I held my phone to my chest and called back to Agnes. "Hey, where's your car?"

Her face crumpled as the panic set in. "They dropped me off down the road a little ways. I thought they'd wait for me, but as soon as I started walking this way, they left."

Despite the phone being muffled, I still heard Phyla's bark of laughter. I raised it to my ear and grinned. "What's so funny?"

"It's just that Agnes is the one who's the practical joker of the club. She's always doing something to somebody. I guess the ladies decided that turnabout is fair play. Do you want me to come pick her up?"

"Yes, sooner than later, please."

"I'll be on my way in about fifteen. And Alex?"

"Yeah?"

Phyla was quiet a minute, apparently trying to figure out what she wanted to say. "She may be the practical joker, but she's also been the brunt of some pretty mean-spirited bullying throughout her life. Not from the Vamps, just in general. She's— Well, let me put it this way: the logs are on fire, but the chimney's sometimes clogged."

I coughed into my hand trying to hide my laughter. I lowered my voice and said quietly enough so Agnes couldn't accidentally overhear, "You mean instead of drinking from the fountain of knowledge, Agnes just gargled?"

Phyla chuckled. "Exactly. She's not really mentally challenged, but emotionally, she's nowhere near her chronological age."

I knew what she was telling me. People like Agnes, who didn't even remotely resemble Venus or Adonis, and who had the intelligence of Yogi Bear instead of Albert Einstein, tended to be treated with little more than veiled contempt by a large portion of society. "Yeah, I imagine the beautiful people didn't treat her very well when she was growing up."

"But you know what's strange? She has an almost eidetic memory for certain things. That's why she's our historian. It's all in her head, but ask her anything about the history of the Vamps, and she'll tell you book and verse. I guess what I'm asking is for you to take it easy on her. She has a good heart, even if she is lacking any modicum of common sense."

"Don't worry, I'm not the bullying type."

"I didn't think you were. I just have an overly developed big sister-protector gene running through my veins. I think if I'd lived in medieval times, I would have been the lady knight protecting the serfs from their cruel overlord or some such thing." She laughed at herself. "Anyway, I'll be there as soon as I wrap up here."

She disconnected and I ambled back to the two women. I pulled out my handcuff key and motioned for Agnes to turn around. "Well, Phyla vouches for you so I'm gonna let you slide." After I unlocked the second handcuff, I stepped around in front of her and made sure I had her undivided attention. "*This* time. No more sneaking around crime scenes. If it had been anyone else in our unit working here instead of us, you'd have been on your way to jail by now."

She nodded and pulled the sleeve of her tee shirt close enough to wipe the tears off her face. "I know, it was stupid." She got a goofy grin on her face. "But what a story to tell around the campfire, huh?"

CHAPTER 7

K ate pulled up just as we got back to our archaeological dung
heap. She sat in her car a while, finishing up a phone conversation with someone she didn't appear to be overly pleased with.

Everyone has some kind of subconscious habit they revert back to
when they're bored, angry or pensive. Kate always broadcasts her irri-
tation by tapping a pen or her fingers on whatever surface happens to
be handy at the time. Right now, I watched her pen playing a staccato
rhythm on the rim of her steering wheel.

I glanced over at Casey who very eloquently widened her eyes and
then turned to make herself busy elsewhere. I grabbed Agnes' elbow
and steered her to the tank I'd been shoveling out prior to her arrival.

I spoke quietly as we walked. "Look, that's our sergeant, and something's got her pissed right now. Just keep your mouth shut, and follow
my lead."

Agnes snuck a peek over her shoulder at Kate's car. "Is she mad
at you?"

I stopped walking long enough to think back on everything that
had happened that morning. "Usually, yes, but I can't think of anything
I've done lately to piss her off." I steered her to where Casey was busy
sifting. "Stay here and keep your hands in your pockets."

I had no idea what had Kate in such a temper, but when her muffled voice rose to an angry shout, I grabbed my trowel and began studiously shoveling dried shit and bone fragments into my bucket. My brain worked furiously as I tried to remember if I'd done anything to piss her off.

I'd interviewed Phyla like she'd asked. I hadn't said anything to any of the other ladies to garner a complaint, and nothing had happened at Gia's that was out of the ordinary. I mean, sure, I'd held a loaded Berretta to Pito's head, but there was nothing particularly noteworthy about that.

I heard the car door slam and my heart started to pound as Kate made her way over to where we were working. It was a conditioned response, like Pavlov's dogs slobbering all over his laboratory at the sound of the bell. I had the unfortunate, slightly panicked reflex of a rapid heartbeat accompanied by the urge to point a finger at whatever innocent person happened to be standing next to me at the time.

"What have you found so far?" Kate must have really been preoccupied because she didn't notice Agnes standing beside me.

Until the woman sprang forward with her hand extended. "Hi!"

Kate's gaze dropped to Agnes' hand, then moved to spear me with a withering glare that I pretended not to notice. I wanted to bat our blanket creeper on the back of the head for not doing as she'd been instructed, but I decided to play the dutiful hostess instead. "Sergeant Brannigan, this is Agnes, a private investigator—kind of—who thinks she might be able to help us with this case. Agnes, Sergeant Brannigan."

Agnes still held her hand shoved in front of Kate's belly and Kate reluctantly took it. "A private investigator, kind of? How exactly does that work, Detective Wolfe?" Normally, Kate would have been genial and easy-going, politely acknowledging Agnes' presence while maneuvering her away from the crime scene. Very few cops trust private investigators and we generally take what information they give us and send them on their way.

I didn't want to make Agnes feel like a fool, even though her hare-brained stunt had almost landed her in jail, so I tried to sugarcoat her qualifications. "Well, she has a certificate from a P.I. school." I held up a finger to emphasize my words. "But more importantly, she worked with Tom on his renovations... occasionally."

"How occasionally?" I could see Kate beginning to relax a little. I guess the appearance of our guest was taking her mind off whatever she'd been discussing on her way over here.

Agnes happily supplied the answer. "Oh, sometimes he'd hire me to take out the windows of whatever camper he was working on at the time. You know, so I could put new butyl tape around the edge and reseal 'em. I'd do the same thing to the vents on the roof, 'cause if you don't, sure as anything, rain'll come pouring into the camper right when you're ready to go to sleep for the night."

Kate glared at me again before turning back to Agnes. "And that qualifies you to help with this case...how?"

Agnes glanced at me, somehow hoping I'd be able to jump in and supply the answer.

I raised my shoulders and my eyebrows, silently asking the same question.

She put her hands in her pockets and began rocking back and forth. "Well, did you guys find his hidden camera?"

Kate's focus sharpened. "Camera?" She looked from Agnes to me and then to Casey, waiting for an answer. "Did you two find a camera I don't know about?"

I grabbed Agnes by the shoulder and gave her a friendly shove toward Jepson's house. "She was just getting ready to show it to us when you drove up. Weren't you, Agnes?"

Agnes got a deer in the headlights look. "Well, n—"

I started talking before she could finish her sentence. "Actually, Agnes has been very helpful with everything she's been telling us." I pushed her again, harder this time to get her to start walking and stop talking.

"Hold it, Alex." Kate stopped me in my tracks. I had to reach out and grab Agnes by the collar, since apparently her brain had finally registered 'go', and 'Hold it, Alex' didn't compute that she had to stop as well. Most cops are pretty bright, and dealing with a not too bright, medieval dwarf was trying my patience. I hauled her back to stand next to Casey.

The pen began tapping against Kate's thigh, and I wondered what was coming. I waited a good while, keeping my expression absolutely neutral so Kate wouldn't read anything in it. I watched her absently watching me, her mind obviously preoccupied with whatever she wanted to talk about.

She finally motioned to Casey. "Would you take Agnes and go collect the camera and whatever recordings you can find?"

Casey nodded and waved for Agnes to precede her. "Sure. Let's go, Agnes. I have some other questions too, and this is as good a time as any."

Kate waited for them to leave before holding her cell phone up and waggling it back and forth. "Any idea who just called me?"

"If it was Lt. Jefferson, I can explain."

Her eyes narrowed. "So explain."

I studied her a minute. "It wasn't him, was it?"

Lt. Jefferson was one of those people who didn't trust his officers to do what they were trained to do. He went to every scene and didn't allow his sergeants to make their own decisions. He even monitored the radio on his days off and came running to the scene whenever he thought the decisions were too difficult for his officers and sergeants to handle. Whenever I had to go to one of his scenes, he drove me completely insane with his micromanaging.

Kate continued to stare at me.

It seemed hotter today than it had yesterday. I took advantage of the pause and pulled out a cold water from Casey's blue cooler. I tipped it back and took a long, much needed drink.

Kate's next words threw my world into a spin. "It was Amanda Kellworth from the six o'clock news." Kate cocked her head as she delivered her bombshell. "She's apparently friends with a woman named Aisla Westhaven and—"

When I took in a panicked breath, a huge gulp of water went into my lungs. I spewed it all out again in an uncontrolled fit of coughing. My throat closed up and the drowning feeling I had only added to my distress.

Kate waited for me to stop choking, which took quite a while since I think I inhaled about half the bottle.

Tears streamed down my face and I reached into my car to grab some extra napkins I had stuffed in my glove box. I dried my eyes and wiped my cheeks, taking a little more time than I actually needed to gather my thoughts. "And?"

Kate leaned against the hood of my car. I guess she'd decided to get comfortable while she waited for me to quit choking. "First, tell me who Aisla Westhaven is."

I looked skyward while I figured out what to tell her. "This is between me and you and that fence post over there, right?"

She snorted. "Depends."

"On what?"

"On whether keeping it between the two of us could cost me my job or land one of us in jail."

"Oh that. I'm not worried about that stuff." I waved away her concerns and watched as her pen began tapping again. "No, this is just some of Gia's personal stuff."

She made a winding motion with her hand, telling me to move on.

"Aisla is Gia's friend and apparently her sometimes lover."

I knew Kate didn't differentiate between gays and straights. Her line was drawn more between good and bad, honest and dishonest, right and wrong.

We stared at each other, the seconds ticking away in my head while she processed the information.

Kate finally pushed her sunglasses up onto her forehead and rubbed her eyes. "Well, that's what this Aisla woman accused you of. She told Amanda Kellworth that you and Gia were in a committed homosexual relationship."

That certainly didn't fit with my impression of Aisla. She didn't seem the type to go running to the press about anything concerning Gia, let alone something so personal and potentially damaging. "So Kellworth was calling you to confirm the story one way or another?"

"Yes. And she kept pushing me for an answer until I finally lost my temper."

So that was why Kate had been yelling inside her car. She rarely lost her composure, and I've never seen her show any kind of anger, publicly at least, with a member of the media. She was always calm and collected when it came to police matters, but when someone started attacking one of her detectives, look out.

She watched me process what she'd said, and honestly, I wasn't really worried. The press walks on eggshells where Gianina Angelino is concerned. She's a powerful woman with influential connections in boardrooms, on the senate floor, at the local horse racing tracks and, luckily for me, in the editorial offices of all the major news outlets.

Kate lifted one shoulder. "Well?"

"Well what?" I wasn't sure what she wanted to know. "If you're asking if Gia and I are in a relationship—" I paused, then waved my hand to erase my last words. "I mean, in a *relationship* relationship, the answer's no."

Kate pushed herself off the car. "Well, just be aware that Kellworth is sniffing around for a story, and that you somehow made an enemy of this Aisla person. And when you're on duty," She caught and held my gaze, "I'd appreciate it if you'd stay away from Ms. Angelino."

My benign gaze morphed into a glare and she held up a hand. "I know, I know, she's your friend, but things are strained in the organized crime world right now, and I'd feel better knowing you were keeping your distance, at least during working hours."

I thought about it a minute, then nodded. "All right, but I need to let her know what game Aisla is playing so she can call Kellworth's editor if she needs to."

Kate began shaking her head. "Oh no, no, no, no. Our conversation is between me and you. The last thing I need is for Kellworth to think I go running to a mafia crime boss whenever a reporter makes those kinds of accusations about you and Ms. Angelino." For the most part, Kate kept her distance from Gia by referring to her by her last name. There had been one or two exceptions, but they were few and far between. "And by the way, steer clear of Kellworth too."

"I need to call her, Kate. Aisla going behind her back could be dangerous, and Gia needs to know about it. I mean, what if Aisla got pissed and gave some compromising information to a rival mafia family?"

Kate glared at me again. "No." Apparently that was the end of the discussion, because when I opened my mouth to argue, she lifted a finger and a warning eyebrow at the same time.

I swallowed what I wanted to say, and she nodded once before walking over to the sieve and shaking it, causing tiny pieces of dirt to cascade down onto the ground below. "Did you two find anything interesting or out of the ordinary yet?" She set aside the sieve and stepped over to the table, holding open the various paper bags and peering inside.

"No. I don't think so, anyway. Well, there's these two skull fragments that have numbers or letters carved in them. We were searching for more when—" I almost said, "when we saw Agnes crawling across the crime scene with a blanket thrown over her" but I decided that was a little more information than I wanted to share.

"When what?" She lifted her sunglasses and stared intently at me.

"When...um, when Agnes showed up."

Her eyes narrowed but after a moment she turned and picked up one of the fragments. She brought it close to her face in order to see it more clearly, then replaced it next to the other. Leaning down to examine the second one, she began reading off the numbers. "There's a 27 on this one and what, lc on here?" She pointed at the second piece of bone.

"No, we think this tiny line here makes it a 15." I swiveled the piece around so she could see it better. I indicated a folded paper bag at the end of the table. "And there's that badge we saw. The crime lab will need to clean it up, but it's definitely an old style T.P.D. badge, number 68. Do you know if that guy, Maloney, is still alive? He must be pretty old if he is, since he was already a veteran cop when you started on the department. I mean, that had to be back in the dark ages." I grinned, then ducked as she playfully took a swat at my head.

Kate shifted her attention to where I'd pointed. Preliminary to storing the badge, Casey had pulled out a paper bag. She'd apparently set it on top of the shield when we'd gone after Agnes. Kate slid the bag aside and lightly tapped the side of the badge with her fingernail. "Micah's been gone almost seven years now. He died fairly young. I think he was about 55 or 56 years old."

"What killed him?"

"He had a massive heart attack chasing some young punk," She took in a long breath and continued speaking on her exhale. "He actually caught the kid and handcuffed him. As he was walking him back to his patrol car, his heart just gave out. It really scared the kid, I can tell you that."

She grinned over at me. "You have to give the guy credit though. He managed to slip his hands around front, grabbed Micah's radio, called for help and started chest compressions." She lifted a shoulder. "It was too late though. The coroner said even if he'd been right there in the hospital, there was no way he could have been resuscitated."

I thought about that a minute. "So, if he died on duty, was he given a full departmental burial? Was he buried in his uniform?"

She studied me a minute before tapping the badge again. "Curious, huh?"

I thought about that as I watched her walk to her car and drive off. Casey and Agnes had been gone a while, so I deposited the badge into the paper bag and secured all the evidence in my trunk for safe keeping. I glanced at the building compound prior to getting in my vehicle. It was too damn hot to walk, so I slid into my car, cranked the air up full blast and drove at about 2 mph to Jepson's house.

When I pulled into the circular drive, Agnes stuck her head out of the main garage and waved me over.

Inside, Casey had flung open every drawer and cabinet, trying to locate the CD player that recorded the video from the hidden camera.

I glanced around the ceiling line looking for a likely hiding place. "Where's the camera?"

Agnes pointed to an air conditioning duct above the desk. "It's up there. I walked in on him once when he was doing something with it." She crossed her arms and studied her shoes. "When he saw me, he jumped down from the ladder, grabbed my shirt and shoved me into the wall." She looked up at me. "He said he'd kill me if I ever told anybody about it. I believed him, too, and I never told nobody." She turned in a full circle and called out, "I'm tellin' now, you asshole! I'm tellin' everybody I know!"

I walked over to Casey, who slammed a cabinet door shut and threw up her hands. "I've checked every drawer, cabinet and closet in this place. We know the camera's up there, but if there's a recorder, I have no idea where it could be."

I thought a moment, "We took a computer when we searched the place. Maybe you should call Kota and ask her to look for the recording on the hard drive. The camera might have been wired straight to the computer. Or I suppose it could have connected through wifi or something."

"Seriously? Wifi? I'm really getting behind the times." Casey shook her head. "For some reason, I had a picture of a VHS recorder stuck in my outdated pea brain."

I pulled out my cell and hit one of my speed dial numbers. The phone rang several times and just before I disconnected, my friend answered.

"Crime lab."

"Hey, Kota, it's Alex. You know that computer Casey and I checked into evidence on the Jepson case?"

Kota, or Dakota Charles as her parents had named her, was a good friend who knew more about processing evidence than anyone I've ever known. She'd come to TPD several years earlier after many years at the CIA, having been heavily recruited by them right out of Loyola University. "Yeah. I haven't gotten to it yet, if that's what you're asking. I'm working on three homicides, ten rapes, I don't know how many—"

"Okay, okay, I get the idea. A dried up femur in a toilet takes a distant second, but maybe since you're working on Jepson's homicide, you could do me a favor? When you get a minute, could you pull out the computer and see if there's any video recordings from the guy's garage, or from anywhere else on his property, where he might have had a camera stashed and recording?"

"What's it worth to ya?"

I grinned, knowing the answer without even thinking. "A bottle of Bailey's?"

Kota has the same rebellious streak in her inner psyche that I have in mine. Actually, I don't see it as rebellion as much as solving problems in a slightly different way than tradition dictated. Well, maybe more that slightly different, but a girl just can't help herself when normal methods force her into a brick wall, now can she?

Kota and I had become close friends shortly after I'd joined the department, and I valued her advice and slightly twisted sense of humor more than that of most people I know.

She didn't hesitate. "Done. It shouldn't take me too long to find any open source camera software."

"Can you send the videos to me when you get 'em?"

"You don't ask for much, do you? Sure, if you throw in a half-gallon of vanilla ice cream and come share it with me some evening. And bring Megan. She's always good for a laugh."

There wasn't much I wouldn't do for a Bailey's and ice cream, as Kota well knew. "You got it. I'll call ya later after I talk to Megan, okay?"

When I disconnected, Agnes, who'd obviously been listening in on the conversation, smiled. "Bailey's is one of the Vamps' favorites. Since everybody's coming into town, you ought to stop by the campground some evening. We usually have food and drinks, and almost always Bailey's." She cocked her head sideways. "And bring your girlfriend if you want."

"My girlfriend? What girlfriend?"

"Megan."

"How could you hear the other side of the conversation?" Apparently Agnes' oversized ears were good for more than just catching wind. I tucked away that little factoid and turned to Casey. "She's gonna shoot us a copy of whatever she finds." I glared at Agnes. "Megan isn't my girlfriend. She's a friend, and I don't usually mix business with my personal life."

"Aw, c'mon. We're a lot of fun, and you'll learn a whole lot more about Tom by drinking around the campfire with the Vamps than by trying to figure it out all on your own."

I motioned toward the car. "C'mon. Get in, and I'll drive us back to the camper. We've got a lot of sifting to do and I'd love to finish sometime today."

Phyla's car had just turned onto the property when we got back to the camper. Apparently not wanting to drive across the desert in her pristine Jeep Grand Cherokee, she parked just inside the property line and walked the rest of the way.

Agnes lit up when she saw her and all of us got out of the car and waited for her to join us.

Phyla walked up to Agnes and playfully swatted her on the back of the head. "What is the matter with you? You know I've told you if anyone dares you to do something, you need to come to me before you actually do it."

Agnes continued to beam at her friend, and when Casey cleared her throat, I belatedly remembered that she'd never met any of the other Vamps. "Oh yeah, Casey, this is Phyllis Ketterly. Phyllis, my partner, Casey."

Casey stepped forward and held out her hand. "I'm pleased to meet you, ma'am. Alex told me earlier that she'd talked to you and that you knew Tom Jepson."

"Call me Phyla. Yes, I knew him." After they'd shaken hands, Phyla walked over and ran her fingers along the side of the camper. "She's still a beauty, isn't she? Even though she's been left out here to rot. Any idea what's going to happen to her?"

Casey stepped over to the open door and stuck her head in to look around. "No, but it needs a lot of work. I think it leaked around that back window. It's pretty obvious where the water rotted the wood, and I'd bet there's some mold growing behind that panel." She pointed to the rear of the camper, then pushed on the floor with her hand. "And if you walk in, you can smell packrat urine and the floor feels kind of spongy."

Casey backed out of the door and Phyla took her turn. "Sounds like you know a little about campers. Yeah, I can see there's a lot of work here, but it wouldn't take a professional restorer all that long to get her into shape."

The day was getting away from us so I opened my trunk to retrieve some more evidence bags, hoping Phyla would get the hint and get Agnes out of our hair. The bag with the badge in it caught my eye, and I wondered if either of these two knew anything about how it might have gotten there. "Did either of you know a cop named Micah Maloney, or do you know if Tom had any reason to ever meet with a detective?"

Phyla shook her head, but Agnes went still and focused her attention on something in the distance. I turned to see what she was looking at but all I saw was dirt and cacti and desert trees. When I turned back, I saw that Phyla had noticed Agnes' reaction as well.

She caught my gaze and inclined her head toward Agnes, lifting one eyebrow as if to say, *Watch this.*

Agnes continued to stare, her brows pulled low. She began to hum to herself, off key, in an unrecognizable melody. We all watched a while, and right before I'd decided she'd checked out and wasn't coming back, she nodded once and began to speak.

"So, about eleven years ago, right around August 12, at 3:30 in the afternoon, I was helping Tom pull some rotten paneling and insulation out of a... let's see, I'm pretty sure it was a 1966 Shasta Super... white with a yellow stripe."

Casey ran her hand through her semi-spiked, pixie cut hair. "I'm sorry, but I don't remember anything about what I was doing seventeen years ago, let alone that kind of detail. You expect us to believe you remember what you were doing on a particular day at a certain time that long ago?"

I watched as a red tint blossomed across Agnes' cheeks, spreading across her nose and continuing up into her hairline. She self-consciously crossed her arms and moved closer to Phyla, who rested her hand on her friend's shoulder.

The older woman spoke slowly, not taking her eyes off Casey. "Agnes has a gift for remembering dates and details. I've never seen anyone with her kind of talent. I wouldn't discount what she's saying just because you've never met anyone with her particular gift."

As far as I'm concerned, there isn't a better investigator on the department than my partner. If there's a stone that needs to be over-turned, she overturns it. If a witness needs to be tracked down, there's no place they can hide. But the one thing she's never had any patience for is someone who wastes our time by giving us bogus information that we either have to prove or disprove before we can move forward with our investigation.

I assumed she'd just dismiss Agnes outright since we had at least another half day's worth of sifting to do, but as always, her innate decency won out. She motioned for Agnes to continue. Casey, more than anyone, was a champion for the bullied and downtrodden, and she'd recognized Agnes' reaction as coming from someone who'd had their fair share of ridicule and abuse. "Go ahead, Agnes. I didn't mean to insult you, and if you can remember back that far, I'm really impressed."

The good natured grin returned to Agnes' face. "Most people don't think I really remember everything, but I do." Her brows pulled together, which, honestly, wasn't that far of a hike. "But sometimes, I feel like I've got too much stuff stuck up here," She tapped her temple with a finger. "And it took me a long time to learn how to organize it all. Like now, when Alex asked if Tom knew a cop, I knew somewhere in my brain files I'd seen Tom with a detective, and I just had to open drawers in my head until I found the right file folder."

Casey answered Agnes' grin with a smile of her own. "Okay then, open that file and read it to us."

The vacant expression returned to Agnes' face, and we waited for her to once more find the right file and continue. "So I was inside the Shasta, and Tom was outside screwing the windows back in." She paused. "You know, with the Butyl tape an' all, when I heard a loud thunk on the side of the camper. I looked out the window, and some big guy was holding Tom up against the camper by his neck.

"I could tell Tom was mad, but scared too. I couldn't hear what the man was saying, 'cause he was kind of growling, but when he twisted his body and punched Tom in the face, I saw a badge on the front side of his belt."

That hadn't told us anything other than some cop had come in to rough Jepson up for some unknown reason. But sometimes information that you don't think is important at the time can blow a case wide open. I wondered how much detail Agnes had seen. "Do you remember anything specific about the badge?"

Her gaze traveled down to where I had my badge secured to my belt. She studied it, taking in the details, then shook her head and glanced over at Casey's badge. "No, it wasn't like yours. I mean, it was the same shape, but the front looked different. There was a number on it, and your badges don't have any numbers."

Casey and I both glanced behind us to the table where we'd been cataloguing the evidence. I remembered I'd put the bag with the badge in it into my trunk. We knew that Agnes couldn't have already seen it since Casey had covered it with the paper bag when we'd gone to investigate the blanket.

I turned back and asked, "What number?"

She thought a second. "68."

Casey and I exchanged looks and Phyla asked, "Is that significant?"

Neither of us liked to talk about our cases, other than with cops we trusted, so I just shrugged. "Maybe. We really don't know what's important and what's not until we get further into a case." I thought a minute before asking Agnes, "What happened after he punched Tom? Could you hear what they were saying then?"

She squinted before shaking her head, looking almost apologetic when she answered. "No, like I said, the cop was growling up close to Tom's face, but when he let him go, Tom kind of got brave and shoved the guy backward. He yelled something about a woman, and told him she didn't have anything to do with anything."

Agnes brightened, her mischievous eyes sparkling. "Well, what he actually said was that a whore's-get like her had no claim on anybody or anything. Whooeee! That cop turned purple and grabbed Tom's throat again and banged him into the camper so hard it rocked up on its wheels."

She tilted her head to the side, apparently reading a different section of her mental file. "I heard what the cop said that time. He said, 'I'll figure out what you're doing, asswipe, and when I do—' and then he kinda squeezed Tom's throat until his eyes bugged out. Then he let him go and left."

The three of us had been listening intently to Agnes, astounded, and on my part, a little skeptical about her ability to recall those kinds of details eleven years after they happened.

Even Phyla looked kind of nonplussed.

Agnes caught the hesitation in the air and once again took a step back so that Phyla's shoulder was between her, Casey and me. "I know, people don't usually believe me when I say those kinds of things. They think I'm making stuff up, but I'm not. I can't help it that I am the way I am. People think I'm kinda slow, and maybe I am with stuff that hasn't happened yet, or like sometimes when I try to figure things out and I can't, but I know what I remember."

Phyla took a step back to once again include Agnes in our little group. "She *was* tested at the U of A. They were doing a study on the correlation between memory and I.Q. The grad students doing the study were able to consistently corroborate specific details Agnes told them, even when the incidents were insignificant and happened when she was a child. It's uncanny, but—" She lifted a shoulder, almost as an apology.

Agnes' information was interesting to me, even if I couldn't testify to it in court. It gave me some new leads to follow, and I always found that having someplace to start, even if it turns out to be the wrong place, is better than having no starting point at all. "Well, thank both of you for your help. Agnes, don't ever let anyone tell you you're not okay just the way you are. Everybody's different. Heck, I give my sergeant nightmares because I usually do things differently than your average cop, but I'm okay too."

Casey rolled her eyes and chuckled with a kind of grunt before walking over to her sieve. "Different doesn't even begin to cover it."

I exchanged grins with Phyla, then turned back to Agnes and stabbed my finger in her face. "Now listen to me. You are *not* a private investigator. And even if you were, you're not allowed to trespass on an ongoing crime scene. That's not just a prank; it can land you in jail. Understand?" I waited for her to nod before I motioned toward Casey, who had begun methodically sifting through the dirt again. "We need to get back to work, so…"

Phyla took the hint and guided a reluctant Agnes to her SUV. Agnes wanted to stay until we'd finished, or until the sun went down, whichever would keep her involved in the investigation for as long as possible. I think she really did fancy herself a private investigator, even if her certificate had been bought from a sham college,

CHAPTER 8

The next morning, I went to the evidence section to see if the papers in the baggie had been processed and whether I could check them out to take a closer look.

The evidence tech, Marla Springer, a perky 20-something Asian woman with golden skin and a heart-shaped face, stood behind the countertop with her chin in her hand, studying some paperwork my friend Ruthanne had apparently just put in front of her.

Marla pointed at one of the items. "So you remember turning in this bag along with all the other evidence you brought in that day?"

Sounding exasperated, Ruthanne tapped the evidence sheet several times. "Not only do I remember turning in this bag, I remember handing it directly to Steve Acres and joking with him about keeping it safe because it was the lynchpin of my whole case! If I don't have it for court tomorrow, I'm toast."

"Okay. Steve's working a narcotics destruction board today, but when he comes back, I'll ask him about it. I've already looked at the shelf where it should have been stored, and then I searched the surrounding shelves just in case he'd misfiled it."

Ruthanne straightened, lifting her bangs with one hand, obviously trying to get a handle on her temper before it got the best of her. "Those destruction hoards last all day. He won't be back until late this afternoon, and if he can't find it then, it'll be too late to search for it. I have to have it, Marla. Can I just come in and search around myself? Can you maybe page him and ask him over the phone if he remembers the bag and where he put it?"

"Where he put it? This case is...let me see..." She turned the paperwork so she could read the date at the top of the page. "It's a ten year old case. Think about that, Ruthanne. He's processed hundreds, if not thousands of bags of evidence since then. There's no way he's going to remember it."

I took a peek at the evidence sheet. "Ten years? I didn't know you guys did cold cases. What's up with that?"

Apparently Ruthanne had been too preoccupied to notice me, and when I spoke, she jumped sideways, throwing her hand over her heart to reassure herself it was still in her chest. "Jeez, Alex, don't sneak up on me like that."

"Sorry, I was just standing here. So why are you working a ten year old case?"

She picked up the evidence sheet and flicked it with her fingers and then began reciting as though she'd told the story a hundred times, which she probably had if she'd had to convince some department commander to re-open a dead case.

"Ten years ago, I was on foot patrol downtown when this kid ran up to me and said there was blood coming out from under a porch. When I went to investigate, I found Laura Woods, one of the local hookers, with her head bashed in. She'd been stuffed under this old guy's raised front deck."

She leaned her elbow on the counter. "Long story short, guess what detective came to investigate the case?"

I raised my shoulders along with my eyebrows.

"Who was the worst detective this department has ever known who rose to through the ranks on the basis of who his brother-in-law was?"

"Oh, shit. Not Fred Beulow?"

"One and the same. He came to the scene, took one look at Laura and elbowed his partner. He said, 'Jesus, she calls us out for a hooker, and not a very good one at that.' The two of them broke up in hysterics like two little school boys. He told me to call the coroner and bag the evidence and call him when I was done. Then those two asswipes went and had their breakfast at Fernandos."

I felt my anger rising just thinking about Captain Beulow and how many cases he'd buried and how many heartbroken families are still wondering what happened to their son or daughter, husband or wife. "So you've been working the case ever since?"

She shook her head. "I've been trying to get permission to re-open it from the first day I got into homicide. I couldn't get anybody to pay attention until you exposed Beulow for the ignorant, impotent, unqualified asswipe that he is."

Ruthanne was referring to a case I'd stumbled on where Beulow's incompetence had almost resulted in an innocent man being executed for a crime he didn't commit. "So you re-opened it, and..." I rolled one hand in the air.

"I had a suspect all along, but unfortunately, all the evidence was—" She corrected herself. "*Is* circumstantial, except for this." She stabbed her finger down onto item number 3RS.

Her handwriting has always been little better than chicken scratch and I had to pull the paper up close to try to decipher the entry. "A rock?"

She nodded. "A rock with the victim's blood on it. The murder weapon, in other words. But I didn't have anything to link it to my suspect until about three months ago. I was bitching to Kota that the asshole who murdered Laura was still walking around free as you please while Laura's mother, who's been diagnosed with pancreatic cancer, can't get closure. Laura's mother was going to die knowing her daughter's murderer never paid for what he did."

I'd never known Laura Woods. In fact I'd never even heard of her. She'd been murdered several years before I'd come on the department. But I knew the frustration of watching guilty people walk because we couldn't put together a strong enough case. "So what changed? Why is the rock all of a sudden such a crucial part of your case?"

"Because, after I explained why I was so frustrated, Kota told me

103

about a new technology, something she called a forensic vacuum. She had a friend at the FBI lab who had one, so she took the rock to him, and they were able to pick up something she called 'touch DNA' from the rock. And voila!" She grinned triumphantly. "It matched the asshole's DNA!"

Marla shuffled through the papers in the case folder. "Wait a minute, I don't show Kota checking that rock out of the evidence room." She stepped over to a pile of papers stacked in a tray labeled To Be Filed.

Her fingers flew through the stack until she called out in triumph and held up an evidence log sheet. "Ah ha! *That's* why I couldn't find it! Kota still has the rock. Get her to bring it to me today, I'll check it back into evidence, and you can check it out again for court in the morning."

Ruthanne had already pushed away from the counter and was halfway out the door. She called back over her shoulder, "I'll get her here with that damn rock if I have to push her in a wheelbarrow! Don't go away!"

Smiling, Marla turned to me. "Crisis averted." A dimple formed on her cheek as she grinned. "So, what can I do for you, Detective Wolfe?"

"I need to check out this paperwork for a little while." I slid the evidence form over the countertop until it rested in front of her.

"Sure, let me go get it for you. I'll be right back."

I watched as she clicked her way back to the evidence room on impossibly high-heeled shoes. Everyone knew they were way outside the dress code for evidence techs, but Marla seemed immune to any kind of censure. Of course, the fact that she had a perfect hourglass figure combined with drop-dead gorgeous looks probably accounted for that. Although, if she ever got a female commander, she might find herself wandering around in black, rubber-soled lab shoes.

She clicked back to me holding the evidence bag. Setting it on the counter, she placed a red lacquered fingernail on the line where I was supposed to sign.

Once the technicalities were out of the way, I tucked the package under my arm and turned to leave. On the way out, I was almost run down by a triumphant Ruthanne, practically dragging Kota and the rock through the evidence room door.

Kota shot me an amused look as I stepped aside to let them pass.

I waved and let the door shut behind me.

CHAPTER 9

Quitting time had come and gone, and most of the detectives had left the building by the time I finally looked up from reading Jepson's paperwork. I rubbed tired eyes as I sat back and thought about the various genealogical lists and scribbled notations I'd found while skimming through the stuff. Unfortunately, even though I'd written three pages of my own notes about the Jepson family line, I wasn't any closer to understanding why the research had been stuck in a bag at the bottom of the closet.

I hadn't realized Kate was still sitting at her desk until she pushed her chair back and stood up to stretch cramped muscles. She called out to me over the glass partition that made up three sides of her cubicle. "Well? Anything interesting?"

"No, not really." I picked up my notes along with the scattered papers I'd taken from Jepson's closet, tapped them into submission, placed them in a manila folder and shoved it into my green canvas briefcase.

Kate walked over and indicated the case with a lift of her chin. "I've been watching you. That's a lot of notes for 'not really.'"

I shrugged. "Sometimes I have to let things sit and jell before I can make sense of what I'm seeing. I haven't gotten it all figured out yet, but I have the feeling I'm missing something. I know a lady who works at the library who's pretty good at genealogy. I think I'll take the notes to her tomorrow and see if she notices anything interesting."

She watched as I packed my briefcase with everything I'd need on the off chance I got called out in the middle of the night. Casey and I were on call, and you just never knew what kind of case was going to turn up out of the blue. Crossing her arms, she said, "What else?"

I looked up at her, curious about why she was so interested in Jepson's genealogy. "Nothing much. Just some notes along the edge of the pages, mostly things relating to who married who, how many kids they had, when they died and where they were buried. I'll let you know if I find anything interesting." I grabbed the briefcase and keys off my desk and waited to see if she had anymore questions.

She turned and walked back to her cubicle. A notebook lay open on the corner and she flipped it closed, turning it minutely so it lined up with the edge of her desk. "Time to head home. I've always found the dead to be very patient victims—or witnesses—whatever the case may be."

We walked to the garage together where I climbed into my car and quickly drove home to let Tessa and Jynx out for their nightly run. When they came in panting and happy, I set their full dinner bowls on the floor before jumping into my Jeep and making my way to Megan's animal obedience school. Megan and I had made plans to get a chilidog and fries at a great little place on the west side of town.

When I pulled into her parking lot, the number of luxury sedans and sports cars scattered about surprised me. Megan's school wasn't exactly in the classiest part of town, and I was impressed that these cars had not only kept their tires in place, but they'd somehow managed to not get stolen in the bargain.

As I climbed out of my car, the driver's door to a Mercedes S-class sedan opened. I knew it was an S-class and that it retailed for around $95,000 because Gia had one that she used as her second car, presumably whenever her $330,000 Bentley was unavailable.

A huge, longshoreman type in a chauffeur's coat and cap stepped out and eyed me suspiciously. The presence of the gussied up gorilla explained how the cars remained untouched, but it didn't tell me why they were here in the first place.

As I walked over to the chauffeur, I absently catalogued the different types of cars parked in the lot. Most of them were black sedans, but I also saw one dark maroon Jaguar, a silver Porsche, and a sea-green Mercedes.

I glanced across the street where a combination of security lights and street lamps lit the sidewalk. Several of the local street thugs, dressed in baggy jeans with long sleeved shirts buttoned up to their chins, stood drooling over the luxury car smorgasbord. I'm sure they were wondering why the not-yet-stolen cars had come to them instead of the other way around.

When they saw me looking, they began making smootchy noises and rocking their hips back and forth while calling out invitations and insults to me in the same breath. They were off to my left, so they were oblivious to the fact that I was a cop.

I stepped around the back of the Mercedes and faced them, giving them an unobstructed view of my badge and gun, which I carried on the right. Within seconds, the sidewalk had cleared and there wasn't a banger in sight.

"Nice trick." The chauffeur spoke with a deep bass rumble, and I turned to study him.

He stood with his arms crossed, his over-developed biceps straining at the fabric of his black uniform jacket. If he'd been doing performance art, he would have been an immovable tree with his perfectly balanced stance, trunk-like legs shoulder width apart, and a thick neck set solidly on beefy shoulders.

I walked over to him and mimicked his posture, right down to the crossed arms and shoulder-width stance. "Thanks. So what's happening? What are all these," I waved in the general direction of the cars, "doing here?"

He indicated Megan's school with a tilt of his head. "The lady who owns this place, and Ms. Masterson," He raised his chin toward the maroon Jag, "are doing a fundraiser for some rescue organization. Everybody brought their dogs...well, except that lady." He once again gestured with his chin, this time toward a shiny black Mercedes SUV.

"She brought a miniature pony, about the size of a Belgian mastiff." He grinned, dropping his arms to his sides and moving aside his jacket as he rested one platter-sized hand on his hip.

I couldn't help but think he could easily wrap his hand around my throat and have the fingers touch in the back as he systematically crushed my windpipe.

"A pony? In there?"

"Yeah, she put a ramp on the back and the little guy walked right down. I've never seen a horse that small." He wiped a drop of sweat off his cheek. "Damn, the sun's gone down and it's still boiling out here."

"You have to wear that jacket? Even as hot as it gets in Tucson?"

He nodded. "My boss' wife, Mrs. Alderson, is old school. From England, no less." He shrugged. "But the Alderson's pay really well."

He looked toward the door of the K9 school. "*Really* well. I used to play pro ball. Mr. Alderson was the majority owner of the team I played for, and I guess he took a liking to me. He offered to match my player's salary if I'd come to work for him as a combo security guard, chauffeur, and jack of all trades.

"I was tired of limping home after every game and spending the next week soaking my battered body in a sauna just so I could jog out onto the turf the next game." He turned suddenly. "Here they come." He hurried toward the front of Megan's building.

He pulled open the door, and to both of our surprise, the miniature pony was the first to come bounding out, with Megan hot on his heels.

He was the cutest thing I'd seen in a long time. I admired his cherubic face, stubby little legs and determined expression until Megan saw me and screamed, "Alex, stop him!"

I remember thinking *piece of cake* just before I grabbed him around his neck and was immediately pulled off my feet and dragged bumping and bouncing off the pavement as he careened down the street completely heedless of the oncoming traffic.

Behind me, Megan ratcheted up to apoplectic and screamed, "Alex! Don't let go!"

I hadn't realized the media had been at the fundraiser until I saw a man with a camera loping down the sidewalk taking pictures. I almost had my feet under me and the pony stopped until the guy's flash caught the little fella in the eyes and he took off running and bucking again with me hanging on for dear life.

Some kind, cowboy type who'd almost hit us with his pickup truck, took pity on me and parked his Chevy in the middle of the street. He chased us down and jumped on board, easily pulling the little guy, and me, to a stop. Of course, I landed flat on my back on the asphalt.

Megan came panting up shortly after that. It was obvious she was working to keep her lips pinched shut as she knelt down to snap a rope onto the pony's halter. Unfortunately, the second she looked down into my eyes, she threw herself onto her back next to me, laughing so hard I thought she was going to pee.

Close on her heels came a plus-sized woman. She race-walked up to us, scolding the pony with all kinds of "snookums" and "ukums" and "bad widdle boys." When she finally reached us, she dropped to her knees and embraced her impish little runaway.

He pushed his muzzle up under her strawberry blonde hair, then peeked out at me with what I could have sworn was a twinkle of mischief in his eye.

The cowboy pushed himself to his feet.

I looked up at his lanky frame from my ignominious landing pad on the pavement. "Hey, thanks for the help. Who knew these little guys were so strong?"

He brushed some loose dirt off his jeans. "Yes ma'am. I've had calves about his size throw me right onto my—" He stopped, realizing he was standing in the middle of three women. "Well, he dumped me, that's for sure. Anyway, have a good day, ladies."

The pony's owner called out in a Julia Child voice, "Here, young man, come back to my car and let me pay you for your help."

He grinned and shook his head. "Thank you, ma'am, but seein' this lady bouncin' down the street tryin' to stop that little fella was payment enough." He sent a saucy wink my way before climbing into his truck and tapping his horn lightly as he drove off.

I stood and helped the heavy lady to her feet.

I also offered my hand to Megan, who still lay on the pavement wiping her eyes with the sleeve of her shirt. "Oh my God, Alex. You're gonna make the nine o'clock news *and* the morning papers." She grabbed my hand and hauled herself up, laughing again as she brushed some dirt off the back of my pants.

I tried to glare at her over my shoulder, but she and the lady began chuckling again. A begrudging smile escaped my determination to recapture my flagging dignity.

When the three of us started back to the parking lot, the large woman pulled gently on the pony's lead rope and called out encouragement. "Come along, Titus. Come along now."

The pony smart-stepped right next to her thigh, picking up his hooves, holding his head high on an arched neck while occasionally glancing at me out of the corner of his eye. Despite the wild ride, I liked his spunky personality. I mussed the mane on the top of his head.

The woman noticed and held her hand out to me as we walked. "I'm Millie MacDunne. I didn't thank you for capturing Titus. I can't imagine what would have happened if he'd gotten lost in this type of neighborhood."

Since I was walking to the right of her, I had to reach across my body to shake hands. "I'm Alex Wolfe. And you're welcome."

As we neared the K9 Academy, a reporter and his cameraman came over and stuck a microphone in Millie's face. "Care to give us a comment on Detective Wolfe's wild ride?"

Most of the luxury cars were pulling out of the lot just as we walked up, and I grabbed Megan and steered her toward my Jeep. "C'mon. Let's get out of here before they ask us for an interview."

Megan pulled her arm out of my hand. "Hold on, I need to lock up first. You go ahead. Meet me at my house so I can drop Sugar and my car off before we go." She started for the door of the business, but I quickly stopped her.

"Megan."

She stopped, probably noticing my "this is important so listen up" expression.

I stepped close and whispered in her ear so no one else would hear. "If the reporters ask you anything about me or Gia, or about my friendship with her, don't say anything."

She shrugged, apparently unconcerned. "Sure, no problem."

She started away and I grabbed her again. "Megan, listen to me. I mean *really* listen, okay?"

I finally got through to her because she leaned her head close to mine and whispered back. "Why? What's the matter? Is everything okay?"

I saw the reporter glancing our way and steered Megan closer to my Jeep. "Some reporter is trying to say Gia and I are... you know." I felt my cheeks go red.

"You're?"

I didn't want to have to spell it out, but the blank look in her eyes told me she had no idea what I was trying to say. I moved in even closer and spoke so quietly I could barely hear my own words. "That we're, you know, in a relationship."

"What?" She yelled the word loud enough that one of the thugs who'd returned to his perch across the street shifted his focus off Millie and the reporter and onto the two of us.

I slapped a hand over her mouth. "Shhhhh. Jeez, Meg. Yell it out to the whole world why don't ya?"

She coughed a laugh, turning in a circle and raking her hands through her mop of frizzy, red hair. "You have got to be kidding me! Oh my God!" She turned toward the reporter, then spun around to face me again, a huge grin spreading across her face. "Are you?"

"What? No!" I gaped at her, shocked that she would even ask. I pulled her close one more time. "Look. I just didn't want you to be surprised into saying anything we'd both regret. So don't even talk to them, okay? Anything about me or Gia is out of bounds. Period."

She sighed, amusement still sparkling in her eyes. "I've got your six, Alex. Don't worry. I'll see you at my house, but then you've got a lot of splainin' to do." She did her best Ricky Ricardo imitation before practically skipping off to grab her golden retriever, Sugar, and lock up her business.

Apparently the reporter had finished with Millie, because he hurried over to waylay Megan.

As I climbed into my Jeep, I sent up a quick prayer to the goddess of preservation that she'd keep her head about her if he started throwing out questions about me. Megan is smart, and I was pretty confident that forewarned was forearmed.

I glanced over at them as I left the lot, and cursed quietly to myself when I saw Megan expounding enthusiastically about something while the camera rolled. I would have crossed myself for good measure except I was afraid God would send down a bolt of lightning or some such thing. I wasn't exactly a practicing Jew, but I was pretty sure that was on some rabbi's list of proscribed religious practices.

By the time Megan jumped into my Jeep in front of her house, it had actually gotten pretty late and I was starving. I drove in the direction of the greasiest, most fat-laden dive this side of the Rio Grande, Pat's Chili Dogs, anxiously waiting to hear what Megan had said to the reporters.

We both began at the same time. "So what did—"

"Spill it, Ale—" Megan stopped and held up her hand to silence me. "Me first. What's going on? Why do they think you and Gia are an item? That guy didn't ask me anything about you two. He was just doing a follow-up on the fund raiser, but what reporter is trying to say you and Gia are lovers?"

I sighed. "Her name is Amanda Kellworth."

"Six o'clock news? I know her, big hair, tons of cleavage, lotta teeth."

"Yeah, that's her. Anyway, this lady who's supposedly friends with Gia went to Kellworth and said Gia and I were a lesbian couple. I think she's jealous or something because she and Gia sometimes...you know."

She put on her worldly face. "So Gia's a lesbian? Could have fooled me."

"I think Gia's whatever Gia wants to be, whenever she wants to be, with whomever she wants to be." As we drove through downtown, I caught a glimpse of a woman hurrying out of the Hotel Congress, the local watering hole famous for its ghosts and wispy apparitions.

The woman caught my attention because she was moving really fast on ridiculously high heels, which would have had my nose planted in the sidewalk after the first step. We pulled up to a red-light and I watched her in my rearview mirror, curious about the coordination needed to perform such a feat.

She hurried to a white BMW and slipped into the back seat, circling her hands in a forward motion, apparently gesturing to the driver to get moving. The Beamer pulled up beside us where I was able to get a closer look. "I knew she looked familiar."

Megan pushed up off her seat in order to see over me and down into the backseat of the other car. "Who looks familiar?"

"Well, you know how we were just talking about Gia's sometime lover?"

"That's *her*?" She practically lay in my lap trying to get a better look.

"Megan, get offa me." As I shoved her back into her own seat, Aisla Westhaven pulled her cellphone out of her pocketbook, listened for a moment, and began yelling at the person on the other end of the line.

The light turned green and the Beamer pulled away.

I wondered what had Aisla so upset. I glanced at Megan, who was intently watching the back of the car. Someone behind us honked, and I quickly accelerated.

When the car made a right turn onto Fifth Avenue, going in the opposite direction of Pat's Chili Dogs, I sighed and began to move into the left turn lane. Megan grabbed the wheel and jerked it to the right, pointing wildly in the direction Aisla's ride had taken. "Alex. Where are you going? Follow her!"

I peeled her hand off the steering wheel and grinned. "I was hoping you'd say that." I turned right at the intersection and positioned myself two cars behind the Beamer. It turned left onto Toole, passed the Southern Pacific Railroad station, took a few more turns and finally headed north on Campbell.

Megan fidgeted in the passenger seat, always anxious or overly excited whenever we did something like this. I put a hand on her shoulder. "You okay? Do you have to go pee or something?"

She sat up and craned her neck to make sure she could see the BMW, which had moved ahead another few cars. "C'mon, Alex. You're gonna lose them."

"I'm not gonna lose them. I'm betting they're headed somewhere in the foothills on the north end of Campbell."

My phone rang and I fished it out of my front pants pocket. I knew it was Kate from her ring so I didn't waste time on preliminaries. "Hey boss. What's up?"

I frowned. Up ahead, a black SUV quickly pulled up alongside Aisla's Beamer.

As I wondered what was going on with the black SUV, Kate said, "I need you and Casey for a call-out. It's—"

Bullets slammed into the BMW, and other cars swerved or pulled U-turns directly in front of me.

"Shit!" I slammed on the brakes, sending my phone flying.

The driver of the Beamer slammed on the brakes, turned a sharp right and drove the car up onto the sidewalk in an attempt to provide some minimal protection to the passengers. Still, the bullets had shattered windows and riddled the shiny black paint with quarter-sized holes.

I yelled "Get down!" at Megan, then punched the gas pedal and rammed into the back of the SUV, moving it forward and away from the BMW. I grabbed my Glock and leapt out.

The driver of the SUV gunned the engine. Smoke peeled off the tires with an ugly stench as it drove off at a high rate of speed.

"Fuck!" Running back to the Jeep, I first checked to make sure Megan hadn't been hurt in the crash.

She'd unbuckled her seat belt and had just grabbed the door handle when I wrenched her door open. She handed me my cell phone.

Miraculously, it hadn't disconnected. "Kate! Someone in a black SUV, license John-King-Tom-3-3-4 just shot up Aisla Westhaven's BMW. We're on Campbell just north of Limberlost. I need back-up and meds, but I don't have a radio. I'm going to check the car to see if there's anyone left alive."

"I'll make the call. Be there in twenty." She hung up before I could tell her I didn't need her. I really didn't want to have to explain why I happened to be a few cars back from Aisla's, or why Megan was with me.

No one else had gone near the car. In fact, there wasn't another vehicle in sight.

The rear passenger door was locked so I covered my elbow with the bottom of my shirt and smashed the rest of the glass out of the broken front passenger window. I reached in and hit the unlock switch. When locks popped, I jerked open the rear door only to see Aisla lying on the floorboards covered in blood. I carefully put my knee on the glass-covered back seat and leaned in.

Megan stuck her head in next to mine. "What do I do?"

I motioned toward the driver with a lift of my chin while I felt Aisla's neck for a pulse. "See if he's still alive. If he is, try to stop the bleeding by putting pressure on his wounds."

As she rushed to the open front passenger door, I said, "Watch out for the glass."

"Right."

A moment later she began pulling in great gulps of air. "Ewwwww, my God! Most of his head's gone!" True to course, she ducked back out the door and retched.

Aisla's pulse beat weakly under my fingertips and I quickly checked for injuries. A bullet had entered the left side of her back at such an acute angle it had exited on the far right side of her chest. Hopefully it had missed anything vital. I put pressure on both holes and visually checked for any others.

By that time sirens were wailing in the distance, getting progressively louder as the cavalry approached. Soon, a vehicle pulled to a stop behind us and almost immediately a male officer began shouting commands at Megan. "Show me your hands! Turn away from me and get down on your knees!"

"But—"

I knew Megan thought everyone should know she was one of the good guys. I didn't have time to be nice. "Goddammit, Megan, do what he says! Just do it!"

I couldn't leave Aisla, so I called out to the cop, "Tucson Police Detective Wolfe inside the car with a victim." I heard cuffs ratcheting and knew they'd handcuffed Megan.

A familiar female voice called out, "You in the car, let me see your hands."

Apparently they hadn't heard me the first time. "I can't. Detective Alex Wolfe. I'm trying to stop her bleeding."

"Alex?" My good friend Terri Gentry stuck her head in the door. When she saw me, she immediately keyed the mic attached to her shoulder epaulet. "Code four here. Send in the meds."

All the sirens from the other police vehicles shut down. They'd turn their attention from an active shooter call to finding the SUV.

The paramedics, who'd been holding off until the police had the scene secured, drove up and parked next to the Beamer.

I'd been so busy up to that point trying not to get shot that Aisla's whispered voice startled me. I bent down to hear better. "What?"

Her voice cracked as she struggled to speak. "Gia." She pulled in a harsh breath. "Wanted to put...bullet proof..." There was another strangled breath and a weak smile. "I said...no." The smile left as she coughed up blood on the last words.

When the paramedic came in from the driver's side door and took over, I got out to allow the one behind me to take my place.

I hurried over to the patrol car where Terri had just taken Megan out of the back seat. She nodded to me as she took her keys off the ring on her belt and unlocked the handcuffs.

Megan's wrists had lines gouged into them. In his hurry to secure the scene, the cop had ratcheted them on a little too tight.

When I walked up, I could see steam coming out of her ears. "You okay?"

She punched me in the arm. Really hard.

"Ow! What was that for?"

Her voice escalated with each of the three points she began to tick off. "For letting him point a gun at me and then letting him strangle my wrists with those things, and then for not letting me out of the friggin' police car!"

"I came over as soon as the paramedics took over. And he had to put cuffs on you until he knew what was happening."

The young officer walked over to us and Terri handed him his cuffs.

He glanced at Megan, who suddenly burst into tears and buried her head in his chest.

Not knowing what else to do, the officer awkwardly put his arm around her shoulders.

She managed to sob out two words. "His head."

He patted her back with a stiff hand, giving me a slightly panicked look over the top of her head.

Terri took over from the young man who beat a hasty retreat to his car. I had other things I needed to do, and seeing that Megan was in good hands, I turned and started for the Beamer.

"Alex."

I froze. I hadn't had time to work out exactly what I was going to tell Kate. More importantly, I hadn't had a chance to tell *Megan* what we were going to tell Kate.

As soon as she finished talking to the patrol sergeant on the scene, she started toward me. On the way, she looked over at Terri and Megan.

She stopped and did a double-take.

I decided this might be a great time to check the damage to the front of my Jeep. Not too long ago, I had added a full grill guard over the front bumper because I thought they looked cool. Now, as I surveyed the damage, or lack of damage, I was glad I had. I was trying to decide whether I needed to mention that I'd rammed the other vehicle when I saw Kate's shoes step up next to mine.

"Hey boss." That was about as good as I could come up with for an opening line.

"Are you okay?" She didn't exactly sound sympathetic, but I didn't hear any edge to her voice. Yet.

"Yeah, fine."

"And Megan?" The edge crept in a little on that one.

"She's fine."

The silence stretched out enough that I gave in and looked her in the eye. I still didn't say anything. I'd learned fairly quickly working for Kate that the less volunteered, the better. I scratched the back of my neck, hoping for an innocent, haven't got a clue look.

The problem with Kate was, she'd perfected the art of interviewing without saying a word.

So we stared at each other.

The muscle in her jaw flexed, and she began tapping her leg with the tips of her fingers.

The paramedic's siren whooped as they left to transport Aisla to the hospital. I caught the gaze of the guy who'd relieved me and lifted my chin in thanks. He was friendly enough and waved as he drove by.

The rush of adrenaline was slowly wearing off, and I lowered my head to rub my eyes with the tips of my fingers. When I looked up again, Kate's arms were crossed and I gave in. "Sure was a good thing we happened on the shooting like we did."

Kate's eyes narrowed.

I tried again. "Too bad about the driver, though."

She spoke very slowly. "Do you know who he is? Or was?"

"Nope. Megan said his head was blown off and—" My voice stuttered to a halt and I felt my stomach drop.

I whispered, "Not Gabe."

When she shook her head, I had to lean against the Jeep to steady myself. In fact, I felt so lightheaded with relief, I pulled myself into the driver's seat to sit for a moment.

Kate followed and rested her hand on the top of my door. "The name on his I.D. was Luca Romano."

My gaze snapped up and I stared into Kate's eyes.

She didn't blink when she asked, "Who is Luca Romano?"

I lowered my head onto the hand I had draped over the steering wheel. "Oh shit. This is not good."

Slowly and distinctly enunciating the name, Kate repeated her question. "Alex. Who is Luca Romano?" Her voice had a hardened quality that told me she had just about run out of patience.

I looked up again. "Luca was...let me see." I had to figure out the relationship in my mind. I drew a diagram in the air with my finger to help me think. "If I have it right, he's Gia's second cousin. Her father's cousin's son."

I thought about the quiet man with a friendly grin who'd nodded in greeting this morning. We'd never really talked. Most of Gia's men were the bulked up silent types, but I remembered he'd also smiled slightly the day I'd dislocated Pito's thumb.

Kate glanced over the hood of my Jeep. "Shit."

I followed her gaze and saw Amanda Kellworth standing outside the crime scene tape focused intently on us. I shared her sentiment. "Shit."

She grabbed my arm, pulled me out of the Jeep and steered me toward her car. I saw Megan watching us and waved her away with a flick of my hand.

Apparently that meant 'come on' to her and she waved goodbye to Terri before jogging over to meet us.

I heard the click of the locks on Kate's car and pulled my arm away just as she jerked the passenger door open. Hot air flowed out, heating the already overheated air around us.

Kate made her way around to the driver's door. "Get in." She started the car, rolled down the windows to let more hot air escape as she turned on the air conditioning.

Megan opened the back door and hopped in as I slid into the front seat. Her voice was somewhat subdued but at least she'd gotten control of her emotions. "Hi Kate. It was awful." She wiped away the tears that began welling in her eyes with a tissue she held wadded up in her fist. Okay, so she almost had control of her emotions.

The air was just beginning to cool, and I aimed the middle vent toward the back seat.

Kate rolled up the windows. She turned and pinned Megan with her glare. "How did you get here?"

Megan reacted with her guilty puppy dog look. "Alex and I were headed to Pat's Chili Dogs." Whenever Megan becomes nervous, her mouth kicks into verbal diarrhea mode. "I don't know if you've ever eaten there, but we wanted their chili dogs and, well, really, Alex likes their fries the—"

Kate held up a hand. "Not interested." She turned to me. "Okay. Tell me exactly why you were following Aisla Westhaven when I specifically told you to stay clear."

The Beamer had ended up off to the right of my Jeep, and I stared at both of them while I came up with my answer.

"Don't think too hard, Alex. We're in this car because I want the truth and I don't want the media's long range microphones picking up what you say."

"I always tell you the truth."

"You tell me what you want me to know."

There was that. "Well, technically, you told me to stay away from Gia, and you said to stay away when I'm on duty." I shrugged. "Aisla's not Gia, and I'm not on duty. So it's all good, right?" I glanced back at Megan who bobbed her head up and down. Apparently she thought the more enthusiastically she nodded the stronger my case would be.

Kate rubbed her forehead, probably trying to stave off the headaches I usually brought on. "So you were following her?"

"No. Well, yes. Kind of. Not really."

"Which is it? It's not a hard question, Alex."

"Megan and I started out for Pat's Chili Dogs."

Megan nodded again. "Best dogs in town."

The one finger Kate held up over the back of the seat silenced her. "Megan, a man just died, and the war between the Angelinos and the Andrulis Mafia is going to ramp up to unprecedented levels. Do you really think it's appropriate for you to be telling me about Pat's Chili Dogs?"

Megan wilted back into her seat. I felt bad for her. She's the most positive, upbeat person I know. If something gets her down, she feels the emotion intensely, then in a few minutes, all is forgotten and she's onto better things. "Megs, I'll tell the story, okay?"

She nodded and mumbled guiltily. "I forgot about the dead guy."

I took a breath and continued. "We were driving down Congress and I saw this lady in ridiculously high heels get into a Beamer. When they pulled up next to us at the light, I could see it was Aisla, and she was pissed and yelling at someone on the phone. So, no, we didn't start out to follow her. When they turned right, away from Pat's, I was curious to see where she went. That's all."

"Why?"

I thought about that for a second. "To see where she was going, I guess."

"Why?"

"Because I don't trust her."

Megan sat forward. "And I wanted to see what she looked like because she thought Alex and Gia were lovers."

The two of us glared at her over the back seat.

Kate pointed a finger in Megan's face again. "You will not repeat that, understood? Not *in* this car, not *outside* the car, and definitely not to the detectives who come to take your statement."

"Statement?" The shocked look on Megan's face would have been comical under different circumstances. She glanced at me worriedly. "What should I say?"

Kate answered for me. "The truth exactly how you saw it." She looked at me. "The same goes for you. You tell them exactly why you happened to be behind Aisla when the shooting happened. Got it?"

I hesitated. "You know... I actually followed her because I saw this lady in high heels and thought maybe I recognized her, and when I saw she was angrily talking on the phone, obviously super emotional, and since I thought I might know her, I wanted to make sure everything was okay. I'm sure I know her from somewhere, but don't exactly remember from where..."

Once again I looked over the back seat at Megan. "Do not mention the connection to Gia."

"Okay. Geez, Alex, I wasn't born yesterday."

I could feel Kate's glare boring into the side of my head. She surprised me when she turned off the car and got out. I'd expected at least some kind of comment to my recollection of the events.

Megan and I got out too.

Relief washed over me when Ruthanne walked up holding a notebook and tape recorder. "Who wants to go first?" With a wave of her hand she invited one of us to accompany her to her vehicle for a preliminary interview.

Megan pushed me forward. "Alex does."

Kate shook her head. "Talk to Megan first while the events are fresh in her mind. Alex can give her statement back at the station."

Ruthanne nodded and we watched the two of them walk back to her car.

As I scanned the area looking for Amanda Kellworth, I just

happened to notice they were loading my Jeep onto the bed of a big green tow truck. "Hey!" I ran over to the tow driver. "That's the wrong car!" I pointed to the Beamer. "That's the one you want."

The driver, who resembled a six-foot emaciated scarecrow with no teeth, glanced up at me with a slightly bored, somewhat dull expression on his face. "Talk ta 'at dude, over there." Apparently he didn't deem it necessary to take his hand off the knob controlling the inexorable forward movement of my Jeep onto the platform of his truck. He simply indicated Detective Andy Montagne with a lift of his elbow.

Andy and I had gone through the police academy together. Throughout the entire eight months of training, all he ever talked about was becoming a homicide dick like his dad, Detective Carl Montagne. Andy had made the grade in record time and right now, he stood about ten yards away grinning at me from ear-to-ear.

I stalked up to him, jammed my hands onto my hips and glared. "What are you doing? I need my Jeep. You need the Beamer."

"Hi Alex. Good to see you too."

"Andy. I need my Jeep."

"You rear ended the suspect SUV, right?"

I shrugged. "Well, technically, but— Wait, how'd you know?" I hadn't intended to mention that if I didn't have to. I wondered how he'd found out and began looking around for potential witnesses.

He stepped to his car and reached into the trunk to pull out a lunch-sized, paper evidence bag. He hadn't sealed it yet and he unrolled the top to let me peek inside.

I shoved my hands into my pockets. "Damn it." My Jeep had apparently broken the rear taillight on the SUV. Nestled down in the bag were small pieces of red plastic that unfortunately I knew probably belonged to the suspect vehicle. "So what makes you think I hit it? What if there was another car that took off?"

He put his hand on my shoulder. "Nice try, but I have another bag in the trunk with parts of a broken tail light cover I took off your front bumper. Nice grill guard by the way. Anyway, I'm hoping to get some paint transfer off your car and maybe identify the make and model."

I brightened. "Oh! If that's all you want that's easy. I gave Kate the license plate number when I called her. Let's see, John King Tom something something something. She'll have it."

We both glanced over to where Kate stood talking to Jon Logan, the homicide sergeant. "Sorry, Alex. If you hadn't rammed 'em, your Jeep wouldn't be evidence, but since you did..."

Sighing, I watched as the tow driver finished wrapping chains around my wheels, peeled off his leather work gloves and climbed into the truck.

"I'll get it back to you as soon as I can."

"I know. Thanks." It occurred to me I hadn't seen him since his dad had died about a month earlier. "Hey, I was sorry to hear about your dad."

He nodded. "Thanks. Pretty bizarre, huh?"

"I heard a little about what happened." I stopped, hoping he'd fill in the details. The only thing I knew was that they'd had to have a closed casket funeral.

He grimaced and rubbed the back of his neck. "You probably heard he died in a car accident?"

"Yeah. Pretty bad, huh?"

He crossed his arms and spread his legs wider as he started the story. "Do you remember how much he loved to surf?"

"He once told me he started as a kid and never stopped."

He bobbed his head. "Yup. That was my dad. He was on his way to Rocky Point to surf like he did just about every weekend in the summer. He had his board tied on his old Mercedes convertible. The nose of the board was sticking out on the front passenger side past the windshield and he'd tied the tail to the trunk with a bungee cord." He paused and took in a deep breath, letting it out slowly as he worked to keep his emotions in check. "Some yahoo going in the opposite direction passed a truck on a double-yellow line not realizing how close Dad was."

"Hit him head on?"

He blinked as a hint of anger flashed in his eyes. "Is that supposed to be a joke?"

Confused, I blinked stupidly back at him. "I'd never joke about your dad dying. You know me better than that."

He looked away. "Yeah I know. There's no reason you should know what happened. I've only just now started telling people the whole story. Anyway, the guy cut it too close, and when he swerved back into his own lane, he hit the nose of the surfboard. The tail whipped around and—" His hands tightened into fists. "Well, it decapitated him."

"His surfboard?" My eyebrows shot up into my bangs. No wonder they'd had a closed casket. I couldn't really come up with anything to say, so I just repeated what I'd said earlier. "Uh, I'm really sorry. That —" I stopped myself before "that sucks" came out. "That is such a tragedy."

His characteristic grin reappeared. "Yeah, it does suck, doesn't it? Knowing my Dad, he'd say something like 'Well Andy, now I'll never be the head of a major corporation.'"

I grinned back at him. "Austin Powers!"

"He loved the guy. Don't ask me why. Anyway, I need to get moving before Jon realizes we're not talking about this case. Like I said, I'll try to rush your Jeep."

I tucked an errant lock of hair behind my ear as he walked over to talk to the tow driver. Watching the two of them discussing where to take my Jeep, I didn't think there was any way this week could get worse than it already was. I should know better than to think things like that. Ever.

CHAPTER 10

Megan and Ruthanne must have had a very short interview because they'd both gotten out of the car and were walking my way.

I'd started toward them when a familiar-looking Mercedes pulled up to the crime scene. Gabe stepped out and motioned me over with a slight lift of his chin. I quickly glanced behind me to see where Kate was.

She and Jon were still talking next to the Beamer and luckily their backs were turned.

Ruthanne, who knows me all too well, stepped directly into my path.

I practically ran her down when I turned to go talk to Gabe. "Sorry." I tried to go around.

She moved sideways to block me again.

"What? I need to talk to him."

She maneuvered around so she was facing the same way as me and whispered, "Amanda Kellworth is behind us staring straight at you. If there was ever a reporter to watch out for, she's it. Anyway, Kate and Jon are heading over to talk to him now. Why don't you come sit in my car and we can pretend we're doing an interview?"

"Why pretend? Let's just get it over with so Megan and I can figure out how we're gonna get home."

The way Megan had inched toward us as we spoke was a sure sign she'd been listening in on our conversation. She pointed in Amanda's general direction. "That's the reporter who's been giving you a hard time? She looks different in person."

About a second too late, I recognized the mischievous, determined glint in her eyes. My heart leapt into my throat as she marched across the lot to where Amanda had taken up her post.

"Oh no. No, no, no, no, no." I quickly glanced at Kate who by now had reached Gabe.

She had her left hand planted firmly on her hip and didn't look like she planned to mince any words. Even though she had to crane her neck to look up into Gabe's face, I knew from the set of her shoulders she was delivering a very pointed message.

Gabe glanced my way.

Kate took a small step to the left so she stood directly between me and him. He must have gotten the message because he immediately returned his full attention to what she was saying.

When I looked back to where Megan and Amanda should have been, dread filled my every pore. Neither of them was anywhere to be seen.

It didn't take long for Ruthanne to figure out why I had gone so deathly pale. "Shit."

We stared at each other, not having the faintest idea what our next step should be. I leaned in close and whispered, "One, if we go searching for them, Kellworth will assume there's a reason and start digging more than she already is. Two," I held up my fingers in a peace sign. "If we do find them, Amanda will try to grab me for an interview, which can't happen. And three—"

"And three," Ruthanne said, automatically matching her volume to mine, "we both know Megan isn't half as scatter-brained as she makes out to be and she'll do just fine."

I couldn't help letting out a quick, albeit panicked bark of laughter.

Nodding slightly, Ruthanne conceded the point. "All right, so maybe she did break in and fill the entire city council hallway with ten thousand Dixie cups full of fake animal urine when they voted no on some animal rights cause."

She raised her eyes to the sky as she thought some more. "And then there was that time she completely outlined that guy who was passed out on the floor with empty bottles of beer and later found out he was actually dead and not just dead drunk. And then—"

I started for the crime scene tape. "We've gotta find her."

There weren't many places they could have gone and we hit pay dirt in the first place we looked.

Megan sat in the news van with huge headphones covering her ears. A tiny bit of her tongue was stuck between her lips and her eyebrows were pulled down in her typical "don't bother me I'm concentrating" look. She was turning a dial left, right and back left again.

A sculpted, rock-hard sound tech leaned over her, practically putting his cheek in her hair. He seemed to be instructing her on the fine art of electronic eavesdropping.

Megan shifted slightly to "accidentally" rub faces with the guy, who didn't seem to mind one bit.

The red, blotchy patina on Amanda Kellworth's face spoke a different story. She stood with her arms crossed, glaring at the back of the sound tech's head. While her eyes glowered with malice, the ubiquitous fear of wrinkles most female journalists have forced her to keep any scrunched up show of anger off her perfectly smooth, doll-like face. "That's enough, Jenks, we have a job to do."

Jenks held up one finger without even glancing at her. "Just one sec." His attention never wavered from Megan. "Are you getting anything?"

Megan's fingers ever-so-slightly and sensuously stroked the control knob. In her sultry, come hither voice, she said, "Not yet. Maybe you can help?"

Jenks covered her hand with his and they slowly twisted the knob this way and that.

Kellworth threw up her hands in disgust, then noticed Ruthanne and me standing at the back of the van. Her sweet public voice we all knew and loved morphed into the evil intonations of Cruella Deville. "What do you two want?"

Megan swiveled toward us, positioning herself deeper into the curve of Jenks' arm. "You guys should see this! They really *can* hear every word the detectives say from in here." She put a finger up to one of the earphones and listened. "Kate is telling someone he needs to leave the crime scene. A man is saying— "

"Enough!" Amanda's face actually spasmed into wrinkles as she stormed over and practically ripped the earphones off Megan's head. She slammed them into Jenks' chest when he reared back in surprise.

She must have realized what she'd done because almost immediately, she composed her features into those of Amanda Kellworth, six o'clock news. She breathed in a steadying breath, then turned and smiled at us. "The three of you really shouldn't be here in the van. If you'd just go, Jenks and I can continue with our work."

Megan indicated Jenks with a thumb over her shoulder. "You remember Jenks, Alex? Spring break our senior year in college? The five of us floating on moonlit waves? The tequila?" She glanced over her shoulder at Jenks and lifted her eyebrows several times. "The—"

Both Jenks and I reacted at the same time.

I held my palm inches from her face. "Stop."

Jenks covered Megan's mouth with his hand. "Okay, okay. That's old news. I'm sure Amanda would be bored with the details."

Amanda twisted a smile into place. "You're right there."

Megan propelled herself out of the chair and hopped out of the van. "Thanks for the tour, Jenks. Give me a call sometime."

"I don't have your number anymore."

"Oh yes you do." She pointed to a piece of paper sticking out of his jeans pocket.

The wrinkles in the paper meant she'd hastily stuffed the note where her fingers probably shouldn't have wandered.

The fact that he hadn't noticed spoke volumes about his muddled state of mind at the moment of delivery. He quickly smoothed out the note, glanced at the numbers, and carefully placed it inside his billfold.

Ruthanne had already hightailed it back to the crime scene tape and Megan and I followed on her heels.

Megan stage-whispered. "Ta da."

We ducked under the tape and the three of us kept walking. I whispered back, "What do you mean, ta da? You got a date, big deal."

"No. Well yes, that too. But," She held up her finger triumphantly. "Did Amanda have the presence of mind to ask you any embarrassing questions while you were standing right in front of her? No. Did she and Jenks have *any* time to listen in on conversations that are none of their business? Again, no."

Both Ruthanne and I stopped to regard our crazy friend. All I could say was, "Oh my God. You are absolutely brilliant."

Ruthanne held her arms out to her sides. "I don't know why I ever doubted you, Megs. You are truly one of a kind."

She preened under the praise. Still speaking in a whisper, she said, "I recognized Jenks over by the sound truck and figured a little diversion was in order. Besides, I didn't really believe Kate when she said they can hear us talking from inside the van. Holy cow. I just had to aim that dish-like thing using that knobby thingamajig at whoever I wanted to listen to and I could hear every word being said."

Technical terms had never been Megan's strong suit, so both Ruthanne and I just nodded.

Megan held up her finger again as though she were a professor making a salient point. "But when you and Ruthanne put your heads together and whispered, I couldn't hear you. That's important."

I heard a car door shut. A moment later Gabe was backing his car away from the scene. When he turned his attention forward, he focused on my eyes, clearly intending to send a silent message. I didn't dare acknowledge him because Kate and Jon were headed our way. As he drove off, he kept his attention locked on me until the last possible second.

Jon pointed to Ruthanne. "Take Alex and Ms. O'Reilly back to the station. I understand you already took Ms. O'Reilly's statement so get Alex's too. When you've finished with that, take them to Alex's house since we towed her Jeep.

Megan piped up. "No, that's okay. My ride's already here waiting for me.

All of us turned to where she'd indicated.

A well-built cowboy leaned against the hood of his Ford F250, his arms and legs crossed, waiting patiently. He languidly repositioned his chew in his mouth, then slowly leaned over and spat on the ground at his feet.

"When did you have time to call Tony?"

"I called from Ruthanne's car after I told her what happened, which didn't take very long because she said to tell her everything I saw." She shrugged. "Since you yelled at me to get down, I didn't see much." Her mouth curved into a smile as she waved to her cowboy.

He lifted his chin in response. Tony had never been much for words. In fact, I think I've only heard him utter a complete sentence on three occasions. Two of those had been to ask me to pass him some food, and the third was when he explained to me why he didn't talk too much. He'd said his granddaddy had a saying: Never pass up a chance to shut up. And he didn't.

Megan headed his way, and with a wave to us, climbed up into the seat of his truck.

CHAPTER 11

The jangling of my cell phone woke me the next morning. I'd programmed in almost all of my friends and co-workers with their own special rings, and since I didn't recognize this one I hit ignore and rolled over for some extra Zs. When the jangling started again, I angrily punched the ignore button and stuffed the phone between my mattress and box springs.

The third time, I didn't so much hear the ringing as feel the buzzing from the phone's vibration. I ripped the phone from under the mattress and punched send. "What?"

Gabe's matter-of-fact, deadpan voice brought me completely awake. "Ms. A. would like to see you."

It took me a minute to clear out the cobwebs. "Why?"

Since in Gabe's universe, it didn't matter why Gia wanted to see me, he remained silent.

I drew out the word. "Okay." After thinking a moment, I continued, "Tell her I can come after work, say around six if nothing else gets in the way."

"Ms. A. wants to see you now."

"No can do. Kate asked me not to talk to Gia on duty for a while, and I have to respect what she tells me."

I could hear Gabe's unasked question floating through the carrier waves, *Since when did that start?* But, as usual, he remained silent.

"So I gotta run. I'll see you this evening."

He must have quietly conveyed my message to Gia because he said, "Ms. A. says to bring her along."

"Ha!" I couldn't help the incredulous bark of laughter that escaped my lips. "Bring Kate along? Is that what I heard? Just a sec. Let me clean out my ears. Did you just say 'bring Kate along'? Because me telling Kate, 'Gia's ordered us to her home' is gonna fly about as well as a pregnant elephant in a tutu."

I listened for a minute, expecting some kind of reply. When I checked my phone to see if we were still connected, we weren't. I chuckled as I tossed the phone on the bed and went to jump in the shower. "Bring Kate along. Yeah right."

Before the water had fully heated up, I heard Kate's siren ring in the bedroom. Normally, I'd finish my shower and call her back when I was done, but curiosity won out. I dripped my way into the bedroom and answered. "Hi Kate."

"Meet me in the garage in twenty minutes. We're going to talk to Ms. Angelino."

"What?"

Kate and Gabe actually have quite a bit in common when it comes to answering questions they deem superfluous. They don't. Answer, that is.

"Well, okay. I just jumped in the shower, but I'll be on my way after that."

"If showering means you'll be late, don't." Her clipped tone left no room for argument, and neither did the fact that when I checked, I saw that she'd disconnected. Another irritating quirk she and Gabe had in common.

When I pulled into the parking garage, I drove around the various levels until I saw Kate's car idling on the third-floor ramp. I found a parking space, then took my time getting my briefcase since I hadn't appreciated rushing out of the house with my hair still wet. As I walked to the passenger side of her car, I noticed her tapping the steering wheel.

We pulled out of the garage and headed west. Gia's home was east. "Um..."

A muscle in Kate's jaw twitched.

Since I knew she knew where Gia lived, I thought it was the better part of valor to stay quiet.

She rewarded my silence with an explanation. "There's no way we're meeting Ms. Angelino at her home. I told her if she needed to see us that badly, we'd meet her at the end of Sweetwater Rd. It's isolated enough we'll know if anyone followed either of us, and if they did, we'll try somewhere else. The last thing I need is for Amanda Kellworth or anyone else in the media to see us talking with the Angelinos."

"Yeah, let alone the Andrulis people seeing us." I could just imagine getting caught in the middle of a firefight between Gia and the Lithuanian mob. Again.

We rounded a curve as we neared our destination. Off to the right, we saw Pito standing next to a Dead End sign. Knowing him the way I did, that sign could definitely have several different connotations.

He held an assault rifle at port arms and I could just imagine how cool he thought he looked holding a weapon any self-respecting SWAT officer would be proud to own.

I glanced around and saw three other similarly equipped men standing at various strategic locations farther back in the desert. I pointed them out to Kate.

"I see them, Alex." She unholstered her Glock and set it on her thigh. "Do you recognize this guy?"

"His name's Agapito Mancini, but they call him Pito. He's one of Gia's. He's also a dangerous, violent asshole."

She nodded slightly, then slowed when Pito waved her to a stop and stepped around to her side of the car. She already had her window down by the time she rolled up to him and I was impressed with how quickly the sights of her Glock were aimed directly between his eyes. I hadn't seen her unclip her badge, but she held it out the window as well.

Her voice sounded hard and clipped. "Back up."

His mirthless laugh irritated me, but he held his hands away from his weapon and took a step back.

Just when Kate opened her door to get out, we both heard a vehicle climbing the hill behind us. I jumped out and had my weapon leveled at the approaching car while Kate kept her Glock trained on Pito. I recognized Gabe and let Kate know. "I can see Gabe driving. Aldo's in the passenger seat. I assume Gia's in the back."

Gabe flicked one finger on top of the steering wheel and Pito immediately turned and walked several paces into the desert. Gabe nodded at me, then made the same motion, only this time pointing toward the end of the road.

I lowered my weapon and spoke quietly. "Gabe says we should go on to the meeting spot." I glanced over at her. "I guess I should have warned you Gia's ramped up her security really high."

Kate rolled her shoulders to ease some of the tension, then lowered herself into the seat and once again placed her Glock on her thigh.

I did the same.

"I'm well aware of Gia's security, Alex. In fact I make it a habit to get daily briefings from Chuck about what's going on with her."

That confused me. Kate and I worked for Special Investigations, sure, but not specifically for the Organized Crime Unit. "Why?"

She shook her head as though the answer should be obvious. "Why do you think?"

"Oh." Because of my friendship with Gia. "You don't need to do that. I can take care of myself."

She put the car in gear and drove forward. "It's not you I'm keeping an eye on."

"Oh." There wasn't much I could say to that, so I kept my mouth shut. I felt relieved that she didn't think she had to keep tabs on me, while at the same time I felt slightly put out that she didn't think she needed to keep tabs on me.

We parked and got out.

Kate turned a 360, taking in her surroundings, then holstered her Glock.

Taking my lead from her, I began to slide the barrel of my gun into the top of my holster, but heard a quiet "Don't" from Kate.

I lowered the Glock back down to the side of my leg and watched as Gabe closed his door, buttoned the bottom buttons on his tailored, black linen jacket and opened the back door for Gia.

Aldo stepped out of the passenger side carrying an assault rifle. He took up a position to the rear of the Mercedes with his back to us. Before he turned, I could see he had his finger resting on the trigger.

As usual, Gia had on a richly colored, designer power suit that didn't even attempt to disguise her curves. Her confident stride left no doubt as to who she believed was in charge of this meeting.

I glanced at Kate out of the corner of my eye and realized her stance and bearing also commanded respect. Here were two alpha females who knew how to take control of a meeting. I doubted either one was conscious of their body language, and I studied them both to try to pick up on the nuances of their movements and posture so I could practice at home in front of my mirror.

Gia spoke first. "Sergeant Brannigan."

"Ms. Angelino."

Apparently that was all the polite chit chat they intended to have. Gia got right down to business. "I need to know what Alex saw." She turned to me. "*Exactly* what you saw."

Kate crossed her arms. Her terse response left no room for debate. "No. This is a police investigation and we'll handle it. You don't cross examine my detectives. Ever."

Gia mirrored Kate's stance by folding her arms across her chest. The only difference between the two women was the thin cigar Gia held between perfectly manicured nails, the body of which was now resting on one of her forearms. A thin wisp of smoke drifted skyward, a metaphorical line drawn between two powerful, opposing forces.

Gia's eyes sparked with aggression before she pulled in a deep breath. When she spoke, her voice seemed deceptively calm. "Listen to me. I normally don't explain myself to anyone, ever, but I'm going to make an exception in this case." She made a sweeping motion with her arm. "Every man and woman who works for me would immediately put their lives on the line if I ordered them to."

She lifted her chin in my direction. "Like your officers, they are loyal, fearless and trained to within an inch of their lives. Yesterday, when I heard what had happened, I almost unleashed a hell storm that would have turned the City of Tucson into a war zone." She stopped to let that sink in and then held up the fingers holding the cigar. "Almost." Dropping the cigar on the ground, she ground it into the dirt with the tip of her black Jimmy Choo high heels.

I couldn't help but think the line separating the two immutable forces had just symbolically been erased.

"In a retaliation the size I had planned, many, many of my people would die." She stared into Kate's eyes. "They are my family." She broke eye contact and stared off into the desert. "Have you ever just *felt* something was wrong, but you had no idea what it was?"

Kate shifted. "Wrong how?"

"I don't know. Wrong enough to stay my hand until I can gather more facts." She felt in her suit pocket and came up empty. Gabe immediately reached inside his coat and pulled out a maroon, leather cigar case. He held it open and she absentmindedly took one, her mind obviously on what she was trying to explain.

"One of my father's teachings has always stood me in good stead. He told me that every mafia don is different. 'Learn each of their habits,' he'd say. 'Know their personality and understand who they are. Here.'" She pointed to her heart before continuing.

"Some capo famiglia believe dead is dead. How the death happens is someone else's worry, not theirs. They order the hit, and go have a scotch on the rocks with their wife."

She half shrugged. "Others make sure the hit is ruthless and in a public place, so everyone knows and fears the one responsible. Tito Andrulis is neither of those. He's someone who uses the unexpected to keep his opponents off balance."

I rubbed my shoulder to ease some of the tension there. "Like attacking you in your home and killing your father."

A line appeared between her brows as she nodded. "Exactly. He doesn't use fear the way most do. He manipulates his opponent's balance. Tilt them off center, and he has the advantage. A drive-by shooting doesn't *feel* like a Tito Andrulis hit. It's too expected for me to know for certain whether or not it came from him. I can't explain it any better than that."

When Kate nodded, Gia continued emphatically. "So you can see why I *need* to know exactly what Alex saw."

Once more, Kate shook her head. "I understand what you're telling me, but I'm sorry, you're going to have to get your information somewhere other than from Alex and an ongoing criminal investigation." When Gia pulled up to her full height and pinned Kate with her piercing, grey eyes, Kate held up her hand. "I will give you this though. The reporter, Amanda Kellworth, called me and said your friend Aisla had contacted her. Apparently Aisla said you and Alex are in an ongoing lesbian relationship."

For the first time, ever, I saw Gia recoil in shock. Her reaction wouldn't have been more dramatic if someone had actually punched her in the gut. She regained her composure quickly enough though.

I suppose you didn't survive in her business too long if you allowed surprises to derail you, but I thought it was kinda sad all the same. When you're the head of a powerful crime family, you don't have many friends you can trust. Now, Gia would have to cut Aisla off of that ever-shrinking list.

But Kate's statement got me to thinking. If Aisla had betrayed Gia to Amanda, who else might she have been talking to? I stepped a few paces away, pulled out my cell and called Ruthanne. When she answered, I turned slightly away from Kate and Gia and covered the phone with my hand. "Hey, it's me."

"Hey Alex. What's up?"

"Did you guys recover Aisla Westhaven's cell phone from the wreck?"

"Yeah, why?"

"Have you checked to see who her last call was from?"

"Yeah, I have it here somewhere. Hang on."

While she looked, I glanced behind me. Kate watched me while she listened to Gia saying something. I turned away again when Ruthanne came back on the line.

"She got a call from an untraceable phone. Well, it was untraceable as far as who made the call, but through some fancy footwork, Andy connected it to another phone used in a homicide in Chicago. He said he couldn't sleep, so he came in early and hit up a Chicago homicide dick he met at a conference a while back. The phone that called Aisla and the other phone used in the homicide were both from a batch of phones stolen in an unsolved business burglary. Let's see..."

While I waited, I pulled my notepad out of my back pocket and fished a pen out of my front.

"The Chicago guy said they had a possible suspect in the homicide, a Sal Morris, but that's all he could give us."

I wrote down Sal Morris, then asked, "Any news on Aisla?"

"She's still in critical condition, but the doc thinks she'll pull through."

"That's good to hear. Listen, thanks for the info on Morris. I'll talk to you later." After I hung up, I quickly found the speed dial for my friend Chuck, the department's expert in organized crime. When he answered, I got right to the point. "Hey Chuck. It's Alex Wolfe."

"Hey, long time no talk. What's up?"

I walked even farther away from everyone and lowered my voice almost to a whisper. "Do you remember a few years ago I asked you about Tancredo Angelino and you told me he brought his family here from Chicago after a rival mafia family killed his son?"

"Well, I don't remember the exact conversation, but I know what you're talking about. What of it?"

"Does your database include gang members from Chicago?"

"Some but not many. You got a name for me?"

"Try Sal Morris." I waited while he ran the name.

"Nope, sorry. I got an Antonio Morris, kind of a midlevel lieutenant in one of the lesser branches of the Chicago mob, but that's as close as I can get."

"Okay, thanks. I'll catch up with you later." I hung up and thought a minute. A possible, tenuous connection to a Chicago mob might be all Gia needed to figure out what Aisla was up to. I wrote on my paper next to Sal Morris, *Aisla's last call has a possible, remote,* I underlined remote several times, *connection to Chicago Mob.*

When I returned, Kate lifted her chin toward my notebook. "What was that all about?"

I stuffed the notebook into my back pocket. "Nothing."

She narrowed her eyes, then held her hand out and curled her fingers several times. "Hand it over."

"It's just something I need to do some follow-up on. It's probably nothing."

When Kate didn't lower her hand, I reluctantly pulled out the notebook and handed it to her. She read it, then looked up at Gia. "I'm sorry, Ms. Angelino, but there is absolutely no way I can possibly help you."

To my complete surprise, Kate tore the sheet of paper from my notebook, crumpled it up and tossed it to the side.

I've never seen Kate litter in the entire time I've known her. She even picked up garbage in the office if someone had missed their trash can.

"Let's go, Alex." She started for her car.

I blinked stupidly a couple of times while I stared at the crumpled paper.

Her voice held the unmistakable tone of command when she said, "Alex. Let's go."

There wasn't much more I could do. Kate had said I couldn't talk to Gia, so I shrugged an apology in Gia's direction and joined Kate in the car. It wasn't until we drove past Pito that the penny finally dropped. I chuckled as I turned to her. "I think you've been hanging around me too long."

Her mouth curved up into a smile.

CHAPTER 12

B ack at the office, I decided to take a second look at Jepson's
genealogy. I grabbed my briefcase and headed for the library.
When I walked in, I immediately saw my friend, Kelly, working her
normal station at the customer service desk.

I'd met Kelly a while ago while investigating a case. In the time I'd
spent with her since then, I'd come to know that she's the type of
librarian who loves to help people with any type of research. If she
can't find what they're looking for, she'll stay late or come in on her
days off to continue looking.

Today, she wore her black hair pulled up into a jaunty pony tail and
when she saw me, she gave me her customary lopsided grin. She was in
her late forties, with very few lines or wrinkles marring her otherwise
unremarkable features. Her brightly colored print shirt and blue slacks
were a perfect complement to her sunny good nature.

Since there was one person ahead of me in line, she raised one
finger telling me she'd be just a minute.

I browsed through the library's newest arrivals. I tend to gravitate
toward fantasy fiction and I read the back cover on several hoping to
find something that caught my attention.

Close to five minutes went by before Kelly waved me over. "Alex,

what kind of adventure do you have for me today? Old school year-
books? Newspaper articles from the 1930's?"

"Genealogy." I pulled the packet of papers out of my briefcase and
laid them on the desk.

"Oh my. That's going to take longer than a few minutes." She
caught the attention of a young man heading up the stairs with an
armful of books. "Bobby, could you work the service desk for a little
bit while I help Detective Wolfe with some research?"

I'd come to admire the friendly work atmosphere at this library.

Bobby nodded genially and placed his armload of books back on a
cart. The easy way he slipped in and took her place and the affable
nods they exchanged didn't happen in many of the work environments
I'd experienced.

We climbed the stairs to the second floor where several small
conference rooms were located. When we entered one, she shut the
door for privacy, even though the floor-to-ceiling windows overlooking
the bookcases afforded us little of that.

"Now, show me what you have." Her blue eyes sparkled with anticipation as she watched me once more pull the folder out of my
briefcase.

I laid the papers on the table and let her scan them at her own
pace. She settled into one of the chairs, pulling the papers close so they
were easier to read. She ran a light blue polished fingernail down the
middle of each page, apparently understanding more than I had on my
first run through.

It took about a half hour, but she finally reached the last entry. She
inclined her head toward the papers on the table. "Okay, this is mostly
straight forward. It's the descendant chart of Jep Abatescianni who
was born in..." She flipped back to the first page. "Well, there's no date
of birth, but since one of his children was born in 1834, you can guess
fifteen to twenty years before that. It gives you a starting place to
begin looking for him anyway. And his wife, Lyudmila Abatescianni,
nee Carrizozo, also no date of birth."

I craned my head around so I could see the papers better.

Pushing with her feet, Kelly thrust herself and her chair out from
the end of the table and scooted around next to where I was seated

and then placed the papers between us. She pointed to an entry. "It looks like this man, Titus, or possibly his wife, Sally, was the genealogist of the family because the more detailed records begin with him."

I smiled over at her. "I figured out that much myself. Does anything unusual stand out to you?"

She sat back and crossed her arms. "Like what?"

"Well, for example, do you have any idea what the numbers beside each of these dates of death means?" There were several dates that had two, three and in one case four numbers next to them.

"No, but I did notice them. They're not in any chronological order, and they don't correspond to any of the genealogical numbering systems I'm familiar with. But they only pertain to the fourth generation. And here, did you notice this?"

She pointed to a woman named Penina Jepson. "She's listed as Sally's daughter, but not Titus'. And then Penina's daughter, Prudence doesn't list a possible husband. And then—" She turned a few pages. "Here. Someone entered Prudence's daughter, Sasha, by hand in this margin."

"So it looks like everyone born in Penina's line was possibly illegitimate."

"Right." She turned over a few pages. "Whoever put this together did a pretty thorough job. If you notice, all eight of Jep's children were born in Italy, but three of them died in Massachusetts."

"So why does their name suddenly change? I was just assuming those three were from a different father or something."

Rummaging through the papers, she found what she was looking for and held up two sheets of paper triumphantly. She grinned excitedly. "I love this stuff. So, here's the cargo list of a freighter where three of the children—well, they were adults at the time, Augusto, Jacoba, and Ottaviano—were all listed on the bill of lading."

"As cargo?"

"Yes. If they were very poor and couldn't afford a passenger liner, some people traveled as freight. The living conditions were usually abysmal, and many of them died on the way over. But if you look, they're listed on the bill of lading as Augusta, Jacoba, and Ottaviano Abatescianni, like their father." She put her finger on the second sheet she'd retrieved. "This is the immigration document for Ottaviano."

I read the name aloud, "Otto Jepson."

"My guess is the immigration officer couldn't even begin to spell Abatescianni, so to speed things up, he asked Otto what his father's name was and voila, Otto and his siblings' last name is suddenly Jepson, or Jep's son."

She pulled out several more sheets from the middle of the pile. "Whoever was gathering this information also gathered quite a few birth certificates, which will give you information as well."

I'd been able to follow her logic fairly well, but I wasn't any further along figuring out why these papers were in a baggie in the bottom of a closet. "Thanks, Kelly. I can see it's gonna take a little more time than I have right now to figure this out—if there's even anything to figure out." I began shuffling the papers into a neat pile.

"There's one more thing I noticed, but I don't have any kind of explanation for it." She plucked papers out of my hand and slid them this way and that, scattering them on the table again, looking for one in particular. "Here it is. This is Penina's birth certificate." She held it next to the descendant chart. "Notice anything unusual?"

I studied the birth record. "No, not really. Penina Prudence Jepson."

She placed a fingernail on the descendent chart.

I blinked several times, then checked the birth record again. "Penina N. Jepson?"

Nodding, she began tapping the chart. "It's interesting that she's one of the ones with the numbers. Maybe a coincidence, but I thought I'd bring it up anyway."

I checked the middle names of the other people who had numbers. "Here's another N, and the other two have Ws. Do we have their birth certificates?"

When I began searching for them, Kelly stopped me with a hand on mine. "I already checked. We don't. Do you think I could keep these for a while to study them?"

"No, I'm afraid not. They're evidence and I probably shouldn't even be showing them to you now."

Picking up the descendent chart, she studied it carefully, then set it back on the pile.

We both neatened the stack and I shoved it into the folder. "Thanks for taking the time to go over this stuff with me."

"Of course. You have my cell number. Call if you have any other questions."

CHAPTER 13

As soon as I walked into the office, Kate motioned me into her cubicle. While I waited for her to get off the phone I helped myself to a hard piece of butterscotch candy from the dish on her desk.

She took the phone from her ear long enough to tell me what she wanted. "Casey's in the back room of the evidence section going through the bones we've collected so far. Go help her."

"Sure thing, boss." I grabbed another candy and went to find Casey.

Marla buzzed me through the door to the evidence section. "Casey's in room three. Here." She held up a box of gloves and I took a couple. "We don't keep the gloves in the rooms anymore because they always disappear."

"Thanks." I headed to the back of the section and joined Casey in workroom three. I call it a work room, but the only furniture in it was a long conference table, a whiteboard with various colored markers in the tray along the bottom, and a desktop magnifying glass about the size of a salad plate attached to a swivel arm bolted to the table.

Casey currently held a skull fragment beneath the lens and was in the process of turning on the little light that circled the underside of the magnifier. She glanced up when I entered and immediately returned her attention to the bone. "Hey. Was your librarian friend any help with the paperwork?"

"A little bit. She showed me a few interesting things, but I'm gonna have to let everything rattle around for a while to see if I can make any sense of it." I grinned at her, then got down to business. "Was this your idea or Kate's?"

"Kate's. She wants us to see if there are any more numbers, and then she wants us to try to piece together the skulls like a big jigsaw puzzle."

"You're kidding. There must be forty or fifty pieces here. How are we supposed to hold them together? What does she think we are, forensic anthropologists?"

Kate must have come in behind me while Casey and I were chatting. "No, I don't. I was just on the phone with a friend, Harlan Taylor, who is though. He asked us to bring the bones to his lab at the University. He's agreed to help us piece together the skulls. I told him at this point, I don't need the skulls fully restored, but because of the numbers you found, I need a general idea how each of the bones go together. Before you go, I want you two to examine each piece carefully to see if there are any more numbers."

She held up a paper bag. "These are some of the fragments Tony and Sam dug up from under the tree Lido hit on. Alex, Marla's bringing in another table and I want you to go through these and see what you can find. Remember, they're from two different areas so we need to keep them separated."

Reaching into one of the bags, she pulled out a baggie containing masking tape, markers and a ruler. "When you're done, take the bones to Harlan. His lab is in the Department of Anthropology at the University. Make sure he knows he has to keep the two digs separate. Questions?"

I massaged the back of my neck, suddenly realizing it had become a habit when I needed to ease tense muscles. Being tense isn't usually something that happens to me, but lack of sleep and all the other things that had happened recently were taking their toll. "How is this gonna help us figure out why the bones were shoved down into the toilet?"

Kate shrugged. "I don't know. But we're going to follow every lead we get until we figure out where the bones came from, and how Micah's badge ended up down in that tank."

The bag she handed me turned out to be heavier than it looked. I almost dropped it when I took it from her and just barely caught the bottom with my free hand. "Whoa. How many old bones did they find?" I peered inside and let out a short whistle. "I sure hope Sam gave Lido an extra treat with his dinner."

I carefully upended the bag onto the table Marla had dragged in. There were about twenty smaller bags, all sealed and catalogued. Kate handed me the property sheets so I could record that I'd opened them and examined the contents.

By the time we'd finished, we'd found numbers on seven separate skull pieces. We replaced each bone in its individual bag, packed everything up and drove to the university where Kate's friend awaited us. I looked forward to seeing how he would identify which pieces fit together since neither Casey nor I had had any luck in that department.

We walked into the lab and a man I assumed was Harlan rose to greet us. I liked him instantly, something that doesn't happen very often.

He appeared to be in his mid-forties, muscular and very polished in a well-educated, professorial sort of way. The amused crinkles at the corners of his eyes and his friendly, half-smile implied good humor instead of the intellectual superiority I'd halfway expected to find. His wavy, shoulder-length brown hair complemented his strong chin and neatly trimmed beard. The tailored, light-blue dress shirt and dark brown chinos definitely added to his overall appeal.

He strode up to me and held out his hand. "Harlan Taylor. You must be either Alex or Casey?"

I shifted the bags to free up a hand. "I'm Alex," I said, then gestured toward Casey with my chin. "This is Casey."

He nodded, then turned to grip Casey's proffered hand. Once the preliminaries were out of the way, he rubbed his palms together while eying the bags we held. "Are these all the bones you found?"

Casey placed her bags on one of three autopsy tables in the center of the room. "No sir. These are just the ones we thought might be skull bones. If you need to see the others, I can get them for you."

"No, no. This is fine for now. And please, 'sir' makes me feel rather older than I actually am. Call me Harlan."

I knew Casey well enough to know she'd call this man 'sir' no matter how many times he reminded her otherwise.

Pulling open one of her bags, she explained Kate's concern. "The bones in these bags came from the waste tank of an abandoned camper." She looked up quizzically. "I assume she told you the basics of the case?"

Apparently her formality amused him because I saw just the hint of a smile before he answered in the same formal tone. "She did. You were sent by an anonymous caller to a camper that appeared to have been abandoned in the desert. When officers arrived, they found a bone jammed down into the drain hole of the toilet. Upon further inspection, you discovered many other fragments of bones in the tank."

She nodded and patted one of her bags. "Yes sir. These are those fragments." She indicated I should set my bags on the second table. "The bones Alex has were discovered when the department's cadaver dog alerted on an area approximately thirty yards away under a mesquite tree. Kate asked me to mention that when you piece them together they need to be marked so we know which bone came from which area."

"I see." He walked to a brown leather attaché case sitting on top of a utilitarian metal desk. "I just came from looking at some bones discovered on the Pasqua Yaqui reservation. Most of what I'll need is still packed in here."

When he opened the case, I noticed he kept his tools meticulously clean and organized. The top tray held five or six brushes lined up according to bristle size and handle width. He pulled that tray out and set it on the desk.

The next tray contained various metal instruments. I could only identify a few of them. There were spreading calipers that I'd seen our lab technicians use to measure the length and breadth of a skull, and a smaller Boley caliper Marla used when measuring teeth. There were also scissors and a scalpel plus a few other items I didn't recognize.

He removed that tray, and I could see larger tools in the bottom of the bag. There was a bone saw, a skull chisel and I think a pair of rib cutters. He spread a cloth near Casey's set of bones and carefully laid out the tools he intended to use.

Casey and I put on some gloves, opened each bag individually, removed the bone fragment it contained and then folded the bag flat before laying the fragment on top.

Harlan had also pulled on his gloves and occasionally lifted a fragment that caught his attention. When we'd finished, he raised an eyebrow. "No lower jawbones?"

Casey shook her head. "No sir, we didn't find any."

Other than the quiet whirring of some type of drill in the next room, the building seemed eerily quiet to me. For some completely irrational reason, the silence coupled with the presence of the skull fragments spooked me. I glanced over my shoulder, expecting to see an apparition floating by.

Harlan chuckled. "You'd be amazed at how many students have that exact same reaction when they come in here. As you probably saw on the plaque outside, this room is called The Calvariam, calvaria being the Latin term for skull."

When I'd first entered, my focus had been entirely on Harlan. I hadn't quite yet registered the large number of skulls safely stored behind the glass doors of the floor to ceiling cabinets lining the walls.

"Believe it or not," Harlan continued, "there are times I swear I can feel a presence here even when I'm the only person in the room. I've been to enough archaeological digs during my lifetime that I don't easily discount those feelings. In fact, I was the first human to enter one of the tombs at the Sheikh Abd el-Qurna archaeological site and I will swear until the day I die something, or someone I guess, kept stroking my forearm as if in greeting."

We were all quiet for a moment, thinking about ghosts and ghouls and such.

Casey finally broke the silence. "We didn't find any lower jaw bones, that we know about anyway. Some of the smaller crushed pieces could have been the jaws, but—" She waved her hand over the shards. "This is all we found in the camper tank. Any larger bones were from Lido's find."

"Lido?"

"The cadaver dog."

"Ah. That makes sense." He picked up two pieces. "So, you have parts from both male and female skulls here. These two pieces are an excellent illustration of what I mean. These are both parts of a parietal bone. That's right here." He rubbed the lower back part of his head. "On a man," he said and raised the bone in his right hand, "skull bones are generally heavier, and usually notably larger.

"Those from women, on the other hand, are smaller and lighter. Also, the parietal bones on men tend to be thicker because we have more rugged muscle attachments."

I picked up two pieces to see if I could tell the difference. He was right. One was definitely thicker and heavier than the other.

"So why do some of the shards have skin left on them and others are only bone?"

He shrugged. "There are a lot of possibilities. The ones with some skin left were probably in the ground for less time than the pure white ones. Also, the methods for preserving the body may have been different. Were they embalmed or simply buried in the dirt or in a pine box? Without knowing the details, it's difficult to tell. I'm surprised the department is treating the discovery so lightly."

Casey looked slightly insulted. "We're not taking it lightly, sir. On our department it's usually the detectives who gather the evidence rather than a crime scene technician. Kate has made sure we've followed protocol the entire time. She's sent samples of the organic material to be DNA tested, but right now she wants us to solve the riddle of why the numbers were carved into the skull."

Once again, amusement crept into his gaze at her formality. "Well then, we'd better get started, shall we? You two use those brushes to get as much dirt off as you can and I'll begin sorting."

We worked for several hours, with Casey and I brushing off the bones and Harlan fitting them together. He wasn't actually gluing the pieces together to make something that looked like a human skull.

Kate had wanted to find out which numbers went together, so he more or less placed each piece next to the one it fit with. Not an easy task, but he kept at it until we had four distinct sets of skull bones laid out flat on the autopsy table.

He pointed to the first pile. "You have the skulls of two women and two men and various other pieces of bone not associated with the skulls. These two on the left are the women and these over here are the men."

Squinting down at the first set of men's bones didn't help me see the numbers. "Can I borrow your magnifying glass?" He'd been working with a pretty sophisticated head-mounted magnifier to allow him to keep both of his hands free.

Opening a drawer, he pulled out a hand-held magnifying glass similar to the kind my mother had for working the smaller crossword puzzles. "Here, this should work. There's an on switch on the handle for the light."

I held the glass over the skull and switched on the light. The numbers came into focus. "Casey, can you write this down?"

"Already on it."

When I looked up, she was holding a notepad and pen at the ready. I looked back at the numbers. "On the left side—"

Harlan interrupted me. "That's actually the right side. You're looking at it upside down."

"Okay, on the right side of one of the men's skulls is 1665. That's on pieces 2a and 2b"

Harlan had marked each piece of skull with a numbered sticker.

I moved the magnifier to the other side of the skull. "On the left side is 31138 point 52. The 3 is on 3a, the 11 is on 3b, the 38 is on 3c and the point 52 is on 3d." I carefully examined the rest of that man's skull but didn't find any more numbers.

"Next guy." I studied each bone several times, then flipped them over and examined the other side. "Nothing on him."

I moved over to the two women. The first one didn't have anything carved on the pieces we had, although, to my untrained eye it didn't seem as though we had all the parts. Moving to the final skull, the numbers were visible even to the naked eye. I held the magnifier over them anyway just to be sure. "On the right side—"

"Left." Harlan crossed his arms and grinned at me.

I smiled back and re-oriented myself. "On the left side of one of the women there's 2724 point 15 with the 272 on 1a, the 4 point 1 on 1b and the 5 on 1c. On the right..." I trailed off while I tried to find some numbers anywhere else on the skull. "Nothing."

Harlan and I carefully flipped each piece over but we didn't find any more numbers written on the inside.

We placed the fragments back into their individual bags and got ready to return to the main station. Not surprisingly, it had taken us all afternoon to clean and sort.

Harlan arched his back, groaning a little as he pushed away from the table. "Too many years of bending over tables and archaeological digs has given me a body full of stiff joints." He walked us to the door and held it open for us. "It was a pleasure meeting you ladies. Tell Kate I'm always available for whatever she needs. She's good people."

We stepped through the door and I looked back over my shoulder. "We will. Thanks for all your help. There's absolutely no doubt in my mind we never would have been able to piece those skulls together like you did."

He gave a quick nod and wave and the two of us made our way back to Casey's car, eventually getting back to the station and returning the bones to the evidence section before calling it a day.

CHAPTER 14

The next morning, I went in early and commandeered an interview room in the back of the office. I spread the papers out where I could easily study them and then leaned back in a chair, unwrapped my bagel and began to read. Unfortunately, nothing jumped out at me.

Sighing, I decided to try again when I had some extra time during the day. In the middle of stacking the pages, I was surprised to hear my cell ringing so early in the morning. I didn't recognize the number, which actually wasn't that unusual considering that I have witnesses to several other open cases returning my calls on a regular basis. "This is Detective Wolfe."

"Alex? This is Kelly, from the library?"

Slightly perplexed, I automatically looked at the number she was calling from. Sure enough, it had the city's 791 prefix, so she must have gotten into work as early as I had. "Hey, you're in early. I didn't expect to hear from you. What's up?"

The excitement in her voice intrigued me. "One of our volunteers came in today and the two of us got to talking. His name's Henry, and he served in naval intelligence during the cold war. Guess what his specialty was."

I grinned, "Genealogy?"

She laughed as she answered. "No, he was a cryptologist. He's agreed to take a look at the genealogy and see if he can make some sense out of the numbers. He can come down to the station now if you want."

"Cryptology?" It hadn't occurred to me there might be some kind of secret code embedded in the paperwork. "Well, yeah, sure. Have him tell the guy at the window he's here to see me and I'll come downstairs to get him."

"I wish I could come with him. This is so exciting!"

I sometimes forget how fun our job can be, and having people like Kelly around served as a good reminder. "I do too. I'll definitely fill you in if he comes up with something."

"Oh I've already threatened him with dire consequences if he doesn't tell me everything that happens."

We disconnected and I began to think in terms of hidden codes and numerical analysis. I searched through my notebook for Phyla's phone number, and when I found it I gave her a call.

She answered on about the third ring. "Phyla here."

"Good morning. This is Alex Wolfe. I hope I didn't catch you too early."

"Not at all. How can I help you?"

"When I saw you yesterday, you mentioned that one of the Vamps is in military intelligence."

"That's right. Sonya Walks With Bears. She's an army reservist."

I could hear the curiosity in her voice and had to admit, from her perspective, I was coming out of right field. "I have a retired cryptologist coming in this morning to look at some paperwork we found at Tom's place. I was wondering if she might be able to come in as well. The more ideas we can toss around the better."

"Hang on, I'll ask her. She's two campers away from mine." I heard a general rustling on the line, then the sound of Phyla knocking on a camper door.

After some general conversation, a new voice came on the line. "Detective Wolfe? This is Sonya Walks With Bears. Phyla said you were wondering if I could come help you with some kind of code or something?"

"Just some numbers on a genealogy chart that don't belong there. I have a retired cryptologist coming and wondered if maybe you could take a look as well."

"Of course. I'd love to. Just tell me when and where."

I gave her directions to the main station and told her Henry was on his way. She said she'd be right down.

When I hung up, I gathered all the papers together and went out to my desk to wait.

It took Henry longer than expected, so I wasn't too surprised when Paul, the front desk officer, told me that both Henry and Sonya were waiting for me in the front lobby. I told him I'd be right down.

As I stepped out of the elevator on the first floor, I noticed a portly gentleman standing with his back to me while he looked at one of several display cases showcasing the history of our department. He had a halo of grey hair surrounding a mostly bald pate, which was covered by a slight comb over of whispy white strands. His green, short-sleeved dress shirt was neatly tucked into tan cargo pants, but he'd absently tucked part of one pant cuff into his honey-colored, leather work boots.

"You must be Henry?"

He turned and held out his hand. "Henry Torrington. Pleased to meet you." A spider's web of red veins crisscrossed his round face and nose, telegraphing his liberal enjoyment of various alcoholic beverages.

I couldn't smell any alcohol on his breath or body at the moment, which was a relief since I didn't want to rely on someone who's been drinking by seven o'clock in the morning to figure out my puzzle. He seemed genuine enough, however, and I decided I'd trust Kelly's friendship with the guy and see how everything panned out.

"I'm Detective Wolfe. Thank you for coming so quickly." I glanced behind me and saw Sonya standing near the sofas in the middle of the lobby. I steered Henry toward her, made the obligatory introductions and then led them both toward the elevator doors.

Sonya remained silent while we waited for the elevator to arrive.

Henry on the other hand spoke with the excitement of a small child on Christmas morning.

"Kelly tells me you have a mystery." He rubbed his hands together in anticipation. "There's nothing I like better than trying to solve a good mystery. I've been out of the navy for almost thirty years now, and I still miss the work. Did she tell you I was in counter espionage? I loved it. The navy made me leave after thirty years, you know. I'd still be there if they'd have allowed it."

The door slid open and we stepped to the side to let a couple of uniformed officers exit. I nodded to them both before ushering my two charges in.

Henry continued talking while I pushed the button for the third floor. "I understand you have some sort of genealogy report with some strange numbers. Kelly said there were also a couple of middle names, or at least their initials, that have been changed."

I didn't answer since he hadn't really asked a question. He simply seemed to be the type of person who needed to fill the silence with good-natured chatter. When the door opened, I waved them out and led them to our office.

When we entered, Kate looked up from the report she was reading. She eyed Henry, who hadn't stopped his monologue, and Sonya, then glanced at me with raised eyebrows. I simply lifted my chin in greeting and led my two guests back to the interview room.

Earlier, I'd locked the door to protect the evidence, so I pulled my keys out and let us in. The door automatically closed behind us.

Before it had completely shut, Henry had gone silent and was already sorting through the paperwork. "Hmmmm. Yes. Interesting. Very. Yes, quite." He continued to make these sounds for a while, sorting the papers one way, then holding one page up against another, before switching them out for a different set.

I glanced at Sonya, who stood patiently watching him. She had an amused expression on her face, which she turned on me when she realized I was looking at her.

I gently extricated some of the papers from Henry's hands and handed them to her. She pulled out a chair and sat before starting on the files.

After about fifteen minutes, Henry seemed to remember I was there. He jerked his head up and gave me a quick smile. "Oh! I'm sorry to ignore you, Detective Wolfe. I just get so involved in this type of project that everything else becomes part of the background noise."

I'd never been called background noise before, but since I'd been called worse on many, many occasions, I simply nodded. "So...did you find something?"

"I believe I did. If I'm correct, this is a very basic cypher used at the beginning of the First World War." He held his hands out, palms up. "The reason I say the first part of the war is because the central powers—by that I mean Germany, Bulgaria, um...the Ottoman Empire and—" He gave me a quizzical look. "I seem to be missing one. Um..."

"The Austro-Hungarian Empire." History had always come easily to me because my father had been a history buff extraordinaire. Some type of revelation about this dynasty or that Egyptian mummy had always been a topic of discussion around our dinner table.

When he blinked at me, he had an uncanny resemblance to a splotchy-faced owl. "Why yes, that's right. I'm surprised—well, that is to say, um..."

"You're surprised a cop would know something like that?"

He had the grace to blush. "Well... I apologize Detective Wolfe. Now where was I? Oh yes, by the middle of the war, the code had been broken and so it was phased out rather quickly."

"So, this is Cryptography 101?" I bent over the paperwork, trying to get him back on task.

Just as he set the papers down to show Sonya and me, Kate stepped into the room.

Henry stood and quickly wiped his palm down the seam of his pants. He visually checked it, then held his hand out to her for a shake. "Henry Torrington."

Her gaze moved from him, to me, and then back to him again. She shook his hand and I quickly introduced her.

"Henry, this is my sergeant, Kate Brannigan. Henry was a cryptologist during the cold war and Kelly, my librarian friend, thought he might be able to tell me what these numbers are beside some of the names."

I motioned toward Sonya. "And this is one of the Vamps, Sonya Walks With Bears. She's with military intelligence. I thought the more experts we can get to look at this the better."

This time Kate offered her hand first. "I'm pleased to meet you." When they'd shaken hands, Kate turned to Henry. "What have you found?"

Henry started right in. "It's actually very easy really." He glanced at me. "Do you have a laptop you could bring in here?"

I left to go get it, brought it into the room and set it on the table.

Henry began his explanation. "I believe these numbers here," He pointed to two names in the fourth generation, "on the twins, Jesse N. Jepson and Michael W. Jepson, are probably related to each other since they died within days of each other as infants.

"Now if I'm correct, the numbers under the burial section for Jesse, 41.27, and the N of her middle name refer to a latitude and the 70.12, coupled with the W of Michael's middle name is the longitude. If you would be so kind as to open your computer and put in this address." He waited for me to get settled and then rattled off a web address. "Go to www.gps-latitude-longitude.com."

I pulled up a search engine and began typing. "Okay, I'm there."

"At the top, click Address of Longitude and Latitude. Now put 41.27 in the latitude and in the longitude put -70.12, that means 41.27 N and 70.12 W, then hit load."

I did as he said and was surprised to see a flag marker set in the middle of Nantucket Island. He and Kate were leaning over my shoulder at this point so I refrained from pointing out the obvious.

Henry pointed to another space on the webpage. "If you look on the map here, the pin is on Prospect Hill Cemetery. The only significance I can see is that's probably where the two of them were buried. It's anyone's guess about why they split the numbers up between the two infants."

My disappointment probably showed on my face. "That's it? That's the big secret?"

Kate turned the descendant chart her way and put her finger on one of the entries. "Put this in. Penina, who died in 1915 has 34.28 N latitude and her brother, Henry W. Jepson, who died in 1918, has 112.72 W longitude."

Henry added, "Remember to make it -112.72."

I did as I was told and read off the results. "The pin is near a little town called Peeple's Valley, here in Arizona."

Kate's startled intake of breath surprised me. She stepped behind me again and pointed to the computer screen. "Zoom in." I did. She impatiently brushed my hand aside and zoomed in several more times.

Henry leaned in and squinted for a closer look. "I'd say that's a cemetery as well."

"It is." Kate crossed her arms while she stared at the screen. "Alex do you have those other numbers you and Casey got from Harlan yesterday?"

At the time, I almost hadn't copied the numbers from Casey's notebook since I knew I could always get them from her if necessary, but I'd written them down anyway and now I was glad I did. I pulled out my notebook and handed it to her.

She in turn handed it to Henry. "What about these numbers? Do they mean anything to you?"

Pointing to me, he said, "Try 24.2715 N longitude and 16.65 W."

I did as I was told. "Nope, that's the middle of the ocean. There was a third number also."

Kate took back the paper and read it out to me. "31138.52 W? What the heck does that mean?"

He retrieved the paper from her and studied it. "My gut feeling is these numbers aren't latitude and longitude. They just don't read correctly. Do you have any other paperwork or clues that might tell us how these translate?" He took my little notebook and handed it to Sonya, who quickly glanced at the numbers before setting it down next to some of the papers.

Ripping out a blank page, she began pointing to the papers and quietly talking to Henry as if Kate and I weren't in the room. She wrote down several words, then scratched them out after consulting with Henry about their possible significance.

They continued for a good while before Henry began shaking his head. "No, this is just gibberish." He handed my pad back to me. "It looks like this is a multiple encrypted code, and you're missing the cipher. Without it, these numbers are complete twaddle."

Sonya nodded in agreement. "He's right. You're definitely missing a crucial piece of your puzzle."

Kate crossed her arms again and began tapping her fingers on her forearm. "If we were to go back to the scene, what would we be looking for?"

"My guess is some type of writing. A cipher is necessary to decode the message. It could be a book, an old magazine, a notebook, sometimes a bible was used.. Those are what I'd be hunting for if I was you."

Exasperated, I slapped the notebook on my thigh. "A book? Do you know how many books are lying around that man's house? How the hell would I know which one is the cipher?"

Henry shrugged. "Once, we had intelligence that a critical cipher was being kept in a home in Brussels. We were sent to find it. We opened every book, slashed every picture, cushion and lampshade. We finally found it in the hollowed out leg of a seven-foot-tall wooden giraffe."

"And how will I know when I find it?"

"You may not."

I shot Kate an irritated look, daring her to tell me to go back to Jepson's house and start our search all over again.

She gathered up the papers and handed them to me. "Take Casey with you."

The papers were completely mixed up, and since I knew I was on the verge of saying something I'd regret, I took a second to arrange them in the order I'd been keeping them.

Kate offered to walk Henry and Sonya downstairs.

I shook both of their hands, thanking them profusely before they followed her to the elevators.

Casey was working at her desk when I went out. "Hey."

She looked up from her computer. "Hey, yourself."

"Kate wants us to go back to Jepson's house to try to find a cipher for those numbers. Sonya said it could be a book, or that poster, or a bible even. How the hell she expects us to know it if we find it is beyond me."

Crossing the I's and dotting the T's was butter to Casey's bread. She loved digging and sifting through anything, so she happily shut down her computer and joined me as I was walking out the door.

It took us about twenty minutes to reach Jepson's house. When we pulled up to the garage, I noticed the grill of a dark blue Ford pickup truck hidden so that the building would shield it from anyone driving past the residence.

I pointed to it and Casey nodded that she'd noticed it too. We got out and quietly shut the car doors just in case the driver of the truck hadn't heard us pull up. The crime scene tape surrounding the property still fluttered in the breeze, and there wasn't supposed to be anyone around.

We drew our weapons, walking slowly up to the truck to make sure no one was in the cab. The hood felt cool, so it was a good guess whoever had trespassed onto the property had been here for a while.

"Psst." Casey hissed to get my attention. She pointed toward the house where the front door stood wide open. We crossed the short dirt yard and bracketed the door, one on either side.

Casey nodded, and Glocks at the ready, we rolled around the opening into the living room. Broken furniture and shards of glass blocked our way. The room reminded me of what Henry and his fellow spies had done to the home in Brussels.

Furniture lay upside down or sideways with cushions slashed open and all the white cotton insides thrown about. All of the camper parts that had been stashed randomly atop tables and desktops were now on the floor along with books from the shelves, and lamps that had been tossed aside and shattered on the hard ceramic tile.

Once we'd cleared the living room, I stepped over and around the mess and took the bedroom, despite the possibility of snakes.

Casey made her way into the kitchen.

I hadn't taken more than two steps through the bedroom door when I heard the explosion of gunfire behind me.

The first shot sounded like a canon. That was answered by several more shots that didn't have the intensity of the first.

"Casey!" Just as I ran back into the living room, the swinging kitchen door slammed open, crashing into the wall with a loud crack. I hadn't seen him up close before, but I instantly recognized the man who'd shot Jepson and the deputy chief.

He fired wildly at me as he ran for the door. I had to dive behind an upturned sofa, rolling as I did and firing off several shots of my own toward his retreating back. When he disappeared through the door I was torn between following him and checking to make sure Casey hadn't been shot.

Torn really isn't the right word. In fact, it took less than a second before I was sprinting for the kitchen and plowing through the door going in the opposite direction of the gunman.

My first sight had me sliding to a stop on my knees next to Casey's inert form. "No, no, no, no, no. Don't be dead. You can't be dead."

The truck roared to life in the yard.

I only peripherally heard it past the blood roaring in my ears. I quickly felt for a pulse. At first I couldn't feel anything, then realized I'd misplaced my fingers on her neck. I adjusted my placement and felt dizzy with relief when blood pumped steadily beneath them.

I snatched my radio off my belt. "9 David 72, officer down. Start meds." Casey had called in our destination when we'd left the office so the next thing I heard was the emergency tone on the radio and the dispatcher sending out a 10-99, or officer needs assistance, call.

There wasn't any blood on her clothes, and as I rolled her onto her side, I keyed the mic again. "9 David 72. Code 4 the 10-99 but keep meds rolling."

The emergency tone stopped since I'd told her the immediate danger had passed but Casey still needed medical attention. I gave her a general description of the pickup truck and shooter and then put the radio chatter out of my mind while I checked her back and legs for any bullet wounds. A bruise had begun swelling on her temple, and I guessed she'd either hit her head on something or the suspect had clocked her a good one.

She groaned and I eased her down onto her back. Her eyes opened just a tiny bit and she brought her hand to the bruise on her head as she sat up. "That bastard shot at me and charged." Her growling tone told me she was more pissed than injured. "I tried to shoot back but he was too quick. He hit my arm while I fired, then cracked me on the head with something."

Resting her elbows on her knees, she put her forehead in the palms of her hands. "I think I'm gonna puke."

I quickly moved out of the line of fire.

Once the nausea had passed, she glanced up at me. "If he'd wanted to kill me, he would have. He shot high to make me duck as he charged." We both looked toward the doorway into the living room. Sure enough, a bullet had entered the drywall near the top of the door, leaving a good-sized hole.

The sirens I'd heard in the distance became more pronounced and it wasn't long before the paramedics hurried into the kitchen with a gurney.

She allowed them to fuss over her for about half a minute before batting away the flashlight one of them tried to shine into her eyes. "I'm fine. I don't need to be fussed over." Without exception, from the first time I'd seen her take a blow to the head from a baseball bat to this incident, Casey had always shrugged off her injuries, intending to immediately return to work.

The paramedics had come to our aid on previous occasions and they apparently knew enough not to argue. The shorter grey-haired man sporting a well-greased handlebar mustache glanced over at me with raised eyebrows, silently asking me what I wanted them to do.

I shrugged, knowing what I was going to say would piss her off. "Well, she was unconscious for a while."

"I was not."

The lady who'd tried to shine her light in Casey's eyes got a look of concern on her face. "How long was she out?"

"About..." I had to think a second. Everything had happened so fast. "Maybe fifteen seconds?"

Casey ground out the words between clenched teeth. "I... did... not... lose... consciousness."

The woman began putting away her equipment. "She should definitely go in and get checked out then."

Kate surprised me by coming through the kitchen door. Her flushed face gave away the fact that she'd rushed to get here, but her outward demeanor was calm and collected. "I'll take her to get checked. Thanks for your help."

The glower Casey turned on her would have cowed most people. "I'm fine. I don't need medical attention."

Kate was not most people. "Good, then once you're cleared for duty I'll bring you back to help Alex and Nate."

I hadn't noticed Nate, who hovered in the background, his concern evident by the intense way he visually scanned Casey's body to make sure there were no obvious injuries. I nodded at him. "How'd you get here so fast?"

Kate pointed west. "We were doing some follow-up on one of Nate's cases not too far from here."

Casey knew when she had no further say in the matter. She pushed to her feet and both paramedics grabbed an arm. It only took one of her pissed off glares for them to immediately release her and step back a pace. She wobbled a little and had to catch her balance by leaning on the kitchen countertop. Nobody else dared lend a hand.

Kate pointed to the door. "Nate, walk Casey out to my car, I need to speak to Alex for a second."

Casey said, "I don't need—" but the look Kate turned on her shut her up immediately.

We watched them and the two paramedics head outside and then Kate turned to me. "Did you see who hit her?"

"I'm pretty sure it was the same man who shot AC Pardo and Jepson. He had the same build anyway, and I think the same short, military style haircut. Casey said she didn't think he was trying to kill her, just get her to duck so he could ram into her. Now that I think about it, he probably could have killed me too if he'd wanted to."

"So is the ransacked house his doing then?"

I nodded.

"He was looking for something, probably the cipher Henry was telling us about. Do you think he found it?"

I shook my head. "I don't think he would have still been here if he had. And he'd been here a while. The hood of his truck was cold when we got here."

"Did you call in the plate as a suspicious vehicle?"

The color rose in my cheeks "No ma'am. I didn't."

Irritated, she exhaled. "Sloppy, Alex. We can't afford half-assed work. Keep your head in the game from here on out."

The embarrassing part about her rebuke was that she was absolutely right.

We should have at the very least written down the license plate number. If we had, we'd have a good lead on our shooter, not to mention that if he'd killed Casey and me, the detectives would know who to go after. I looked her in the eye and nodded.

That was apparently the correct response because she returned to the business at hand. "You and Nate need to search for that cipher. I don't know what it has to do with anything, but I want it."

I didn't see any need to search through a bunch of books when we didn't have any idea what we were looking for. "You want us to look through every book in the house in the hope we find a cipher. I don't even know what a cipher looks like, how do you expect me to recognize it when I come across it?"

"I'd say there's a pretty good chance it wasn't in any of those books in the living room since it looks like he did a pretty thorough search. Walk around. Note anything that strikes you as odd or out of place. It could be one of those pieces of your internal puzzles you're always talking about."

We returned to the living room. She took a quick look around and then went out to where Casey and Nate waited by her car.

I wanted to get the search over with, so I began by first noticing what hadn't been disturbed. Pieces of the piano lay strewn about, but the majority of the guts lay on the floor where the whole piano had been before.

Interestingly, the shadow box containing the Vietnam War medals had been taken down from the wall, but it hadn't been smashed like everything else. It sat open on the exposed strings of the piano. If the medals had been disturbed you couldn't tell by the neat way the killer had put them back into the display box.

The framed cruise ship flyer had been placed next to it. I would have expected the killer to simply break the glass like he'd done to every other picture in the room, tear out the flyer, and throw the remains of the frame on the discard pile.

But just the opposite had occurred. The frame remained intact, glass and all. When I thought about dusting it for prints, I flashed back on the white, rubber gloves the shooter had been wearing. So much for that. When Nate came into the room I pointed to it anyway. "Will you dust that for prints? And be careful with the powder, I'd rather it not get all over the flyer."

"Sure thing."

I suddenly remembered why I enjoyed having a rookie in the squad. While he took care of that chore, I did a quick tour of the rest of the house. The man had been thorough. Every room had been systematically torn apart.

By the time I returned, Nate had finished. He held up two fingerprint cards in triumph. "I found two partials. Maybe we'll get lucky."

"I think I remember the guy wearing gloves, but you never know." I pulled a pair of gloves out of my back pocket and put them on. "Can I see that?" He handed me the frame and I flipped it over. It was the old fashioned kind, with metal clips stuck into the wood and then bent over to hold the backer board in place. They all flipped up easily and I set the frame down, glass first, on the piano keys. I carefully lifted the board off the flyer.

I'd been hoping there might be something inside screaming 'Me, me! I'm the cipher! Right here!' but all I saw was the back of the poster. Not wanting to damage the old paper, I gingerly picked it up between my thumb and forefinger and flipped it over. Holding it up to the light, I examined it carefully, thinking there might be some hidden message or numbers somewhere. Nothing.

For whatever reason, I replaced the flyer in the frame and gave it to Nate to bag as evidence along with the shadow box full of medals. Kate had said to look for the unusual, and these two items lying unbroken amidst the total chaos of the room definitely fit the bill.

We searched all the outbuildings. Two of them had been ransacked, but the third one with the showroom looked as though it had either been untouched, or the killer had appreciated the quality of the car and camper. He had broken the lock off however, so at least we didn't need the keys to get inside.

Nate let out a sigh of relief as he walked over and lovingly ran a hand just above the paint on the trunk of the Mercedes. "Thank God she's all right."

"She? How do you know it's a she?"

"All cars and boats are she's. It just wouldn't be right to say "Thank God *he's* all right. C'mon, Alex, even you know that."

Rolling my eyes, I stepped up into the camper and carefully searched the interior for clues. I didn't turn up anything so I climbed down. On the off chance there might be something obvious in the filing cabinet, like a folder labeled Cipher, I searched that again while I sent Nate back to the work shed to find a new lock to secure the building. Not that the first one had done any good, but I figured we needed to lock up anyway.

Since Nate had ridden with Kate to check on Casey, when we were done I gave him a ride back to the station. Casey wasn't at her desk, which was something of a surprise since I knew Kate wouldn't have let her go back on duty after getting knocked unconscious. There were several people working at their computers who could probably answer my question. "Hey, anybody know where Kate and Casey are? Did they get back from the hospital?"

Shelley Cummins from child abuse yelled from the back of the room. "Kate gave her a ride home. Boy was Casey pissed when they stopped by here to get her stuff."

"Wow, and Casey actually went?"

"Kate had to give her a direct order, but she went."

Just then my desk phone rang. I set down the two evidence bags I'd been carrying and grabbed the receiver. "Wolfe."

"Alex, it's Kota. I found that computer drive you were looking for. I'll be here for another hour or so if you want to come watch it."

As soon as I grabbed the Jepson folder out of my briefcase, I hurried down to the crime lab. It took me about two minutes to get there, and another ten for Kota to be able to leave whatever she was working on to come escort me back to her lab.

"Did you watch it?"

Kota brought out the laptop we'd confiscated from Jepson's house and set it on the small conference table. "No, that's why I called you. I haven't had any time since they've put Assistant Chief Pardo's case on the front burner."

"I heard he's gonna make it."

"Yeah, I guess they lost him twice on the operating table but were able to bring him back." She accessed a folder on the screen. "Anyway, these are the videos you were asking about. The ones from the security camera in the garage? They're filed by date, and there's a ton of 'em."

"Damn, they go all the way back to 1999. How can that be? Weren't they recording on VHS back then?"

"No, by then they were using DVR, which can be converted to digital. The conversion is what you're seeing on those early ones."

Sighing, I sat down and began searching through the files at high speed, only slowing the recording down whenever a person came into the field. Quite often, an older man I assumed was Mick Jepson came into the garage with Tom. The two of them did very little other than argue and flail their arms at each other, and then leave.

After seeing about eight of these interactions over a period of several months' worth of video, I began to notice a pattern. I sat back for a second to gather my thoughts. "Huh."

Kate came up behind me. "Huh, what?"

I'd planted my elbow on the armrest and had my cheek resting on my left fist. Using my right hand, I rewound what I'd just been watching. "Watch this."

Kate leaned over my shoulder so she could see the computer better.

I planted a finger on each man's face. "I think this is Tom's father, Mick—I'm not one hundred percent certain though—and that's Tom. I've watched almost six months of tape, and they've only come in together about eight times. Various other people come in, but usually when Tom or Mick are giving a tour of the camper or Mercedes. Now watch this."

On the tape, Mick walks over to the filing cabinet, opens one of the drawers and reaches in. The tape flickers slightly, but not enough so you'd notice if you weren't watching for it.

I looked up at Kate. "Did you see it?"

She slowly shook her head. "No, I don't think I did. What are you seeing?" She turned the laptop slightly so she could get a better view.

I'd gone back and recorded all the times where Mick and Tom came into the garage. After checking my pad, I rewound to the previous time stamp. Once again, Mick walked to the filing cabinet, reached in, we see a slight flicker, and the tape resumes.

This time when I glanced up at Kate she nodded slowly. I could see by the furrows in her brow she hadn't quite put it together. I ran the tape back several incidents, then started it forward again. "This is about two months before the one you just saw. Now, Mick is always in the same place before and after the flicker, standing there with his hand in the filing cabinet drawer. But watch Tom."

When the recording flickered, I could tell the penny had dropped for Kate. She stepped back a step and nodded. "You're right. He's not in the same place, is he? He didn't move enough to initially draw my attention, but once you told me what to look for, I see it."

"That's happened eight times so far. Usually Tom is somewhere around the Mercedes. But now watch these two again." I played the last two. Both times Tom was kneeling behind the car polishing the floor.

"That's as far as I'd gotten when you walked in. I have no clue what it means other than for some reason they turn off the recorder for a while and then switch it back on."

"How well did you search the car the second time around?"

"Nate searched it while I did the camper, so I'm not sure."

She crossed her arms and began waggling her pen up and down between her fingers. "What don't they want us to see?"

It was a rhetorical question so I didn't answer.

Kate's a lot like me. She prefers working through the evidence silently, and doesn't appreciate being interrupted while she's doing it. She finally gave up. "Casey's going to be on light duty tomorrow. I'll put her on this while you continue to work on the case from your side."

I shrugged. "Fine with me." There was something I'd been meaning to ask her but hadn't had the right opportunity. "Hey, I was wondering something. Do you remember when I said the latitude and longitude coordinates were in that little town, um..." I couldn't remember the name of the place.

"Peeple's Valley."

"Right, Peeple's Valley. Why did that get your attention and why didn't you want to say something in front of Henry?"

"I don't like bringing civilians in on a case. I will if I have to, but I don't like it so I keep my cards close to my chest."

She hadn't answered my first question, which I thought was kind of odd. "And Peeple's Valley?"

Her lips thinned and I wondered whether she'd answer or just leave the room. Finally, she blew out a long breath. "There's a small cemetery there. Micah's wife's family is from there and she grew up in the community. When he laid Sasha to rest up there, he told me he wanted to be buried on top of her. Each grave can hold three people, one on top of the other."

"Sasha?" I nearly bowled her over going for my briefcase. If my memory was correct, Kate just added not one, but two pieces of my puzzle. I pulled out the genealogy folder and quickly scanned the descendants' chart. I looked up in triumph. "Sasha!"

Kate grabbed the folder out of my hands, her eyes moving back and forth as she scanned the names.

I pointed excitedly to a name in the current generation. "Sasha!"

Kate's intense gaze met mine. Neither of us knew yet what we'd discovered, but I could feel that the outside edges of the puzzle were just about complete.

CHAPTER 15

A ltogether, other than Casey getting knocked unconscious, it had
been a productive day. I wasn't too surprised to see Megan's
Toyota Tacoma parked in my yard since I knew she was dying to hear
an update on all that had happened. Megan and I have a symbiotic
relationship. I often use her as a sounding board to flesh out ideas, and
she gets the vicarious thrill of helping me out with my investigations.

When I walked through the door, my two dogs came barreling
toward me, but her golden retriever, Sugar, sat with a biscuit balanced
on the top of her nose. Sugar glanced at me out of the corner of her
eye, careful not to tip the biscuit onto the ground.

Megan pointed down, and Sugar carefully lowered herself onto her
belly. "Atta girl. Hup." Sugar immediately flipped the biscuit skyward
and caught it deftly between some very sharp teeth. Megan had used
me as a suit-protected perp to train Sugar as a protection dog and I
knew only too well how strong those jaws could be.

"It's about time you got home. I've been working with Tessa and
Jynx on the basics. Jynx gets it. Tessa..." She trailed off as we both
looked over at Tessa who was laying on her back with all four paws in
the air, her tongue lolling to the side waiting for me to scratch her

belly. She'd never been a particularly bright dog, but she'd once saved the life of a young friend of mine and I'd come to love her fiercely.

My mother had given me a hanging grandfather clock that bonged once just as I glanced at the time. "It's only seven thirty. I didn't know you were gonna be here, and I needed to watch the first few months of security tapes from Jepson's garage."

"And?"

"Can I grab some dinner first?"

"No. But you can buy me a burger and tell me all about the tapes. I wish you could have brought them home so I could watch them. Second hand is only as good as the source, and you usually leave so much out I'm in the dark most of the time."

"Fine, but you're driving. I don't have my Jeep, remember?"

My cellphone rang halfway to the Patty Palace. "Wolfe."

"Alex? Phyla here. Do you remember you asked me to tell you when Mick's widow arrived?"

That was a little abrupt. "I'm fine. Thanks for asking. How are you?"

The snort on the other end made me smile. "Sorry, sorry. I've always been a bit too short with people. I'm not much for pleasantries."

"That's okay, neither am I really. Anyway, yes I remember. She's in town?"

"Pulled in today at lunchtime. Listen, I realize you're probably off duty, but she's willing to talk to you, but not at the station because she's from the Columbian Andes, and has a definite mistrust of anything to do with the government. Can you come to the campground at Catalina State Park?"

I looked over at Megan who'd been leaning toward me trying to eavesdrop. Did I really want her to meet the Camp Vamps? No. Did I have much of a choice? No. "Sure. We can be there in about fifteen minutes. How do I find you?"

"Oh," She chuckled. "I don't think you'll have any problem figuring out which ones are us."

She disconnected and I pointed behind us. "I need to make a quick detour to talk to some a lady about the case. Can you hold off on dinner?"

She gave me a conspiratorial grin that set off my warning bells. "Hell, yeah!"

Sighing, I put my head against the headrest and silently prayed nothing would go wrong. "Catalina State Park."

If someone had told me you could do a 180-degree turn in a pickup traveling at 35 miles per hour without rolling I wouldn't have believed them. Megan did it without even checking for oncoming traffic. I grabbed the dashboard and held on. "Jesus, Megs! Are you trying to kill us?"

Her eyes shone bright with anticipation. "Who are we going to see at the park? That's where you and Casey got shot at a few years ago, isn't it? Don't worry, I'll keep behind you and keep my head low. Are they dangerous?" She threw in that last with such enthusiasm I knew I'd made a big mistake.

"Listen. You just stay in the truck, okay? Promise me you won't do anything to get me in trouble with Kate."

She crisscrossed her breasts with a finger. "Promise."

We pulled into the park entrance and I showed the ranger in the guard shack my badge. He was a friendly old guy with greying hair and a disarming smile. He waved us through with a jaunty salute.

It didn't take long for me to understand exactly what Phyla had meant about how easy it would be to find them. Every type of vintage camper imaginable filled the entire first loop of the campground.

There were twenty or thirty ladies and quite a few men in various groups laughing, drinking and generally enjoying themselves around a large, glowing yellow campfire. Picnic tables had been pulled into the middle near the fire, giving the general impression of 19th century settlers circling their wagons. The difference being that instead of protecting themselves from attack, they'd loaded every flat surface with food, beer and wine that they were attacking with gusto.

Megan pulled into an empty space, threw the gear shift into park and jumped out.

I let out a long sigh as I watched her walk up to the first group of women she came to and immediately engage them in friendly conversation. She pointed back toward the truck as I climbed out of my side, and I wondered exactly what she was telling them.

One woman turned and yelled for Phyla, who'd already started walking my way. She waved her thanks before acknowledging me with a lift of her chin. Her eyes sparkled with amusement as she drew near and held out her hand. "I told you you'd find us. We're kinda hard to miss."

I shook her hand warmly. "Is this an unusual number of people or are your gatherings usually this crowded?"

"Are you kidding? A chance to help solve a murder of one of our own?" A chagrined smile appeared on her face when she realized what she'd said. "I don't mean that the way it sounded. I like to think that if any of us had really liked Tom, the festivities wouldn't be quite so animated."

That made me a little uncomfortable. "What? You guys are celebrating his death?"

She waved a hand in front of her face. "Oh heaven's no. Tom's skills were an asset to the vintage camping community. No one wanted him dead, but as you can see," She indicated the feasting behind her, "no one's really grieving either."

A woman with a heavy accent spoke from behind me, off to our left. "He started life as a bottom feeder and has been slithering downward ever since."

When I turned, an older, dark-complected woman wearing blue jeans, a red tank top and an open, white, button down shirt stepped up beside me. The two of us were about the same height. She wore her white hair twisted into two neat braids that hung down like snakes on either side of her back.

It wasn't a long stretch of the imagination to realize this was the woman Jepson had stolen from her Andean home. I could see why Phyla had described her as an exotic beauty. Her strong, erect bearing belied her age, which I thought was somewhere in her early eighties. Judging by her high, angled cheekbones and flawless face structure, in her youth she must have epitomized Mick Jepson's every fantasy.

She raised her chin defiantly as she glanced at me with fiery, black eyes that held more than a touch of triumph. "With his death, he will continue his journey and join his father in the darkest pits of the underworld."

Phyla made the introductions. "Detective Wolfe, meet Cuxi Uarcay, Mick's widow."

Cuxi nodded, closing her eyes to slits as she peered deeply into mine.

I dipped my chin in response. Phyla had said she was a bruja, an Andean witch, and this witch obviously wanted to see deep into my soul. The intensity of her gaze sent chills down my spine.

I decided two could play at this game. I upped the intensity of my own gaze, tuning out the surrounding activity and diving into the darkness of her dilated pupils.

After a short time, she broke eye contact and actually cackled. She indicated me with a flick of her thumb. "This one has a strong spirit." She poked Phyla in the chest with a long, slightly arthritic finger. "Maybe even stronger than you."

I glanced at Phyla, then smiled and turned back to Cuxi. "I take it from your previous comments you didn't like Mick or Tom?"

Her face twisted with contempt and she spat on the ground. "I curse them with every breath."

Okay then.

"Hey, Alex!" Agnes St. Germaine came hurrying over. "I'm glad you decided to bring your girlfriend."

"What?" It took a moment for me to switch from witches' curses to girlfriends.

"Megan. Remember? I heard you talking about her on the phone and said you should invite her to come."

"Megan's not—" I glanced over to the campfire and watched Megan lean back while one of the campers poured beer down her throat. "Oh no."

I started over, but Phyla stopped me with her fingers on my chest. "I'll take care of it. Dammit, they know if they get too wound up the ranger'll kick us out of here. You stay and chat with Cuxi. C'mon Agnes." She put her arm around Agnes' shoulders and led her to the campfire.

Without saying a word, Cuxi walked out of the circle of light toward a darker area on the periphery of the campsite.

I followed, grateful that the din of friendship quieted out here.

She led me behind a cute little white camper that had an aqua blue stripe running around its middle. A metal emblem near the door had the word Trotwood engraved on it.

"Is this your camper?"

She nodded.

"She's a beauty. What year?" I thought I'd break the ice with a little casual conversation.

"1966." She picked up a folding chair stored next to the tires, pulled it open and set it next to a small table. She found a second chair, settled it onto the aqua outdoor carpet she'd laid out in front of the camper and motioned for me to sit.

I watched her settle into the nearest one, leaving me to walk around the table and sit with my back to the camper. She didn't appear interested in engaging in polite formalities, so I jumped right in. "Thank you for taking the time to speak with me. I understand you were married to Tom Jepson's father, Mick Jepson?"

She nodded.

"Do you have any idea who might have wanted him dead?"

Amusement lit her eyes as she blew out a puff of air.

"Ms.—" I pulled out my notebook to check her name and immediately gave up. "I'm afraid I can't pronounce your last name, Ms?"

"I am Cuxi."

"Cuxi, then. Who do you think might have killed Tom?"

She lifted a shoulder.

This was getting me nowhere so I decided to change my tack.

"Hang on a second, okay?" I jumped up and ran to Megan's truck, pulled out my genealogy file and jogged back to the camper. I laid the descendants chart on the table and pointed to the names. "Do you recognize this?"

She glanced at it and nodded.

"Okay, so, I know what these numbers are for." I indicated the names that had numbers after the date of death. "They're coordinates for cemeteries. One in Massachusetts and one here in a place called

Peeple's Valley." I needed to back up a little bit. "Actually, before we get into that, do you know anything about bones in the old abandoned camper on Tom's property?"

Her eyes narrowed as she thought about the question. "No. But I know those papers—" She gestured with her thumb thrust between her middle and ring fingers. "They're evil. Mick stared at them all the time. His anger boiled, always, until one day, he and Tom disappeared."

She waved her hands palm down across the table. "When he came back, he went into that old camper and stayed. He told me he'd kill me if I ever went in." She lifted a shoulder. "Why would I go where he goes?" Leaning forward, she whispered conspiratorially, "I set the curse on his camper and pretty soon, he was dead." Her knowing smile and sharp, hawk-like stare was more than a bit disconcerting.

Although the mechanics of cursing someone intrigued me, I tried to stay on topic. "What was he doing in the camper?"

She lifted her shoulder again. "After Mick died, Tom took the papers and they possessed him too." She tapped my folder. "This is an evil bloodline. Cursed once before me, and now cursed twice, because of me."

A chill ran down my spine. I pointed nervously at the paperwork, staying on topic be damned. "So, should we maybe uncurse it or something? You know, wave burning sage over it or sprinkle holy water on these and maybe on the tires of that old abandoned camper, too?"

She leaned over and spat on the ground again. "I set the curse on those two bastards, father and son. The camper was only to hold the demons captive. Once they did my bidding, the spirits were free to leave." She sat back with a knowing look on her face. "I knew the instant each man died. I knew when the demons fled."

Breathing out slowly, I stared at the genealogy before deciding to move on. "So, you have no idea where those bones in the camper came from? I mean if you maybe used them as part of your curse, now would be a good time to tell me."

"No. In the Andes, the bones of our ancestors are sacred, not evil. We keep them on shelves in our homes. I would never bind evil to something I consider sacred."

We sat in silence for a while. I couldn't think of much else to ask until I remembered the missing cipher. "Did either Mick or Tom have a notebook, or a special book, or maybe that poster of the ship on the wall that they spent a lot of time with?"

She spoke derisively, as though she'd tasted something bitter. "The poster." She shook her head. "I tried to burn it when Mick first stole me from my ancestors and brought me into his prison. All the evil of this family—" Her nose wrinkled and she repeated the strange gesture with her thumb between her fingers. "I feel it strongest there."

"In the poster? The poster is evil?"

"What's *in* the poster. I know nothing more. There is evil on it, evil in it, evil around it."

"They stared at the poster a lot?"

She blew out an impatient puff of air. "No, but I felt the evil coming from it. The boats and the water, did they draw you in when you first saw them?"

I thought back to when Casey and I first searched Jepson's house. As I stared down at my hands resting on the table, I remembered the floating sensation, as though I'd really been treading water.

When I looked up, she held my gaze and nodded. "You did. I sensed your connection to the spirit world when we first met."

Not quite sure what to say to that, I figured I'd stick to my original question. "Was there anything else they might have studied? Some other papers or..."

"There was a book...yes." She pointed to her eyes. "I hid and watched. Over and over they'd turn the pages. Backward, forward, back again."

I felt the familiar excitement that came over me whenever another piece of the puzzle was about to fall into place. "Where did they keep the book?"

She lifted her shoulder again. "Hidden."

"Where?"

When she didn't answer, I wondered if the hiding spot might be too difficult to explain. "Can you show me?"

Without another word, she pushed to her feet, walked over and stood patiently next to Megan's truck.

I unlocked the passenger door and let her in before getting behind the wheel. I had just started the motor when Megan came running over.

She jerked open the passenger door and almost threw herself onto Cuxi's lap before realizing the old woman was there. "Whoa! Sorry about that!"

I could smell the alcohol on her breath clear across the seat. "I'll come back to get you when I'm done, Megs."

"Oh hell no you won't! You're not leaving me out of anything!" She rushed around to my door, yanked it open and threw herself across me, wriggling this way and that, and jabbing my jaw with her knee several times until she'd landed between Cuxi and me.

Cuxi leaned forward to catch my attention, a slight grin lifting the corners of her mouth. She tapped the folder I'd set on the dashboard. "She pushes the evil away from you."

The hairs on the back of my neck stood on end. I'd never met anyone like her and wasn't exactly sure how to respond.

Cuxi sat back. She remained silent during the rest of the drive to Jepson's home.

I wish I could say the same about Megan, who chattered non-stop the entire trip. "I want to get an old camper and join the Vamps. They're some of the coolest ladies. Well, ladies and their husbands if they want to tag along. They travel all over the country and go to rallies, but they don't go to every one, just the ones in the states they want to visit. Did you know some of those campers are over seventy years old? Seventy! Can you believe that? Did you meet Agnes? I like her. She's interesting in a simple kind of way."

She turned to Cuxi. "She says you're a real witch. That is so cool! What do real witches do anyway? I mean, I know it's not like you pull rabbits out of hats or anything like that. Can you talk to dead people?"

When she paused for a breath, I glanced over at Cuxi and was relieved to see Megan still amused her.

Megan continued with her monologue until we slowed at the entrance to Jepson's land.

When I pulled into the driveway, I very carefully checked for any vehicles that didn't belong. The place appeared deserted, but with Cuxi in the truck, my spidey senses were tingling. She'd gotten my imagination going by talking about evil this and evil that, and now it seemed like there was a black presence floating around waiting to eat innocent detectives and their chatty, redheaded friends.

Cuxi turned and met my gaze. Megan's chatter drifted into background noise as we stared at each other. The bruja nodded slightly. "You feel it. It is very real."

It was all I could do to keep from throwing the truck in reverse and backing out of there. I could always come back tomorrow when it was daylight. I'm pretty sure ghosts go into hiding when the sun comes up.

Megan must have sensed my hesitation because she suddenly stopped talking and glanced nervously around. "What? What's wrong?" She turned to Cuxi. "What do you mean it's real? What's real?"

I forced myself to open my door and got out. "Nothing."

Cuxi opened her door and slid out as well.

Megan hesitated, looking around with wide-eyed trepidation before she, too, slowly exited the vehicle. She'd gone silent, which for her was completely out of character. Her head moved as though on a swivel as she looked this way and that, trying to see what had me spooked. She'd never liked doing things with me at night because darkness tended to scare her. That was the main reason I'd wanted to leave her back with the Vamps.

Cuxi calmly walked to the front door of the house and let herself in. The fact that she still had a key surprised me, and I watched her reaction when she flipped on the light and saw the room in complete disarray. For all I knew she'd been the one who came in and trashed the place, but when she barked out a laugh I knew she hadn't done it.

Glass crunched under her feet as she moved into the room, carefully stepping around broken pieces of furniture on her way to the bedroom where I'd run into the snake.

I followed her, with Megan following me so closely she could have been glued to my back. "Back up, Megs." I elbowed her, trying to give myself a little maneuvering room should anything unexpected happen.

Cuxi went straight to the closet and pulled open the door. "The papers were here with the guardian. El cabron fed her, and she stayed and guarded them."

El cabron. The bastard. "Right. You mean the rattlesnake. I already met her and got rid of her, but where did he keep the book? The one that they were always studying?"

She didn't answer, and for the next half-hour, Megan and I shadowed her through the rest of the house, expecting at any moment for her to open a hidden compartment and produce the cipher. Instead, she'd pick up various items and chuckled before flipping them into the air and watching them crash down onto the ceramic floor at our feet.

When we entered the master bedroom, she immediately and vehemently spit on the bed, muttering some weird incantation while flexing her fingers in bizarre, intricate movements above the bare mattress. There was a glass object on the floor that hadn't yet been broken and she lifted her leg high and violently smashed it underfoot.

I'd finally had enough. "Hey! This is still a crime scene. I'm bending the rules just having you here. You can't destroy evidence like that."

"No, she can't."

I whirled around to see a very pissed Kate standing in the doorway with her arms crossed over her chest.

"What? How?" Those were the only words my panicked brain could come up with on such short notice."

She held up a card. "Business cards, Alex. If you hand them out to neighbors, they call when they see suspicious activity. Amazing how that works."

My panicked brain could definitely have done without the sarcasm. Gathering my wits, I decided to try the "this is perfectly normal" routine. "Sergeant Brannigan, may I introduce you to Cuxi...uh...well, I can't pronounce her last name. Cuxi, Sergeant Brannigan."

The two women stared at each other until Cuxi poked me in the shoulder. "Stronger than even you."

I mumbled under my breath, "Yeah, no shit."

Megan decided it might be safe to make her presence known. She poked her head around my shoulder from where she'd been hiding and waved. "Hi Kate."

Kate had locked her gaze onto me and didn't even bother to acknowledge Megan.

I indicated Cuxi with an upturned palm. "I can explain."

The venom in Kate's voice dripped dangerously with all kinds of directed meaning. "I'm waiting with bated breath."

"Right. Well, Cuxi is, or was, or I suppose she still is, Mick's widow."

Cuxi spoke with unconcealed disgust. "He is dead to me and I am nothing to him. *Nothing*." She waved her hand sharply in front of her body to emphasize her point.

Ignoring her protest, I continued. "Anyway, I'd asked Phyla to call me when Cuxi got into town, which she did tonight. Megan and I were on our way to get a hamburger—" I stuttered to a stop when Kate rolled her eyes. "What?"

"Why is it that whenever you and Megan go out to eat, I end up getting called to a crime scene?"

Megan helpfully chimed in. "Just lucky?"

I put my hand on her face and shoved her behind me again. "Anyway, we detoured to the campground so I could meet Cuxi. When Cuxi said she'd seen Mick and Tom always studying a book, she couldn't explain where the book was, so I brought her here to show me where she'd seen it." I turned and glared at the witch. "Something she hasn't done so far."

Outside, the sound of music and laughter rose above the rumbling of a diesel truck. I hurried to the front door, finding myself speechless as two pick-up trucks came barreling along the driveway, music blasting from open windows and women stuffed inside the cabs and hanging out on either side of the truck beds.

"What the—" Kate pushed past me and stood in front of the lead truck holding her arms up to stop the parade. The music stopped when the engines were turned off. When truck doors began opening, Kate barked an order. "The first person to set foot on the ground is going to jail!"

Everyone froze. Some women hastily pulled their feet back in the trucks while others stopped seconds before climbing off the tailgate.

I recognized Darla England when she stuck her head over the cab of the red Dodge Dakota. "It's okay, honey! We're here to help Alex with her case."

Kate's eyes flashed as she spun around, growling at me through what looked to be painfully gritted teeth.

I took a defensive step back, shaking my head and waving my hands in front of my body. "No, no, no, no. I did *not* invite them to come down here!" Panicking, I looked to Cuxi for help. "I didn't invite them. Tell her!"

Cuxi smiled and lifted a shoulder while Kate advanced on me with a murderous expression on her face. I backed into the house and she followed me, slamming the door behind her.

"Kate, I did not invite them. I don't even know most of them. They just showed up. I need to find that cypher. That's the only reason I brought Cuxi."

"Cuxi *and* Megan, who, correct me if I'm wrong, is shit-faced drunk!"

"Right. Well, she jumped in the truck as we were leaving and I know that when she has a little too much to drink she can be kind of belligerent and I figured it was just easier to let her come along as long as she stayed out of the way."

I'd assumed Megan had originally followed us outside, so I jumped when she popped out of the master bedroom holding a box. She sounded thoroughly insulted by Kate's words. "I am not shit-faced drunk." She stumbled on her words, which actually came out as 'I am not slit-faced dunk.'" Pulling herself to her full height, she tried to look as dignified as possible. "As if shotgunning one can of beer is gonna get me drunk."

Kate held up a finger as she glared at Megan. "One can?"

Megan deflated a little. "Well, I only shotgunned one. Maybe I chugged another."

Kate brought her hands to her hips, cocking her head while waiting for Megan to continue.

"Okay, so I chugged two. But one of the Vamps poured the first one down my throat, so that one doesn't really count."

I threw my hands in the air and, thoroughly exasperated, let them drop to my side. With Megan in my corner, there was no way I was going to get out of this in one piece.

She stepped toward Kate, holding the box out as a peace offering. "Here. I thought you might be interested in this."

I rolled my eyes.

Growling again—I really hadn't heard that particular growl in quite a while—Kate grabbed the box and quickly glanced inside.

I had no clue what was in it and had no intention of getting close enough to find out. I waited anxiously near the front door.

Kate glanced up at Megan. "Where did you find this?"

I watched Megan actually blush, something she rarely does. "In the closet. One of the floorboards creaked when I stepped on it. It was loose and I pulled it up and found the box."

Shooting me a dirty look over her shoulder, Kate ground out her words as she grilled Megan. "And what were you *doing* in the closet? This is a *crime scene*, Megan! Why do you think you can just root around wherever you please?"

Megan shoved her fists in her pockets and mumbled like a petulant child. "I wasn't rooting. When you growled and ran outside, I figured the safest place for me to be was in the closet. You know, out of sight, out of mind?"

"I didn't growl."

"Yes you did." Megan studied the floor.

When Kate looked back at me, I shrugged. "You did. It wasn't your 'I'm a little ticked off' kind of growl. It was more like that time you snarled at me after Megan and I went down into the projects in the middle of the night. Remember?"

Megan perked up. "I remember! You chased Shelley through those yards and she clotheslined you with a board."

I felt the blood drain from my face when Kate turned toward me. She hadn't known about that little detail since I hadn't exactly told her that I'd actually seen Shelley that night.

Kate pushed past me and headed out the door. She held the box under one arm and I still wasn't able to see what was inside.

I mouthed, "What is it?" to Megan.

She whispered back, "Thumb drives."

My eyebrows shot up and I hurried after Kate, who by now was standing face-to-face with Phyla, who must have arrived after we went inside. Everyone else had stayed in the trucks. I could see Agnes on the passenger side of Phyla's Toyota peering out over the dashboard.

Kate spoke in that deceptively quiet tone she had when she was trying to rein in her anger. "I told all of you to stay in the trucks."

Undaunted, Phyla simply shrugged. "I must not have been here when you said that, and I do apologize for everyone. I had no idea they were going to follow Alex and Cuxi here. However, now that we *are* here, all of us knew Tom in one capacity or another for years. Maybe one of us knows something that might help with the case."

A blonde woman, whom Phyla had previously introduced as Leslie Schuman, spoke up from the bed of the nearest truck. "For instance, did you know he built a secret compartment inside the Covered Wagon?"

Darla England, who had her elbows propped on the roof of the truck, piped up. "I'll bet you didn't find that, did you?"

I walked over and spoke into Phyla's ear. "Is there any way to muzzle her or something?"

Phyla chuckled quietly while Kate gave a big sigh and turned to me. "Alex, have that woman show you where that secret compartment is, then come on back so we can see what's on these thumb drives."

"Sure thing, boss." I glanced over at the ladies in the truck. "Leslie, isn't it? Would you come show me that compartment, please?"

Leslie sat down on the tailgate and lowered herself to the ground. "I'd love to. C'mon."

All the other ladies began cheering as Leslie and I headed for the garage. Darla called after us. "Hey Leslie! Turn around."

Both of us turned, and before I knew it, Leslie had her arm around my shoulder and Darla's camera blinded me with an ultra-white flash. "Got it! That'll go in our Camp Vamp newsletter. Camp Vamps help solve a major murder for the Tucson Police Department."

Kate stood next to Phyla rubbing her eyes with her fingers. The amusement in Phyla's eyes was catching, and I smiled back at her before turning and leading Leslie through the door to the garage.

Agnes came trotting after us a few seconds later with a huge, excited grin on her face. "I told you we could help. Didn't I?"

"You've already helped us a bunch, Agnes. We wouldn't be nearly as far along without the info you gave us." I hoped Leslie would pass that little tidbit onto the Vamps so Agnes would have something to crow about around the campfire.

For her part, Agnes' chest puffed out and the most gratifying smile spread across her face. "Really?"

"Absolutely. I wouldn't say it if it wasn't true."

"Agnes, your P.I. license paid off after all!" Leslie moved up a few notches on my likeability scale when she walked over and slapped Agnes on her back. "Wait until the Vamps hear about this! C'mon, let's go show Detective Wolfe that hidden compartment."

The two of them preceded me into the camper. Leslie immediately moved toward the head of the bed where she reached under the lip of the intricately carved maple headboard.

I hadn't noticed the detail work on the bed on my first trip into the camper. I stepped closer and ran my fingers over the mother-of-pearl inlay of white swans floating on an iridescent lake. A forest of hand carved trees full of individual, delicately chiseled leaves, surrounded this. "Oh my God. Can you believe the work that must have gone into carving this?"

Leslie nodded. "The story goes that the heiress who commissioned the camper, Holly Marceau, flew in a Chinese master carver from some Buddhist temple to do the work. In exchange, she had their sixteenth century monastery completely restored to its original splendor. If you read about her, you'll see that she converted to Buddhism during the renovation process."

She pushed a hidden button under the headboard, and a thin, oblong box rose up from the end of the bed. When the box stilled, a small door popped open to reveal a key lying on a red velvet pillow.

I blinked first at the key and then at Leslie. "How did you know that was here?"

She shot me a cheeky grin. "Let's just say Tom and I enjoyed each other's company one afternoon. During a rather acrobatic maneuver, I accidently grabbed the headboard and voila." She gestured to the little box. "More than I'd expected popped up."

I returned her smile, shaking my head at the man's abilities to please multiple women in a multitude of ways. "I don't get it. Almost everything I've heard about the guy—"

"Is that he was an asshole. That's true. And he was a first class bastard, most of the time. But when he focused on giving a woman pleasure, those times were extraordinary." She got a far-off look and I decided it was past time to change the subject.

"Do you have any idea what the key opens?"

She shook her head. "Sorry, no."

I grabbed the key and herded the two of them out the door. We arrived back at Kate's car just in time to see her plugging a thumb drive into the laptop she brought with her to every crime scene or investigation.

She'd set it on the trunk of her car and glanced up as we approached. "Find anything?"

Nodding, I dug the key out of my pocket and held it up.

A pensive look came over her face before she returned her attention to the laptop. While we waited for it to load whatever was on the thumb drive, I noticed the Vamps gathering behind Kate to see what we'd found. Ten or fifteen file folders popped up and Kate clicked on one. There were several .wmv files and she picked one, opening it with her Windows Media Player.

As soon as I saw a pair of extra-large, dark lady's legs wound around a man's fishy-white, hairy back I slammed the lid down on the her computer. I was hoping Kate hadn't had time to register exactly what was on the screen, but several of the Vamps began hooting and laughing behind us.

One woman shouted, "Yup, that was Tommy all right." The laughter escalated as the ladies called for Kate to open her computer again.

Leslie's eyebrows came down low as she worriedly looked into the box. There were close to twenty thumb drives in there. I could just imagine her thoughts.

I stepped away from the crowd as unobtrusively as possible and when I caught her attention, motioned her over with a little jerk of my head. When we were far enough away not to be overheard, I whispered. "Those probably aren't evidence, and if they're not, I'll make sure they're destroyed. You don't have to worry they'll get out."

She reared back and gasped, "Destroyed? I want them!"

Blinking several times, I digested that little gem. "Um, well...look Leslie, I really don't want scan through all those thumb drives looking for your trysts with Tom."

"I'll do it."

"No, you won't, because the other women on there have a right to their privacy. I'll tell you what, if I do have any reason to watch them, and *if* I see you in there and *if* they don't somehow become evidence, I'll get permission to release those particular ones to you. Okay?"

She shot me a conspiratorial grin. "Deal."

Kate put the lid back on the box and placed it and the laptop in her trunk. Once the trunk was closed and locked, she turned to face the nine women standing in a group behind her. "Does anyone think they know something else that might shed light on Tom's death?"

There was a general mumbling of "No" and "I can't think of anything" so Kate asked the next logical question. "Do any of you have information about bones being in that old camper parked over there?" She turned and pointed across the desert at the abandoned camper.

Darla England dismissed the bones with a wave of her hand. "Oh that was just a leg off an old bull Tom kept around the place. It really has nothing to do with anything and if you're spending time on that you're just wasting your time."

Phyla glanced over her shoulder at me and rolled her eyes. Since I was facing Darla, I kept any hint of scorn off my face.

Kate's cell phone rang. As she moved to answer it, she growled in my ear, "Ask Phyla to get them out of my crime scene, please."

I clapped my hands and then with arms outstretched, began herding them toward the trucks. "Okay everybody, thanks for your help, but it's time to head back to the campground." I continued talking as they piled back into their respective rides. "You need to remember, this is an ongoing investigation and coming to Tom's house is strictly prohibited."

Cuxi climbed up into Phyla's truck and I hurried over to intercept her. "Hey, you didn't show me where Tom kept that book."

She motioned to the showroom with a lift of her chin. "In there somewhere, but I don't know where. I only saw him reading it, I never saw where he got it from."

That made me more than slightly irritated. "Why didn't you just tell me that back at the campground?"

A knowing grin was followed by the weird, closed-fist, thumb between the fingers gesture she'd done twice before. "I needed to finish the curse so neither of them *ever* escape the underworld." She leaned her head on the headrest, closed her eyes and sighed. "I am finally finished with this house and those two cabrones." When she opened her eyes again, I shivered at the venomous look of pure hatred she turned on the house. I definitely wanted to keep on this lady's good side. "I never will come here again! Never!"

Phyla climbed in behind the wheel and pulled her door shut. She leaned around Agnes who was sitting between her and Cuxi. "Thanks for all the fun, Alex. If you need anything else, or if you just want to come hang out with the Vamps, you know where to find us."

I nodded, then shut Cuxi's door and stepped back to give the trucks room to turn around.

"Alex." Kate stood next to her car and I could tell by the tiredness in her eyes that we were done for the night.

I was surprised when she focused on the end of the driveway and muttered, "Now what?"

I turned in time to see a fresh set of headlights coming onto the Jepson property. As the car neared, I recognized Casey's work car, but when they pulled up next to us, I could see it was Terri Gentry, Casey's girlfriend, driving. Terri's a patrol officer in team two, which explained why Casey had let her drive her department ride.

Casey opened the passenger door but before she could exit, Kate put her hand on the window frame and held the door partially shut. "I thought I told you to stay home until the doctor releases you to come back to work."

Subconsciously reaching for the lump on her head, Casey's shrugged, "I know, that's why Terri's driving, but we found something on the recordings and I needed to come check it out." Her chagrined expression changed to confusion when she saw me standing a short ways away. "What are you two doing out here, anyway, and why did we pass three truckloads of people leaving the property?"

Sighing, Kate stepped back to allow Casey room to get out. "It's too long a story to go into right now. What did you find?"

Both Casey and Terri started for the showroom and Kate and I joined them.

Megan must have been staying out of sight because I'd completely forgotten she was there. She caught up to me about halfway to the showroom and I jumped slightly when she came into my peripheral vision. "Whoa, Megs. You scared the shit out of me."

Megan snuck a nervous glance at Kate before whispering. "Sorry, I've been keeping out of the way, but I don't want to miss this, whatever it is."

Terri reached the door first and held it open for the rest of us to enter. She had a shit-eating grin on her face. They'd obviously discovered something good.

Casey stopped and waited for her to join us in the middle of the room. "Actually, Terri's the one who saw it. I was dozing on the sofa and she kept watching after I went to sleep." She lifted her chin in her friend's direction. "Tell 'em what you found."

"Well, we kept replaying those scenes over and over, you know, the ones Alex found with the one man next to the file cabinet and the younger one near the car. I didn't see anything the first five times through—"

I groaned. "Five times? You went through them five times?"

Terri nodded and smiled at Casey. "You know how bullheaded she can be when she's trying to find something she knows has to be there. I knew her head was hurting, so when she dozed off, I kept looking, hoping to find something, anything, so she could rest easier."

Kate, Megan and I all nodded. Tenacity was Casey's middle name when it came to investigating a case.

"Anyway," Terri walked over to the trunk of the Special Roadster. "I know it's not much to go on, but do you see this gap between the tongue of the camper and the bumper on the Mercedes?"

All of us dutifully nodded.

"Well, some of the time it's this far away." She held her thumb and forefinger about two inches apart. "Other times it's this far." She opened the gap between her fingers. "So I went back again to each of the times the video flickered, and each time, there was some kind of change in the distance between the two. Not much, and I could just be grasping at straws, but I thought, what if they turned off the recorder every time they moved the car? And why would they do that?"

We all edged closer, immediately grasping the implications.

Kate tapped the trunk with her forefinger. "Because they have to move the car to get at something underneath. Something they didn't want a record of."

Terri and Casey spoke at the same time. "Exactly."

I pulled Jepson's keys out of my pocket and found an odd shaped one that looked like it might belong to the Mercedes. I held it up to Kate to see if she wanted to be the one to move it.

She shook her head and motioned for me to get on with it.

The door opened from the front, and I slid into the driver's seat, careful not to scratch anything with my holster. It took a minute to locate the ignition switch, but when I did, the key slid in perfectly. I stared at the ivory knob on the gearshift, hesitant to touch it for fear of leaving any kind of mark. I very carefully slipped it into neutral, took a breath and turned the key. The car started like a dream.

I depressed the clutch, shifted into first and slowly moved the car forward about ten feet.

When I turned the car off, I could hear the disappointment in Casey's voice when she sighed, "I don't see anything unusual."

I walked around to the trunk and saw Kate on her hands and knees carefully examining a mosaic of floor tiles that served as a platform for the car. I hadn't noticed the tiles before, but when I glanced back at the camper, a second mosaic had been set into the tiled floor beneath it as well.

I stepped up onto the tongue of the camper, which allowed me to get a better overall view of the design. A beautifully rendered copy of the White Star Lines poster that had been hanging on Jepson's wall had been artistically crafted onto the tiles. Each twelve by twelve tile held a portion of the poster and I let out an appreciative whistle. "That's absolutely fantastic."

All of us joined Kate on the floor, practically putting our noses into the grout to check for a hidden compartment of some kind. By the time we'd finished, I knew there were seventy-two tiles laid out in a rectangle almost the exact dimensions of the Roadster, none of which seemed to hold a secret hiding place for our cipher.

I climbed onto the camper tongue again. "Can everybody move off the mosaic please? Maybe I can see something different from up here."

They all stepped to the side. Kate knelt again to change her vantage point while Casey and Terri circled slowly, doing the same.

Megan, who'd never been very good at holding her alcohol, sat with her back up against one tire, her arms circling her bent knees with her head resting in the crook of her arms. She'd lost interest a while ago and I knew she couldn't wait to get home to bed.

I carefully studied each square, and then realized I'd narrowed the parameters of my search to the grout between the twelve by twelve foot tiles. I'd been thinking that one of the squares had to lift off, but once I shifted my expectations, I immediately saw what we'd been looking for.

Hopping down, I strode straight for the "L" in the words "White Star Lines." I pushed on each corner of the letter individually, but nothing happened. While I stared at it, I tried to think of a way to hide a mechanism, even if someone should accidentally step on the tile not knowing the lock existed.

The mechanism had to be something precise. I put my ear down onto the floor and studied the letter from top to bottom. From that angle, two spots, one at the center top and one center bottom appeared shinier than the rest of the tile.

I put one thumb at the top, and the other on the bottom and pressed them both simultaneously. I heard a click and felt the letter drop a fraction of an inch. Keeping my thumbs where they were, I first pressed harder, thinking that maybe more pressure would release the letter to swing upwards. When that didn't work, I let up a little, hoping the panel would follow my fingers up. No luck.

This had to be the answer, so I sat with my thumbs pushing down, thinking.

Kate knelt next to me. "Swivel it."

I did, and was immediately rewarded by the letter sliding around and disappeared beneath the rest of the tile, revealing a flat, rectangular door directly underneath.

The little door showed just as much artistic talent as the entire mosaic itself. The rowboat from the poster, with a man rowing and a woman standing in the prow holding up a basket of bread, had been carved into the wooden lid. I bent closer and sniffed because I'd detected the faint odor of cedar wafting up when the panel had slid away. "Cedar."

Casey chimed in. "To keep any bugs out would be my guess. My dad built my mom a cedar closet when we were kids to keep her wool clothing from getting moth eaten."

Kate held out her hand and I fished the little key out of my pocket. She unlocked the door, which then popped open on tiny, spring-loaded, copper hinges.

I punched my fist in the air in triumph. "Yes!" There, nestled spine-up in a red-velvet padded compartment, was an old, yellowish-green book. I leaned sideways and read To Love a Leprechaun. Under that was a fleur-de-lis and below that I read Sinclair.

The book had obviously been well used because both ends of the spine looked wrinkled and frayed. Kate carefully pulled it out, set it on her knee and opened it to the first page. "Published in 1906. Probably worth something all by itself."

I didn't care about that. "Hopefully it's our cipher."

A man spoke from the doorway to the showroom. "You won't have to worry about that anymore, Detective Wolfe. I'll take the book."

The deep, throaty voice didn't sound familiar, but even though the person was wearing a ski mask, I recognized the bulky shoulders and muscular body of the man who'd shot Assistant Chief Pardo. He wore a grey, body-hugging short-sleeved shirt stretched over a wide chest and tight biceps. With his feet shoulder width apart, black military pants tucked into combat boots, and the way he held his M-16 pointed directly at me, it didn't take much imagination to know he'd had extensive combat training.

All of us immediately moved away from each other to present less of a single target. All except Kate who still knelt in front of the floor safe holding the book.

I stepped in front of her to shield her.

Casey slipped behind the camper and Megan, still totally oblivious, dozed behind the Mercedes. That left just Terri and me fully exposed to his weapon.

He'd caught us all flat footed.

I raised my hands out to the sides to try to give Casey time to get into a good position to fire. "You keep turning up like a bad penny. You must want something really bad to take on all four of us at once."

With a definite irritated bite to her words, Kate stepped around me, shoved the book into my stomach and faced him while drawing her fingers across the top of her brow. "I've had it up to here with you. You killed a man, shot Deputy Chief Pardo, and gave one of my detectives a concussion. Now you think you're going to just walk in here and take something from the four of us that doesn't belong to you?"

"It does belong to me. To my family anyway. And I'm sorry about your Deputy Chief." If anyone had asked, I would have sworn his discomfort was genuine. "Collateral damage that I deeply regret. It was the only shot I had, so I took it and I'm sorry for it. Now give me the book."

He hadn't come in guns blazing. And honestly, I knew that if he'd wanted to kill Casey and me the last time we'd met, he would have. I decided to take a risk and stepped back two paces. When nothing happened, I knelt, shoved the book into the safe, closed the door and locked it. When I looked up, the man was striding angrily toward me.

I quickly stuffed the key in my pocket, rose to my feet and held my hands out to my sides once again. The gunman seemed momentarily unsure of his next move, so I decided to add a little fuel to his uncertainty. "The book is useless to you anyway. Obviously you know what the code represents or you wouldn't have been willing to kill for it. We don't know everything yet, but we do know it's a multiple encryption code, and unless you have all the parts, like I said, the book is useless."

"Give me the key, Detective Wolfe."

"Come and get it."

He took two steps forward before Kate stepped in his way. She'd managed to pull her Glock halfway out of its holster before he grabbed her wrist and twisted it to the right. Her weapon went flying. With one smooth jerk of his arm and sweep of his leg, he sent her flying as well.

I used the momentary distraction to dive for the M-16 and managed to wrap my body around his arms for an instant before he snapped my head back with a direct strike under my chin with the palm of his hand. The blow stunned me and I let go of the weapon, but not before I felt the man's feet go out from under him as Terri took out his legs with a perfectly executed sweep to his lower extremities.

As soon as he landed on the floor, Kate dove on his head and pinned it down with her body.

My addled brain hadn't quite caught up with my body, but when I realized Kate had once more been thrown across the floor, I leapt toward him. I hadn't formed a coherent thought about what I'd do once I landed on him, which turned out not to be that important because before I hit him, he brought both pile driver legs up to his chest and mule kicked me in the stomach, knocking the wind out of me and sending me flying.

I heard him grunt when Terri landed a fist to his groin, but it didn't slow him down. He kicked her away from him, and then all hell broke loose.

The Mercedes engine unexpectedly roared to life. Megan had climbed into the car intending to do God knows what. She jammed the gearshift into first and gunned the engine, causing the wheels to spin and squeal on the tiled floor. When they caught, the car took off like a shot. Megan had the wheel cranked all the way to the right and she slid the car around until it was aimed directly for our assailant.

When he realized what was happening, the man swung the barrel of the rifle up until it was pointed directly at Megan, whose eyes were as round as two sugar coated donuts. Thankfully, he didn't have time to get off a shot before the Mercedes was on him. He leaped in the air and did a perfect somersault over the roof, hit the trunk hard and landed in a heap on floor.

Unfortunately for him, I landed on his back shortly after that. Unlike Terri, I didn't have a shot at his groin, so I rammed my knee into the side of his thigh and heard a gratifyingly painful intake of breath through gritted teeth.

I'd managed to land with both hands on the barrel of his gun, but he'd obviously had weapons retention training because before my weight fully came down on him he'd wrenched it out of my hands.

Luckily, Terri had also taken a flying leap at the same time I had. She landed on top of both of us and managed to wrap her arms around his, effectively, for a short time at least, pinning his arms together between her own.

Kate's voice echoed commandingly off the metal walls of the garage. "Stay!"

I glanced back and saw her pointing at Casey, who was running full tilt, hell-bent on diving straight into the melee.

Casey slid to a stop, her face reflecting the feverish internal debate she was having while weighing the consequences of disobeying a direct order.

Meanwhile, the man was throwing Terri and me around like ragdolls, with both of us hanging on to one body part or another.

Suddenly, all motion stopped. While we were struggling, my face had been smashed into his rock hard abs. When I looked up, I saw Kate pushing the barrel of her Glock up against the man's forehead, right between his eyes. She'd also jammed her knee into his Adam's apple and was ruthlessly pushing down with all her weight.

He must have released the M-16, because Terri slid it out of his grip and threw spinning it across the floor to where Casey stood angrily rooted to the spot where Kate had ordered her to wait.

She stopped its forward momentum by catching it under the toe of her boot.

Kate grabbed a handful of the man's hair and between my wrenching his arm almost out of its socket and her ripping his hair out by the roots, we jerked him onto his stomach. Both Terri and I cranked his arms behind his back and pulled them up as far as they would go.

Angrily, Kate jammed the Glock into his temple and nodded toward his wrists. "Cuff him, Alex."

It was silent for a second while I wondered how to tell her I hadn't brought any cuffs with me.

Casey immediately knew what the problem was. "I've got a pair in my car. Hang on." She jogged out the door and I glanced up at Kate and shrugged. I had to force my words out in between my gasping attempts to pull in some air. "Sorry, boss."

Kate pushed the Glock down harder onto his head. "Give me an excuse, asshole. Any excuse."

Casey returned and handcuffed him, and then secured his ankles with flex cuffs.

A definite ringing sound echoed throughout my skull, and I was still having a hard time catching my breath around the indentation his boots had left in my breadbasket. I halfway sat, halfway lay across his back, trying to breathe.

Casey helped Kate and Terri to their feet. I only realized she'd come over to me when I saw her knees resting on the floor next to my face. I heard her chuckle quietly and looked up to see what she found so funny about my injuries.

Her attention wasn't on me, however. She was looking over at Megan, who stood behind the Mercedes with her arms crossed and her chest puffed out like a proud little banty rooster.

Her self-satisfied smile said I'd be hearing the story of how she'd saved all of us during a fight for our lives for the next thirty, forty, or possibly even fifty years of my life.

I forced a weak, painful grin onto my face, then lay my head back down on the suspect and closed my eyes to keep the room from spinning and the contents of my stomach firmly within the confines of my aching body.

CHAPTER 16

K ate had followed the patrol car with our suspect to the station. Megan hadn't been fit to drive yet, so Terri and Casey had followed me to her house. I'd dropped her off with her truck and then Terri had driven me the rest of the way home.

This morning, I'd come to work early to do a little research. I'd also been eager to study the book to see how it related to the second set of numbers we'd come up with. The research had produced some interesting results, but so far, nothing from To Love a Leprechaun had jumped out at me. As I painfully leaned back in my chair, I looked up to see Chuck striding up to my desk. I grinned and motioned for him to pull up a chair. "Hey, you slumming or what?"

The organized crime unit had its offices out near the airport, and unfortunately I didn't get to see him all that often. I loved the friendly, yet always slightly cynical smile he gave whenever we saw each other around the department. He offered one now as he pulled up a chair and made himself comfortable. "I was in the building and thought I'd come up to say hello. Always glad to see your smiling face." He looked more closely. "Although, damn, what'd you do? Get into another fight with a bull?"

"Something like that." I rubbed the underside of my chin where a horrendous bruise had formed overnight. "But I know you. You don't do social visits, so what's up?"

He stared at me for a second, the wheels of his sometimes inconvenient, above average intelligence churning away. "You remember the other day when you asked about the Chicago mob? Why'd you ask?"

I didn't want to tell him about our meeting with Gia, so I shrugged and gave him a little bit of nothing. "I don't remember the exact connection, but I was talking to Ruthanne who happened to mention that a phone they'd found on a case possibly had something to do with the Chicago mob. I decided to check it out, that's all. You know, helping her track down some loose ends."

He continued to stare at me. I knew he believed there was more to it than that, but I was also betting he'd rather not know the entire story. After a while, he nodded. "Uh huh. Okay. Well, I thought you might be interested to know that over the last two days, something like twenty Chicago mobsters have turned up either floating in Lake Michigan or rotting in various dumpsters around town. My contact says the mob's running around like a roiling hive of pissed off yellow jackets."

I blanched. I'd always known Gia's power was far-reaching, but I guess I never really wanted to know just how powerful, and how ruthless, she could be. There wasn't much I could say, so I decided to act like it didn't have any special meaning to me. "Shit. Somebody must have pissed off the wrong person. Damn."

He slapped his knee and stood to his full 6'5" height. "Yup. Somebody must have all right." As he turned to leave, he casually waved over his shoulder. "See ya, Alex."

That wasn't the kind of information I'd expected to hear this early in the morning. I swiveled around in my chair and stared numbly out at the fire station next to our building.

As Chuck opened the door to the office to leave, Kate walked in looking like she'd had a full eight hours of sleep instead of the five or six I knew she'd actually gotten. They exchanged pleasantries, and when he left, Kate stepped into her cubicle without looking in my direction.

I turned back around and pretended to study the book again. After about a half-hour with no insights into using it to translate the code, I gave up and called Henry and Sonya to see if they could come in.

I couldn't reach Henry, but Sonya said she'd be right over.

At around nine-thirty, Casey walked through the door and handed Kate what I assumed was her medical release form.

Kate leaned forward and motioned for me to join them in her cubicle. When I eased my aching body down into one of her very uncomfortable office chairs, she started right in. "Our shooter invoked his Miranda rights last night when Ruthanne tried to interview him. We ran his fingerprints and got a match from the military database. His name's Patrick Jepson, which wasn't too much of a surprise considering he said the book belonged to his family. He's retired army. Alex, could you bring me the genealogy, please?"

The papers were still in my briefcase, which I'd left on top of my filing cabinet. I went over and grabbed them, then hurried back and placed the folder on the edge of her desk.

She scanned the paperwork for a second. "Here he is. He's descended from Samuel Jepson. Tom and Mick descend from Samuel's brother, Tomás Michael Jepson Sr." She abruptly stopped speaking and her head jerked forward for a closer look at the paperwork. A far-away expression came into her eyes and I guessed she was trying to recall some elusive fact or hopefully retrieve some small piece of our skeletal puzzle.

Casey and I sat quietly waiting.

After a short time, Kate pulled her keyboard closer and began typing. Google must have supplied the answer she was looking for because she decisively tapped on her screen. "That's it. I thought Patrick's father's name sounded familiar. Hunter Jepson was recently in the news for running his multi-million dollar company into the ground." She glanced over at us. "Now that just might be a motive for murder, but we still have to connect the dots and figure out why."

I sat back and crossed my arms. Try as I might, I couldn't keep the shit-eating grin off my face. "That explains why Patrick was willing to kill to keep the family secret. My guess is that it was probably coincidental that he or Hunter saw Tom talking to police and they couldn't risk the possibility that he would spill the proverbial beans under pressure." I proudly pointed my thumb at my chest. "And I know what that family secret is."

A glower followed Kate's surprised intake of breath when I didn't immediately dish on my information. I wanted to savor the moment, but apparently she didn't. "Anytime today, Alex."

I held up my hands in surrender. "Okay, okay. I came in early to do a little research this morning. I'd noticed that both the tiles under the Mercedes and the little locked safe had pictures from that poster, remember? The one from the White Star Lines we found in Jepson's house?

"I started thinking that maybe that meant either the poster held the key to what we're looking for or, what the poster was about, did. I decided to look up the ship on the poster, the RMS Republic. Turns out, it sank off the coast of Nantucket, Massachusetts in 1909. A different ship, the SS Florida, accidentally rammed it during a heavy fog."

By now, both Kate and Casey were listening intently to my story.

"Guess what was on the Republic?"

Both of them sat silently waiting.

"C'mon, guess." When Kate rolled her eyes and sighed, I relented. "Okay, Jeez, you guys aren't any fun." I pulled my notebook out of my back pocket. "There are several rumors about what the ship was carrying. One says she had $265,000 in American gold coins to be used as payroll for the US Navy's Great White Fleet. I did some checking. At today's prices, that would translate into millions of dollars."

I flipped the page. "But, that's nothing compared to the three million in gold coins she was carrying as part of a loan to the Imperial Russian government. That's three million in 1909 when gold was $20 an ounce. Today, gold's running somewhere around $1250 an ounce, making the treasure worth over a hundred and eighty-seven million dollars."

I glanced up from my notebook and grinned. "Now, guess who was a deckhand on the RMS republic?"

Casey leaned forward. "Who?"

"Titus Jepson."

Kate raised her chin. I could tell the light bulb had just come on for her like it had for me. She nodded. "If he grabbed a pocketful of coins and hid them once they reached shore, and then paid a cryptographer to devise a code giving the latitude and longitude of the buried treasure, those coins could be worth a fortune to future generations of his family."

My cellphone rang, and when I answered, Paul told me Sonya was waiting for me at the front desk. I stood up, but remembered I still had some more information to impart. "I also went back into the Arizona historical land records database. Those coins explain how Titus, who was a deck hand in 1909, was able to pay cash for a 5000 acre ranch near Tucson in 1915."

Kate stood as well. "Okay, obviously we still need to solve the puzzle of the numbers in order to understand what Tom Jepson was doing with those bones in his camper. We know the numbers in the genealogy were the latitude and longitude for two separate cemeteries. My guess is as members of his family died, Titus carved the numbers in their skulls as hints to where he buried the treasure. Sick bastard."

She bent over her desk and studied the genealogy again. She put her finger on a name. "Here, look. Remember I told you my friend, Micah, was married to Sasha Maloney?" She pointed to me. "And then you figured out that Sasha was a Jepson? Well look at this. Sasha is descended from Titus through his daughter Penina. Penina is one of the people who has the numbers next to her name."

Suddenly I understood where she was headed. "I remember you saying Micah was buried on top of Sasha in that cemetery in Peeples Valley, so maybe Sasha was buried on top of Penina. In order to get to Penina's skull, Tom had to go through Micah, and then Sasha. He probably stole the badge on his way down. And since he was a sick son of a bitch, he might have also stolen some extra bones as souvenirs."

Casey spoke up for the first time. "Or as a fuck-you to Micah. Remember Agnes said Micah had roughed Tom up? And Tom had said something like, 'a whore's-get like Sasha has no claim on anybody or anything.' What if Micah knew there was family lore about treasure and he wanted to get Sasha's share?"

All of us rolled that around a while before I remembered why I'd stood up. "Sonya's downstairs. I thought maybe she could help figure out how To Love a Leprechaun is a cipher." I blinked for a minute. "Titus sounds like he may have been a man with a sense of humor, since a leprechaun is a tiny little man who buries a pot of gold at the end of the rainbow."

With a pleased smile on my face, I headed downstairs to get Sonya. When we returned, Kate and Casey followed us into the interview room. I gave Sonya everything we'd gathered so far, including the book.

She brought out a notebook and began looking back and forth between the numbers and the book. After making several notations on her pad, she looked up at me and smiled. "This is a very old, very basic code that makes perfect sense once you have the cipher."

She waggled the book to illustrate her point, then set it back on the table and continued. "On one side of the man's skull, you found the numbers 1665, and on the other side, the numbers 31138.52. On the woman's skull, you found 2724.15 and nothing else." She opened the book. "Let's start with the number 1665. One way these codes worked —and actually I'm betting this is the way this one does—is to follow the simple sequence: page, line, word. So, we know it's not page 1 because you can have a line 6 but there can't be 66 words on that line.

She sat back a minute, then shook her head. She flipped to page 16. "Let's try this." She quietly read the numbers to herself. "On page 16, line 6, the 5th word is 'hundred.'" She wrote that down. "On the other side of his skull are the numbers 31138.52. My guess would be page 31 —" She flipped to that page. "Line 13, and the 8th word, which is '11'. That leaves .52. So you would have 111.52." She switched over to the genealogy. "And the middle initial for the man who has the numbers is W. So it's 111.52 W."

Kate pulled out a chair and sat while Sonya worked on the rest of the numbers. "Alex, go get your laptop. It looks like we might have another latitude and longitude."

By the time I returned, Sonya had extrapolated the rest of the information. I pulled up the map and entered what she gave me.

"Put in 111.52 W and 34.15 N." The map pinpointed an area somewhere in the Prescott National Forest. Casey and I looked at each other with raised brows.

"Don't even think about it." Kate began gathering up all the paperwork. "We'll give the information to the attorneys and let them figure out who it belongs to."

Sonya gently removed the genealogy from Kate's fingers. "Don't forget, you had two sets of numbers. Do you have the skulls from the two infants who died just days apart?"

Kate shook her head. "No, and I doubt we're going to find them, either. I've been mulling the infants over for a few days, and yesterday I made a call to the Nantucket Police Department. It's a really small department so I dealt with the chief. I asked him to see if there were any records of criminal activity at their cemetery. He did some research and found that in 1943 someone dug up the two infants, Michael and Jesse Jepson, who were buried together. Only their skulls were taken. The rest of the bodies were left in the coffin."

Disgusted, she shook her head. "Titus died in 1942. My guess is, after he died, someone figured out the number system." She pointed to a name. "Possibly Tomás, Titus' oldest son. He probably inherited the book and maybe the family secret from his father. Tomás died two years after Titus."

Kate pulled out a chair and sat, steepling her fingers while she thought. "What if Titus had bequeathed the secret of the treasure to his oldest son? Tomás would have gone to get the numbers carved into the infants' skulls, and those numbers, combined with the cipher, would have made him a very wealthy man.

"We know Tomás died fairly young, and probably unexpectedly, in 1944, only two years after his father's death. That means it's possible he passed on his newfound wealth, but maybe he didn't have the time to pass on the secret of how to locate the second treasure to his eldest son, Thomas Michael Jepson II, also known as Mick."

Excited, I picked up on her narrative. "Cuxi said Mick and Tom were both obsessed with the book. She said at one point they left, and when they came back, they went straight to the camper. Maybe they figured out the first part of the puzzle and went and dug up Penina and

Henry's bones. Then they got stuck, and couldn't figure out how to use the cipher to find the second treasure."

Sonya added her two cents. "It's a simple cypher for a cryptologist. They were probably too paranoid or too greedy to show the book to a professional. They were afraid he'd take the information and steal the treasure." She grinned over at me. "Boy do I ever have a great story to tell around the campfire with the Vamps."

CHAPTER 17

The weekend finally rolled around, and for the first time in a long time, I had nothing to do. We'd solved the mystery of the bones, and we had the person who'd shot Deputy Pardo behind bars. I cleaned my bedroom, did a load of laundry and was just getting ready to do the dishes when I couldn't stand it any longer.

I picked up the phone and called Megan. "Hey, whatcha doin'?"

"Nothin', why?"

"Can you get to my house? And wear some hiking boots and stuff. We're off to the Prescott National Forest."

"Hiking? Are you kidding? Since when does either of us go hiking?"

I grinned. "Since I know where to find a buried treasure." The line went dead. I knew she'd be on my doorstep before I could finish the dishes.

The doorbell rang as I put the last cup in the dishwasher. I flipped the dishtowel off my shoulder and went to answer the door. Megan and Sugar stood there just long enough for Tessa and Jynx to come flying out of the bedroom where they'd been sleeping. The three dogs took off out the front door and began chasing each other full tilt around my yard.

I watched them for a second until Megan pushed me inside. She could barely contain her excitement. "You figured it out!"

"Yup."

"Does Kate know?"

I had to think about that a minute. "Yeah, but she said the attorneys will have to figure out who owns the treasure. So if we find it, it's not ours, okay? If there's really anything buried there and you sneak a coin into your pocket and—" I held my fingers up in quotation marks. "You 'accidentally' forget you put it there, that's a felony and you'll go to jail. Understand?"

She drew an X on her chest. "Cross my heart and hope to die." Bouncing on her toes had always been her go-to outlet when she was too excited to contain her enthusiasm. Watching her jiggle up and down at an unprecedented speed made me question the sanity of my decision to bring her along.

"I've got some sandwiches in the kitchen. C'mon." The peanut butter and jelly sandwiches were still sitting on the countertop, mainly because Sugar had kept Tessa occupied while I'd been out of the kitchen. I wrapped them in baggies and placed them in my backpack next to a collapsible shovel I'd inherited from my dad, a flashlight, a couple of gallon sized baggies to hold any coins we found, and my Ipad, which I was going to use to guide me to the treasure.

Tessa and Jynx began barking outside, while Sugar came into the kitchen and sat in front of Megan, like she'd been taught to do whenever visitors arrived. Megan reached down to pet her on the head. "Are they here, girl?"

I whipped around in time to see Megan's back disappear through the kitchen door. "They who? Megan! They who?" I chased after her, afraid of what, or rather who, I'd find on my front lawn.

By the time I got to my door, Megan was busy ushering Phyla, Sonya and Agnes inside. My jaw dropped practically down onto my chest and I stared dumbfounded at Megan's grinning face.

"Oh come on, Alex. They helped us figure it out after all! They deserve to come along. Besides, Phyla knows how to read a map, something I know for a fact you have no idea how to do."

"Us? There *was* no us!" I looked first at Sonya, who'd helped with the cryptology, then at Phyla, who'd introduced me to Cuxi, and then at Agnes, who'd remembered Micah bullying Tom. I took a deep breath. "Okay, you're right, without them we'd probably still be chasing our tails." I lifted my chin toward Phyla. "You know how to read maps?"

She smiled and pulled a rolled up topographical map out of her backpack. "I do. I used to compete in expedition racing where we hiked through a wilderness with just a compass, a topo map, and a canteen full of water."

I mumbled, "Of course you did." I retrieved my backpack from the kitchen table. "Well, I brought my Ipad. It has a GPS on it that should lead us right to the coordinates we're looking for."

Phyla nodded. "Sure, as long as you have Internet service."

Sighing, I looked down at my technological rock. "I hadn't thought about that."

She smoothed out the map on the table. "So, what are the coordinates?"

We spent the next hour planning our trip. I hadn't realized how big Prescott National Forest actually was, and began to be secretly relieved that Megan and I weren't going in alone.

When we were ready, we all piled into Phyla's truck. Several hours later, we'd reached the end of the dirt road that took us into the middle of the forest. The mood in the cab had almost become festive, with everyone telling stories about their various adventures and camping fiascos.

We'd climbed in elevation and I was thankful the temperatures weren't as extreme here as they were in Tucson. I was also relieved when Phyla announced that the back road brought us to within about five miles of our destination. I was envious of the large packs full of water the three of them had brought. They each slipped one on their back and adjusted the positions of the sipping tubes on their front shoulder straps.

Sonya saw me eyeing my pitiful little canteen and patted me on the shoulder. "Don't worry, we've got you covered. Megan told us you two don't have a lot of hiking experience." She reached into the cargo container behind the cab of Phyla's truck and pulled out two extra packs. "Here you go. You can sling your backpack over your shoulder and wear this on your back."

Relieved, I gratefully accepted her offer and soon the four of us were following Phyla as she set off into the tall pines.

Agnes and Megan kept us entertained the entire way with their mindless chatter about nothing and everything in particular.

I smiled as I listened to Megan's excited yammering. After working pretty serious cases week after week, I loved her for the enthusiastic, happy-go-lucky balance she brought into my life.

Phyla finally stopped at the base of a granite outcropping. She pulled out her map and unfolded it on a large, flat rock. Setting her compass down on the map, she pulled out a notebook and pencil and worked out some calculations while the rest of us took a water break. She looked up at the rocky slope, and then back at us. "Well, we're at your latitude and longitude. Now all you need to do is find your treasure."

I looked around, then held my arms out wide. "I guess we spread out and see if we find anything unusual."

Phyla grabbed Agnes' upper arm when the shorter woman began to head out on her own. "You stay with me. Everybody else make sure you stay within eyesight of each other. It's easy to get lost up here."

We each took a direction and began searching. I had no clue what to look for so I contented myself with walking several paces, then turning in a circle to make sure I could still see everybody else.

After about an hour of climbing over downed logs, turning over flat rocks or peeking into other potential hiding places, like hollow tree trunks and such, I heard Agnes call out from about a quarter of the way up the rocky incline. "Over here. I mean, up here! I think we've found something!"

Shielding my eyes from the afternoon sun, I glanced up to see her and Phyla leaning against a particularly large boulder. Agnes waved one arm back and forth while hanging on to the protruding roots of a plant with her other hand.

The slope angled upward at a fairly steep incline, and rocks of various sizes littered the pathway up to them. Sonya, Megan and I slipped and slid our way up to them.

As my head topped over the boulder they were standing on, the opening of a cave that had been hidden from down below came into view.

Phyla gave me a hand up.

Since they'd discovered the cave, I thought it was only fair they should go in first. I motioned for them to enter.

Agnes excitedly started for the entrance, but Phyla held her back. "No, wait a minute. This is Detective Wolfe's case. I think she should go first."

Agnes's shoulders drooped and her obvious disappointment was more than I could take. "No, you know what? I think Agnes needs to go first. Go on, Agnes, lead the way."

Agnes brightened immediately, turned sideways and just barely squeezed through the opening, which was a slit about four feet high and two foot wide in most places.

Before she was halfway through, Phyla grabbed her arm. "Watch out for snakes. Here." She grabbed a flashlight hanging from Agnes' belt and handed it to her. "Shine it around first and let us know if the cave is big enough for the rest of us."

Once inside, Agnes called out to the rest of us with a voice that had a hollow, echoing sound to it. "It's big enough. It opens up to about the size of your pick-up truck, Phyla."

I'd already grabbed my flashlight out of my pack. I tossed the pack inside, then tried to slide through the opening, scraping my back and chest in the attempt. I knew if Agnes had gotten through, I certainly could, but I became a little concerned when a protruding rock stopped my forward motion. I tried to back out and found couldn't.

Before panic could completely set in, Sonya put her hand on my arm. "Easy Alex. Let all your breath out and squeeze the rest of the way through. You're not stuck, you just picked the wrong height to get through."

I'd inherited my grandmother's fairly good-sized 36C chest and I hoped doing as Sonya said would reduce it enough to allow me to slip inside. Without thinking, I accidentally inhaled in anticipation of exhaling, which wedged me tighter and caused me to panic. Just a little.

Until Sonya chuckled and broke the tension. "Out, Alex, not in."

I nodded nervously, formed my mouth into an O and exhaled. The instant I felt movement, I lurched inside, landing on my knees in front of Agnes. I shined my flashlight up into her widely smiling face and breathed a sigh of relief. "Okay, next."

I carefully checked the rest of the interior for snakes or other critters, and was gratified to find we were completely alone. One by one the others squeezed inside. The floor of the cave was solid rock, so each of us took a section of wall and began shining our flashlights up and down.

Phyla and Sonya moved in a methodical up and down pattern while Agnes and Megan were all over the place in their unbridled enthusiasm.

I went to the back and began at the bottom, moving left to right and back again. I hadn't realized I had a smattering of claustrophobia, but every now and then, it felt difficult to breathe. I glanced over my shoulder at the opening, reassured by the rays of sunlight streaming through.

I stared at the motes floating in the sunshine for a little while and then saw something out of the corner of my eye that didn't quite fit with my brain's notion of "usual." I quickly brought up my flashlight and shined the light on three good-sized rocks that had been jammed into a hole about a quarter of the way up the back wall. "Hey, I've got something."

Everyone crowded around as I gingerly pulled out the first rock and let it drop to the floor. I pulled on the second, accidently dislodging the third in the process. Both rocks went tumbling to the floor and five flashlights simultaneously lit up the interior of the little crevice. The disappointment from everyone was palpable when I pulled out a single sheet of paper lying on top of an old gold coin.

I quickly checked to make sure nothing else had been stuffed inside, then turned and sat with my back up against the wall. I brought up my knees and rested the paper on them while I read aloud:

August 18, 1939

My dear son, Tomás,

If you are reading this, then I am dead and I have passed along our family secret to you. Hopefully you have found the first hiding place and the few coins I left have helped you somehow. I know you're here to claim the rest of your inheritance. I'm sorry to say this coin is all that remains. When I first came off the Republic, I had fifty gold coins stuffed in my pockets. More riches than you can ever imagine! I buried 15 in Nantucket, and 15 here. The rest I spent on our home in Tucson.

Unfortunately, as you know, I enjoy a small bit of gambling. Not much, but over the years I had to return to Nantucket and now here to retrieve the coins to pay off some debts.

I love you my son, and wish I could have given you more.

Good luck and good life.

Your loving father,

Papa

I held up the coin so everyone could see.

My disappointment must have been written on my features because Megan, who knows my every mood, immediately knelt down and made sure I was looking her in the eye. "This is so cool, Alex! What an adventure!" She hit me on the arm and grinned up at the other ladies who immediately took the hint.

Sonya took the coin from my hand and studied it while Phyla and Agnes both spoke at once.

The corner of Phyla's mouth quirked up and I saw the glint of amusement in her eyes when she spoke. "We couldn't have asked for a better adventure, Alex. Thank you for bringing us along."

Agnes spread her arms wide. "I'm gonna be telling this story until the day I die. Maybe even after that!"

I smiled up at her and accepted Phyla's extended hand as she pulled me to my feet. Once everyone had a chance to examine the coin, I wrapped it in the letter and placed both in a baggie, which I tucked down into my backpack.

Just as I was about to slip out through the opening, helicopter blades roared overhead. I peaked out and saw a Forest Service 'copter landing a little ways away from the base of our incline.

Two rangers climbed out of the back seat and carefully donned their Smokey the Bear hats. But what really started my heart racing was seeing Kate slide out of the front passenger seat and look around. "What the— What's she doing here?"

Megan pushed me aside. "What? Who?" She stared for a second, then turned her terrified gaze onto mine. "Oh shit. What are we gonna do? We can just wait in here. Maybe they won't see the cave."

I peeked out again. The chopper's blades had stopped spinning and I could tell from the steadily decreasing thrum of the engines that the pilot had begun shutting them down. One of the forest rangers pointed up at us, and I realized they'd probably spotted the opening from the air. I sighed, blew out my breath and slipped out of the cave. There wasn't much else I could do, so I plastered a big smile on my face and waved down at Kate.

Even from that distance I could see her face harden and every muscle in her body tightened as she put her hands on her hips and stared up at me. Then, miraculously, she covered her eyes with a hand and began to laugh.

I slid down the incline and she met me at the bottom, still chuckling and shaking her head. That is until she took a double take up to the opening of the cave. We both watched as Phyla, Sonya, and Agnes squeezed through the opening and began climbing down to join us.

I'd rarely seen Kate rendered speechless, but seeing those three coming out of the cave had done the trick.

I thought maybe I'd play the "this is completely normal" card I'd used back on Jepson's property. "Hey boss. You'll never guess what we found." I slipped the pack off my shoulders and produced the letter and coin.

She stared at it for a second, then took it from me and smoothed open the letter. Her lips moved slightly as she read Titus' last words to a son who'd never read them. When she finished, she reached up under her sunglasses and rubbed her eyes, hopefully trying to get a handle on her temper.

She looked up when the other three women joined us, then surprised us all by yelling up to the cave. "Megan! Get your ass down here, now!"

Pretty soon Megan stuck her head out of the slot and waved down at us.

By the time she started down, my curiosity was killing me. I had to find out what Kate was doing here. "I thought you said the lawyers had to figure out what to do with the coins."

The glare she turned on me was actually frightening until Phyla spoke in her quiet, authoritarian way. "We just came out on an adventure, Sergeant Brannigan. We had every intention of turning over every coin we found. No harm done."

It took a few minutes, but I was relieved to see Kate relax a bit. I really didn't want her blowing a gasket way out here in the forest. She took a deep breath and surprisingly, began chuckling again. "Okay, you're right. I can deal with Alex later."

That wasn't exactly what I wanted to hear.

Kate glanced back at the helicopter. "We're here because late yesterday afternoon, the judge ordered me to use whatever resources necessary to locate the treasure. She said she couldn't make a determination on the case until she knew what she was dealing with."

One of the rangers walked up with a metal detector. "Should we start looking, ma'am, or did these ladies already find what you needed?"

Just then Megan tripped the rest of the way down and just happened to "slide" into his outstretched arms.

He caught her and set her back on her feet. "Whoa there, young lady. That's quite a slope. You need to be careful."

I shook my head when she looked up into his face and batted her eyes. Some things just never change.

Kate sighed and held up the baggie. "We have it all here. Let's get back before it gets dark, shall we?" Without even a backward glance, she and the other three climbed into the helicopter. They didn't waste any time in lifting off, and even though the sun was in my eyes, I could just make out Kate's head leaning on her hand as they flew out of sight.

THANK YOU FROM ALISON

If you enjoyed this book, please take a minute of your time to leave a review. Your opinion is important to me and to other readers and I appreciate the help getting the word out. If you didn't like it, please feel free to send me an email from the contact page on my website and I'll be happy to chat with you about it.

"If you don't like to read, you haven't found the right book."
J.K. Rowling

Alison, who grew up listening to her parents reading her the most wonderful books full of adventure, heroes, ducks and puppy dogs, promotes reading wherever she goes and believes literacy is the key to changing the world for the better.

In her writing, she follows Heinlein's Rules, the first rule being *You Must Write.* To that end, she writes in several genres simply because she enjoys the great variety of characters and settings her over-active fantasy life creates.

There's nothing better for her than when a character looks over their shoulder, crooks a finger for her to follow and heads off on an adventure. From medieval castles to a horse farm in Virginia to the police beat in Tucson, Arizona, her characters live exciting lives and she's happy enough to follow them around and report on what she sees.

She loves all horses & hounds and some humans...

For More Information
AnHolt@Denabipublishing.com

ACKNOWLEDGMENTS

Editor: Harvey Stanbrough
http://harveystanbrough.com
Cover Art: Kat McGee
https://daringcreativedesigns.com

ALSO BY ALISON NAOMI HOLT

Mystery

Credo's Hope - Alex Wolfe Mysteries Book 1

Credo's Legacy – Alex Wolfe Mysteries Book 2

Credo's Fire – Alex Wolfe Mysteries Book 3

Fantasy

The Spirit Child – The Seven Realms of Ar'rothi Book 1

Duchess Rising – The Seven Realms of Ar'rothi Book 2

Mage of Merigor

Psychological Thriller

The Door at the Top of the Stairs

Alison Naomi Holt

Manufactured by Amazon.ca
Bolton, ON

19009280R00125